Amy Morrison held
many summers diving in
her sister's farm back in '
to the blue fabric before h
navy velvet curtain rippl
aboard this luxury cruise liner, the curtain, which would
be dropped soon enough, was rich and deep. Gold vines
scrolled above the hem, just above a line of matching
gold fringe. Even the ship's name sparkled: *The
Cullinan Diamond.* The library aboard ship glowed in
the soft light of the evening through its picture windows
and the gold pendant light fixtures above her. Leather-
bound hardbacks in shades of wine and whisky lined up
neatly on the polished oak cases beside her. A thrum of
voices preparing for the gala event lay over the constant
hum of the system that controlled the heat and humidity
in which the books were kept. But Amy focused on
little else beyond what was hidden behind the velvet.

# Venus Rising

by

Tammy D. Walker

**Venus Rising**

Cover Art by *Kim Mendoza*

The Wild Rose Press, Inc.
PO Box 708
Adams Basin, NY 14410-0708
Visit us at www.thewildrosepress.com

Publishing History
First Edition, 2023
Trade Paperback ISBN 978-1-5092-4708-0
Digital ISBN 978-1-5092-4709-7

Published in the United States of America

## Dedication

For Brandi, sage travel companion, dear friend

Chapter One

Amy Morrison held her breath like she had so many summers diving into the creek that ran through her sister's farm back in Texas. She held out her hands to the blue fabric before her. Beneath her fingertips, the navy velvet curtain rippled and swayed. Like so much aboard this luxury cruise liner, the curtain, which would be dropped soon enough, was rich and deep. Gold vines scrolled above the hem, just above a line of matching gold fringe. Even the ship's name sparkled: *The Cullinan Diamond*. The library aboard ship glowed in the soft light of the evening through its picture windows and the gold pendant light fixtures above her. Leather-bound hardbacks in shades of wine and whisky lined up neatly on the polished oak cases beside her. A thrum of voices preparing for the gala event lay over the constant hum of the system that controlled the heat and humidity in which the books were kept. But Amy focused on little else beyond what was hidden behind the velvet.

She was careful not to touch the curtain too firmly, too closely, which was something she'd avoided since she arrived on *The Cullinan Diamond*. As the ship's librarian, the duty fell on Amy to host the debut of the painting that hung behind the curtain. A painting even she had been forbidden to see before the evening's gala one night after the ship had departed from London, that British city she'd longed to see since childhood, bound for New York. They were in the Atlantic now, 2,500 passengers and the thousand staff and crew members with them. Just before she'd come to the library, she'd run up to the deck to watch the waves dance in the warm August evening surrounded by the wide blue sky that reminded her of home. She'd wanted to witness the kiss of salt water against the metal of the ship. She'd needed to steady her nerves. August here in the north Atlantic was calm and mild. Amy reminded herself that she needed to be calm, too.

"Curiosity and cats. Remember the maxim, Amy?" Beatrice Taylor, the ship's assistant entertainment director, stood with her matronly arms across the bodice of her beaded cobalt gown. Most days, she looked every bit the housekeeper she might have been had she gone into service on some stately aristocratic manor a hundred years ago. Now, though, with her amber hair swept up and the dazzle of gemstones at her ears and neck, she was even more imposing. "We must wait with the others. Per Mrs. Lewis's request."

"Of course, Mrs. Taylor." Amy stepped back from the curtain. Wait staff moved quietly behind her, setting up a small bar where her librarian's desk usually sat. Ice crashed against the steel container. "Have you spoken with Mrs. Lewis this evening?"

Beatrice looked down at her tablet. "Ms. Westgrove sent a message along for her sister," she said, a veneer of standard British pronunciation just covering the twang of her working-class Manchester accent. "They'll be along after dinner, which they are taking in their suite. Lucia is seeing to them." She looked at Amy again, surveying her appearance, she guessed, by the squint Beatrice delivered to her. "Do notify the salon staff before the next event." The assistant entertainment director patted her own hair, then bustled over to the bar.

Amy looked down at her own dress, floor-length cobalt satin above her sensible heels. Her dress must have wrinkled a bit in the strong wind from her excursion to the deck. Too late to change now. Too late to go back to her room and fix her wind-tousled hair and the mascara that had smudged in the humidity. She picked up her laptop where she'd left it on the armchair that was to be Mrs. Lewis's in half an hour. Amy looked at the curtain over the painting again. This was her gala to steer, not Beatrice's.

In the doorway, a staffer in a navy blazer tapped the side of his scanner. Then he hit it.

Amy rushed over. "Having trouble?"

He nodded. "These scanners don't work when you need them to."

"Let me see." Amy took the scanner from him and pressed the trigger to scan her badge, but it flashed an error message. "Have you tried resyncing it to the server?"

"What?"

"Is there a cable that came with it?"

Again, the staffer nodded, and he held up the case in which the scanner had been. Amy sat down in a nearby chair and opened her laptop. She'd wrinkle her dress further, but function was more important than appearance, she knew. She hooked the cable up to both the scanner and her laptop and opened the application to resync the scanner. Again, it beeped an error message. "One more thing to try," she said to the nervous staffer. The first guests would be arriving shortly. "You did bring a backup, just in case, didn't you?"

"Montague from IT was supposed to bring us backups," the staffer said.

"But that didn't happen?"

The staffer shrugged. "Haven't seen him."

Amy sighed and attempted the technical maneuver that usually fixed the scanners in her former library in Dawville, her tiny Central Texas hometown. "There," she said after she unhooked the scanner. "Try it again."

The staffer scanned her badge as a test, and the scanner beeped its success. "How did you do that?"

Amy closed her laptop and stood up. "I was pretty much the only IT for the library I worked at for the last twenty years. Small town Texas life, I suppose. We're resourceful there."

"What if it happens again?"

Amy looked down at her laptop. "If you're going to be here all evening, then let's leave this under your chair. If you run into any more difficulties with the scanner, send someone to find me. It won't be the first time I've had to work my technical magic twice in one day. Just keep an eye on the laptop."

A laugh echoed behind her. "Technical magic, Amy?"

"All right, Penelope," Amy said to the older woman coming down the hallway with her husband toward the library's open doors. Together, they made a dashing pair, the retired academics who gave lectures aboard ship. Even the entry to the library was an experience, and the academics seemed in place in the hallway, with its nubby gold silk upper walls, the gold toile below, and the line of sapphire tiles between them.

"Technical expertise. You're the one who knows about magic."

"I know about belief systems *about* magic," Penelope corrected her. "In northern Europe, anyway."

Her husband, Richard, took Amy's hand. "Ah, the librarian turns into a swan for the evening."

"Are you insinuating that Amy is an ugly duckling during the day, Richard?"

Amy squeezed his fingers then let go. "No, it's fine. Everything is fine. Feathers might be ruffled a bit. But fine." She smoothed her hair again, or tried to, anyway.

"Not quite convinced?"

Amy shook her head. "Everything is in place, though. Beatrice is seeing to that."

"Well, good," Richard said. "We're early. Come to say good luck and all."

Amy thanked them, and the staffer scanned their badges. They were on the guest list, of course, along with all the Diamond-class passengers, the officers, and a few other guests Diane Westgrove Lewis had personally invited. Which meant her ghostwriter. Which also meant her nephew, Raymond Entwhistle. She'd appointed him as the guardian of her painting, and he'd overseen the staff's installation of the artwork in the library. The painting, *Self-Portrait as Venus Rising from the Sea*, hung just above the glass case in which a copy of Mrs. Lewis's memoir had been locked. Like the painting, the memoir had been off-limits. Amy had enough to worry about tonight to not wonder at what reasoning the publisher, Brent Detweiler, had for enclosing the book in the glass case.

Guests swirled around her. For the first time in her

career, and maybe in her life, Amy Morrison stood in the middle of the sort of event she'd dreamed about hosting since starting her library science degree over two decades earlier. She spotted Brent at the doorway.

Brent excused himself from the guests with whom he'd been speaking. "Ten minutes until the unveiling. We want Venus out the window for the official portrait. Memoir, Diane, Venus, and, well, Venus."

"Will the photographer be able to do that? Get Venus with everything else?"

Brent shook his head. "We can edit it in. It's the experience we want to create for everyone here. It'll be the story everyone takes away and tells their friends, their social media connections, the world. Trust me."

"Oh, I do."

"Everyone will be talking about how impressive the painting is alongside the rebirth of Venus, so to speak." Brent checked his watch, a sleek digital band that barely rose above his wrist.

"I hesitate to ask," Amy said in a low voice. "But isn't Venus technically setting right now?"

"Details." Brent waved his hand. "It doesn't matter which way the planet is going. It's the story that's important."

"But not the book?"

"The book." Brent seemed to stop himself from saying something. Which is what Neil had done too often. Amy pushed her pale coral thumbnail into her bare ring finger and told herself to stop it. No thinking about the divorce tonight. No thinking about Neil. "The book is what it is."

"All part of the magic, right?" Which had been Neil's favorite thing to say when things were going not as well as planned. She pushed her thumbnail into her ring finger again. "Speaking of the photo, we're missing our guest of honor. But I see Mr. Entwhistle now. If you'll excuse me?"

"Of course. Nine minutes."

"Nine minutes."

Too much was going on. Amy thought she'd seen Mrs. Lewis's nephew ducking out into the hallway. Toward the restroom? She peered out the library's glassed in doors and saw a man half-waddling down the hallway. Though she'd been on ship only a few weeks, she knew that walk meant nausea.

A hand on her shoulder brought Amy back to the party. "Help, Amy." Gemma smiled and spoke in a low voice. "It's that art collector, Curtis Jenkins. He's everywhere. Can you steer me somewhere that he isn't?" Gemma, not much over thirty, but genuinely confident, must have been backed into a corner by him. Her dark hair was swept up, leaving her neck bare above the boat neck of her sea green gown. "He keeps talking about our common love of art. As if speculating on paintings had anything to do with my collection. It's enough of an insult having my collection overshadowed by this." She gestured at the painting, the crowd, the beautiful surroundings.

"What a beautiful dress," Amy found herself saying. Gemma Williams was beautiful in her gown, but also in the white graphic t-shirts and dark pencil skirts and boots that seemed to be her day-to-day uniform. She was an art expert, the curator of the collection aboard the ship. A collection that was making its debut aboard the ship on this voyage. And which was being overshadowed by the unveiling of the

7

painting by a woman whose wealth could make the careers of all the artists whose work Gemma had selected for the ship. "No, I mean, yes. Let's get you away from Curtis." As quickly as she could, Amy spotted Penelope and pointed her out to the disgusted young woman. "Tell her I said you could talk to her about the Temple of Zeus. She'll get it."

"Clever. Thanks." Gemma nodded and glided away as quickly as she could as Curtis came over bringing two champagne flutes.

"Shame," he said. "She left without her drink."

Amy smiled as brightly as she could manage. In the many author events she'd managed at the Dawville Public Library back home, she'd always had the problematic person or two in the audience, those poor souls who'd either want the author to read their own manuscript or who'd want to argue the very fine point of a detail within an inch of its existence. She'd become used to steering conversations (and people as necessary) back to safe ground. Which was useful training ground for the moneyed set on board the ship. Curtis Jenkins's reputed fortune could buy the collection of her home library several times over without feeling the impact. "Well, you know how these parties go. You're a figure in the art world yourself. She needs to make her knowledge of painting available to the laypersons among the guests, don't you think?"

"Of course." Curtis looked at the champagne bubbling in his glass. "Part of our business."

"I knew you'd understand."

Outside the doorway, Raymond Entwhistle listed in the hallway. "If you'd excuse me for a moment, I need to act the host just outside the door for a bit."

He looked up at Amy. "You wouldn't happen to want to join me in a toast to the rise of Venus?"

"That's very kind of you to offer," Amy said, trying not to wrinkle her nose. "But I'll wait for the official toast in a few minutes."

Amy slipped out the door, thankful that Mr. Entwhistle was wiping his forehead visibly with a handkerchief. Once at his side, she spoke softly. "Do you need a doctor?"

"No, hale and hearty, reporting for duty. Has my aunt arrived?"

"Mrs. Lewis?"

He let out a short laugh. "That's the only aunt I have aboard ship. I'm her husband's sister's stepson. Diane's sister Wellie wouldn't let me come with the two of them to the unveiling. I would have thought Diane and Wellie had arrived by now." Amy moved to take his arm, but he shifted himself up and trotted back toward the party. A waiter between them offered him a chocolate truffle from the tray he carried. "Oh, heavens, no," Raymond said, his eyes wide. He took a step back, righted himself, and strode toward his aunt's painting.

Brent caught her eye and pointed to his watch. Amy looked outside. Venus was coming up over the horizon, brighter than she'd ever seen it. Or it seemed to be coming up, anyway. And with more company, too, since the skies at sea were darker than she'd been used to on land. A waiter brought Amy a champagne flute and a fork, and she dinged the glass a few times to get the room's attention.

Beatrice stood behind her. "The lady is in the hallway."

Indeed, she was. Mrs. Lewis stepped forward

slowly, leaning on the arm of the ship's captain. In her sea blue pleated gown with its high neck and long sleeves, she looked the part of the lady. The gold of her wedding ring and a brooch in the shape of a sharp-beaked bird in flight glowed in the soft light of the library. Something seemed off about her gaze, though. Amy shrugged off her worry. After a lifetime of such events, they might become tedious, even if they were meant to celebrate this already much feted philanthropist, Diane Westgrove Lewis. Then there was the jet lag she must have felt flying to London from her home in Los Angeles days ago. And Diane was in her early eighties, after all, too. Behind them was Wellie Westgrove, Mrs. Lewis's younger sister. She held a cane in the arm left bare by her one-shoulder sapphire velvet gown. Fire from her diamonds flashed into the crowd. Wellie needed no escort.

"Good evening, ladies and gentlemen," Amy said. "If we might have your attention, please. I'm honored to have Captain Patel at the library tonight, who will say a few words about our esteemed guest Diane Westgrove Lewis before her painting *Self-Portrait as Venus Rising from the Sea* is unveiled for the first time in over sixty years."

The captain nodded his thanks to Amy, then cleared his throat. He escorted Mrs. Lewis to her seat next to the glass encased book and the veiled painting. Wellie sat down in a chair on the other side of the case. Mrs. Lewis gestured slowly, and Raymond stood near her. She took his hand. "It gives me great pleasure to reintroduce the world to the seminal work of Diane Westgrove Lewis. As I'm sure you all know, Mrs. Lewis gave up a career in art in favor of a life committed to family and philanthropy. We'll all be able to read more about that soon in her book, which Brent Detweiler tells me is a winner." Brent raised his glass to the captain. "But what very few people know about Mrs. Lewis is that she never stopped painting." A wave of low voices echoed the constant rumble of the ship's engines. "It's true. Tonight, we'll see just one of the many paintings Mrs. Lewis created in a long life of art, even if she wasn't a 'career artist.'" Another wave rumbled through the crowd. "At the end of this voyage, Mrs. Lewis and her companions will disembark for the esteemed Weiser Gallery in New York City. There, a lifetime's worth of her art will be auctioned for charity, to benefit the many causes she has championed throughout her life." The guests applauded. The captain began to speak again, but the cheers from the guests overwhelmed his voice.

Mrs. Lewis, still sitting, gave her nephew's hand a visible squeeze. He winced out a smile and left her side. When the guests were quiet, the captain spoke again. "Esteemed guests, may I present, as we witness the planet Venus near the horizon, Diane Westgrove's *Self-Portrait as Venus Rising from the Sea*."

The velvet curtain slipped from the top of the painting, landing in a dim puddle on the floor. Amy realized her eye had followed the cloth instead of staying on the painting, when she heard Diane Westgrove Lewis gasp.

"What's wrong, Di?" Wellie squinted at the picture. "It's charming, I'm sure."

"Well, for one, it's not my work." Diane Westgrove Lewis pushed herself up out of her chair and stood square in front of the painting. Brent moved to reposition her into the frame they'd set up earlier, but she shrugged him off. "And for another, it's not charming. It's facile. Who did this?"

Amy found her backbone again and took Mrs. Lewis's arm. "Someone put up the wrong painting?"

"But we hung the one in the case you gave me, Diane." Raymond Entwhistle listed again. He leaned against the oak bookshelf which held leather-bound versions of maritime classics.

"Someone hung up the wrong painting." Mrs. Lewis inhaled sharply. "Raymond, you were here when the workers opened the case."

Raymond nodded weakly. "Of course, I was. But this was the painting in the case, Diane. Wasn't it?"

"Oh, Di," Wellie said. She maneuvered her sister back into the armchair. "You're tired. Let's go back to our suite and let everyone here have a good look at the charming painting you did when you were just a girl. I'm sure it's just the shock of letting everyone see your juvenilia for the first time in ages. Come on."

"I will not be herded back into my bed like a doddering old woman, Wellie."

Amy stepped in. "Shall I arrange for a drink, Mrs. Lewis?"

"Ms. Morrison, you believe me, don't you? Just look at that," Mrs. Lewis pleaded in her soft voice.

Amy stepped closer to the canvas and briefly looked at the painting. A line had formed behind her to examine the artwork. A few jolts of laughter struck from the queue. "There's a young woman coming out of the ocean in a long silver gown. She looks like a rendering of Venus in modern form to me." Which was the case. There was a young woman who looked vaguely like Diane Westgrove Lewis of about sixty years ago dressed in a long silver gown stepping onto the beach. But there was something about the picture that it created that lacked the defiant sensuality of the young woman—that was the description Brent had printed in the invitations sent to the gala's guests. The young woman in this picture might have just stepped out onto the beach for a pleasant stroll through the sand. She'd have to find Gemma later and ask her about it. Or Curtis, though Amy was loath to do so. "It's late. The lighting in here is less than flattering, and I apologize for that. Maybe in the daylight, it'll be more as you remembered it?"

Mrs. Lewis shook her head. "Come on then, Raymond, Wellie. Let's go."

The crowd moved past the unremarkable painting quickly, then mingled through the bookshelves with canapés and champagne. Amy tried to salvage what she could of the party, but really, at this point, it was out of her control. With Diane, Wellie, and Raymond gone, she focused her attention on the guests staying in the elite suites, on the captain, and on the officers. Soon, the crowd dwindled.

After the last guest left, Beatrice Taylor ordered the lights to be raised. "Well, nothing left for us tonight but the tidying. I'll notify the staff to begin their cleanup."

Cleanup. That word slapped into her like an unexpected wave. "Yes, Mrs. Taylor."

For the first time, Amy Morrison stood in the middle of the sort of author event she'd dreamed about hosting for decades. And as she watched the lights in the library shudder on to their brightest, she knew that it had utterly sunk.

Chapter Two

"Sometimes I wonder why I tried so hard to get you at the elites' table for breakfast." Beatrice, prim in her blue-gray suit, was back to managing the staff. She held her clipboard to her blazer tightly. No outside light made it into the assistant entertainment director's waystation between the staff's living quarters and the passenger decks above, but Amy felt the glare of it nonetheless. "At least those lovely lecturers are good company for our Diamond-class guests. Good thing the art curator is on board, I suppose. She'll do your job for the morning."

Amy nodded. She'd had a strange mixture of exhaustion and disappointment dragging at her as she emerged from her shared room on the staff-level of the ship. Mascara had embedded itself in the crease that was the beginning of crow's feet, and she hadn't bothered wiping it off. "I do apologize for being late, Mrs. Taylor."

"Your predecessor would never have allowed himself to be tardy," Beatrice said. Amy had guessed by the number of times Beatrice had mentioned the previous librarian that Beatrice held him in higher esteem than he might have liked. "You're not fit this morning to hold a conversation with a groggy hedgehog."

"I'm perfectly capable, Mrs. Taylor. I'll be fine.

With hedgehogs or passengers."

"You're not fine, and it's shameful you saying so. Don't get used to eating the passengers' food." Beatrice looked down at her clipboard and made a note with the pen that she'd attached to it with a fine golden chain. "I'll send you a tray to the library. A *staff* tray."

At her desk in the library, Amy picked at the stale danish and the fruit cup filled with bruised grapes. At least the coffee was coffee-like. The orange juice had been watered down and yet was still pulpy. She ate quickly what would have to do for calories this morning. It wasn't that Amy had slept particularly badly last night. No sooner had she climbed into her thin twin bed had she fallen asleep. She hadn't even heard her roommate Roisin, the resident morning pianist, leaving in the pre-dawn hours as Amy usually did.

Strangely, Amy had slept, and she'd dreamed quite vividly too, those dreams that stuck with her enough to convince her that she was someplace else in some other time. Not here aboard a cruise ship, but back at her house in Dawville, soon to be woken by the alarm Neil set too loudly. Angus would be waiting at the table, not really for her or for breakfast, but for, she realized, himself. Waiting to figure out life.

In reality, she thought he had. Her only child, off to college in a few days. It seemed hard to imagine. That she was aboard ship when he was leaving for Texas A&M, going off to be a freshman electrical engineering major, hurt her, but she knew Stacey would take care of him. Stacey's first two were already at A&M, so it wasn't like Angus was going alone. And he had practically grown up on his Aunt Stacey's farm anyway, thrown in with Stacey and Rick's four kids. So it was almost like Angus was with whom he should be with right now. Amy would call her older sister sometime today and ask how Angus was.

No one came into the library this early. She learned that pretty quickly during the first two legs of her journey, a trip around the Nordic countries, and another circling Great Britain and Ireland. They'd come back to London, watched the previous set of passengers disembark, watched a new set of passengers embark. The new set of passengers had more or less the same taste in books as the last.

Good taste, she reminded herself. Everything aboard ship was in good taste, refined, elegant. The library had been modeled after those she might have found in British country estates, had she been able to convince Neil and Angus to tour them with her. Warm oak bookcases lined the wall, reaching almost to the crown molding. Between them hung long silk curtains in the darkest blue of the ocean, the fabric just puddling on the floor. Amy recognized that this was a mark of refinement, curtains longer than necessary. There were thousands of details she knew were in place but that she wasn't aware of beyond the luxurious whole they made. Each morning, she found more details—the way the shelves in the middle of the floor created cozy nooks, the way the roses were arranged under the pendant lights. But she couldn't focus on that this morning. Not with the painting and the memoir here now.

Amy got up from behind the heavy wooden desk on which her empty breakfast tray sat. Beatrice must have seen to the desk's replacement back here last night. Morning sunlight caught the gloss on the desk.

The painting still hung where it had been last night. The memoir—the only copy allowed near the public—was still in its glass case.

What had happened last night? She tried to go over it again, but she only heard Mrs. Lewis's shock at the painting. What was hanging in the library wasn't bad. But was it something that could have launched a career? Each summer, she'd convince Neil to take the family down to Houston to the Museum of Fine Arts there. Angus would move listlessly by the canvases, thinking about something else. Amy had tried to focus on the art, but her eye would follow her son or her husband instead. Her newly ex-husband, she reminded herself.

The door creaked. Penelope rushed in toward her. "What a night, Amy. Congratulations."

"I suppose the ship didn't sink, so there's that."

Penelope laughed. "You're in a good mood." She sat down in the armchair where Mrs. Lewis had sat the night before. "We missed you at breakfast. The passengers in the Grand Diamond Suite held forth for a good twenty minutes on the intricacies of wine. You should have seen Richard feigning fascination. He's had to go lie down for a bit for the strain of it. It's a good thing I know a Shiraz from a Syrah."

"Was Mrs. Lewis at breakfast too?"

Penelope sat up. "Oh, you're not in a good mood, and you're distracted, I see. You know, it was the strangest thing. Wellie was there." She laughed again. "What a terrible nickname. Anyway, but Diane wasn't. Wellie said she was too tired from the party. But we did get to see Raymond, the nephew again. He's an odd duck, isn't he?"

"Seasick?"

"Sick with something, I'm afraid. He nearly fainted at the mention of a *pain au chocolat* Richard ordered." Penelope sighed. "Not the first time we've had the company of a queasy guest. It's true what they say, that summer is the best time of year for the trans-Atlantic crossing. Seas are much calmer now than they are in winter. But some people still succumb to the tossing of the waves."

"Poor guy. Nausea's the worst, isn't it? Last night as I was watching him come back from the bathroom the third time, it looked like he had to ask where the library was again. The person he spoke with pointed it out, anyway."

"Which goes to show that Britain might be a sea-faring nation," Penelope quipped, "but not all Brits have sea legs."

Amy looked out into the ocean. Waves pushed up against the morning air. "Even so, he'd spent most of the previous day here, didn't he? They locked the door and chased me out of the library for the entire day while they were hanging the picture and installing the glass case." She looked back at the well stocked shelves around her. "Doesn't matter. I just keep thinking about what I could have done to ease Mrs. Lewis's shock. We'd often have quick run-throughs for authors at the public library. I should have pushed Brent and Beatrice for that too."

"Don't worry, Amy. The lovely thing about the ship is that you stop at a port and, well, all change. No one knows of yesterday's slip-ups. No one has heard yesterday's lecture." Penelope leaned her head against her hand, her elbow nestled into the arm of the velvet chair.

"That must be getting pretty dull for you and Richard. Giving the same talks week after week."

Penelope was quiet for a moment. "It has been three months for us, Amy. We've been given the option to stay on as long as we'd like, but it seems like the adventure has run its course."

"No, not yet," Amy said before she could stop herself. She'd met Penelope and Richard on the second morning of her journey. They'd both taught at some leafy New England liberal arts college before retiring to a life at sea, and they sat next to her at the large round Officer's Table for breakfast. The occupants of the three Grand Diamond suites for the Nordic leg of the journey had chosen to stay up to watch the auroras and took breakfast late in their suites. Aside from a couple who were very much interested in the first officer's experiences in his home country, they were alone at the table. Amy had depended on them since then as her guides to life aboard the ship. "What's life without adventure, though?"

"You're right. We've had our share. We could retire to the English countryside, where Richard grew up, but where's the adventure to that?"

"I would have loved that," Amy said. "Neil never managed to get us anywhere much outside Birmingham, if you don't count going to and from Gatwick Airport."

"I don't." Penelope stood up from the armchair. "You don't think last night was a success, do you?"

"Now it's my turn to say I don't."

"Well, I'll say this. I think we all have this idealized version of ourselves when we were younger packed away in memory. What we were capable of. What we wanted. And when we're confronted with the reality of who we were, then I think we're in for a shock."

Amy looked at the painting of the pretty young woman stepping out of the water. "So you think that really is Mrs. Lewis's famous painting. The one that could have made her career?"

"You don't?"

"I don't know," Amy said. "There's a lot I don't know right now."

"Change is hard."

"Do you know that they don't even have a section on contemporary art in this library? There's every thriller released in the past two years, biographies of every American president, copies of everything Winston Churchill ever even thought about writing, a whole section of what looks like sweet romance novels in Polish translation, but no 21st century art." Amy walked around surveying the books, every one except the Polish translations hardbacks, and many leather bound. Nowhere to be found any of the mass market westerns Neil loved or the weird science fiction Angus gravitated toward. To be fair, there were multiple copies of all of Jane Austen's work.

"You ought to talk to Gemma about that. The art curator. Lovely young woman, even if she's furious about the painting. I spoke with her last night. Richard and I walked her back to her room after the party since that Curtis fellow still had her in his sights."

"There's one passenger I won't mind seeing disembark."

"You and a lot of others, I'm sure." Penelope

knocked against the shining desk. "Let's say this. You meet Richard and me for dinner in the Sapphire Lounge. Our treat. No talk about art or parties or anything. You can find out from your sister this afternoon about how Angus is faring, and we'll trade parenting stories over the best chocolate mousse to have ever sailed any ocean."

"Are you sure? Mine are mostly dull."

"Fair enough," Penelope said. "Why don't you send her a message now, at least. We're, what, six hours or so ahead of Texas? Tell her to voice chat with you as soon as she's awake."

Amy promised to do so, and Penelope went back to check on Richard.

As the morning progressed, more and more passengers filed into the library, most to take a look at the painting hanging by the window. Maybe that hadn't been the best place for it, since it was now back lit by the morning sunlight off the water. At least the weather was clear last night and today. Some passengers browsed the books, opening a few here and there, or took books from the library to their balconies, or to the lounges by the pools. Really, there wasn't much for Amy to do day-to-day. She'd make suggestions about books, show readers where to find books, check out books on the ubiquitous wristbands everyone wore.

They were elegant things, gold-tone bands with the name of the ship in letterpress on the front. Even so, she'd been happy to find out that she'd get a lanyard with an ID badge. That was more like home for her. How could she be homesick here?

Amy walked down to the staff canteen. She opened the staff stairwell with her badge and left the dream world of her library and the passenger area of the ship for the concrete drabness of its inner workings. Inside the steel and laminate canteen, she grabbed a take-away sandwich and fruit, neither of which lived up to its name. She ate while walking through the staff hallway. The blank white walls gave her a moment to ponder the painting and memoir. Voices echoed off the hard walls. She'd have to look more closely at both away from the glow of their surroundings.

Back at her desk, Amy sat down to send a message to Stacey. A voice took her away from her computer. "Is this where all the fashionable young ladies are taking their lunches now?"

Curtis Jenkins stood with his leg pushing into her desk, the linen of his summer trousers bunching up against its shining surface. At some point, he might have been what Stacey had called "paint-can handsome," the kind of guy that looked good on the surface until you saw what a piece of junk the fresh coat was covering up. Even that shine had worn off. Not that Amy was young herself. At forty-five, though, she felt pretty naive about things all the same. But not about unwanted attention from patrons. That she'd had enough of early on to get the routine down pat.

"May I help you find a book?"

"That Texas accent of yours, oh." He closed his eyes and breathed in as if he were smelling something naughty and delicious. "Gets this old city boy worked up every time."

"We don't have much of a selection on the dialects of American English." She rolled her chair away from her desk, away from Curtis. "We do, however, have an assortment of roguish fantasy."

Curtis breathed out audibly. Cigar funk hung in the air between them. "My dear, I'm not looking for reading material today. I'm hoping you can help me with Mrs. Lewis's painting."

"You'll have to speak to Mr. Detweiler regarding the painting. It's in his company's custody until it reaches New York to be shown with the others at auction." She took a long sip of her coffee, stalling. "It's not for sale, though. I'm afraid there's nothing I can do for you."

"That I don't agree with. Look, if you can't get me the painting, you can get me an interview with the painter." He leaned toward her and lowered his voice. "You see, I've purchased a number of Diane Westgrove pieces over the years, and this one, such as it is, will make a nice centerpiece for my collection."

"Wait." Amy fought against the stink of his breath to lean toward him. "You own other works by Mrs. Lewis? I thought she'd given up showing or selling paintings."

Curtis smiled. If this had been one of the patrons at the public library, in to pass the time with her, she would have wriggled her way out by now, particularly if she had a long line at the checkout counter. But her curiosity got her. And Curtis knew it. "Have dinner with me and I'll tell you all about it."

Amy looked over at the painting. Was the young woman in the painting warning her away? "I already have dinner plans, thank you."

"All right. You're in demand, aren't you? What a lucky young man to have you as a companion tonight. Well then, have dinner with me tomorrow, and I'll show you the few Diane Westgrove pieces that ever made it to market."

"Okay. Where?"

"My suite. Eight p.m. I'll order. It's formal, of course."

"Formal."

"Formal." Curtis winked. "See you tomorrow."

Amy checked out a few of the Jane Austen copies to the passengers waiting behind Curtis. After the queue cleared out, she logged on to the web portal for staff to check her email. A yellow warning box popped up. "Be advised: You are nearing your daily data usage limit." Nearing? She'd just logged on for the day. A few emails in her personal box popped up. She scrolled down. A message from Stacey, one from their parents, and another from her best friend and fellow librarian, Tiffany, in Dawville.

Just as she opened Stacey's message, a red box popped up: "You have reached your daily data usage limit. Please log back on tomorrow to resume your internet usage." Amy closed the web portal.

She'd figure this one out later. Back home, she always had figured out the technical problems. And she had done it quickly. But that system was one she knew, front end and back. This system, like so much aboard *The Cullinan Diamond*, was new to her. New and daunting.

\*\*\*\*

At dinner that night in the posh Sapphire Lounge, Penelope and Richard were already seated at a table for four. Beatrice had made special arrangements for the lecturers' dinner preferences in the passenger decks, since any guest who'd seen their lectures would be welcome to ask follow-up questions, she'd reasoned.

Grudgingly, Beatrice allowed Amy the same privilege, but only if she paid for her meals.

Shortly after Amy sat down, a flustered Gemma flopped into the remaining seat next to Amy. "You'll never guess who tried to invite me to his suite," she said as she opened the menu. "Oh, how do you decide with all this on offer?"

"Curtis?" Amy ventured.

Gemma closed her eyes and leaned back. "Let's not talk about him, Amy. Please."

"Good idea," Penelope said. "I'm glad we found you in the lounge."

"Where else would I be?" Gemma's voice echoed against the metal plating behind them, a gold-tone depiction of a garden near the sea. She sat up and blinked. "I'm here to act as the docent for the debut of the most expensive art collection ever to be displayed aboard a cruise ship. The most important. The most socially relevant. A collection I put together, mind you. And it's all been overshadowed by an amateurish rendering of a college-boy's idea of the goddess of love."

"Venus?" Amy ventured again.

"Let's not talk about her, either." Gemma ran her finger down the menu.

"Surely, it's not amateurish," Penelope said. "Maybe youthful?"

Gemma shook her head. "By the time Diane Westgrove painted that piece, she'd studied under some of the best teachers in America for years. Supposedly, she'd taken painting lessons since she was ten. If her professors were talking about her, then, there should have been something there. Unless, well. Unless."

"Unless what?" Penelope laid her menu down on the table and signaled for the waiter to come over. Really, they weren't that much different, were they? The wait staff, Penelope, Richard, Gemma, and Amy herself—they were all there to make sure the passengers aboard ship were well taken care of, weren't they?

"Was it as bad as she feared?"

"Yes, Richard, I'm afraid so."

"So there wasn't much she was giving up, then?" Amy wanted to say more, but the waiter strode up to their tables to take their orders. Amy gulped, thinking about the prices her paycheck would be docked, but how often would she have the chance to eat steak in the middle of the Atlantic again, especially steak this perfectly prepared? As soon as he left, she continued. Who was more invisible, the waitstaff or her? "So it was true that she wasn't all that talented after all, and that all the buzz around her was just because she was already famous?"

"Famous for being famous, yes." Gemma twirled her pendant around her finger. When it flashed again, Amy looked at is more carefully: a blue sapphire surrounded by diamonds. Something classical and conservative that didn't go with Gemma's chartreuse boots or the angry slogan on her t-shirt. "It's a pretty well-known fact that the art school was struggling even then."

Richard raised an eyebrow and chuckled. "Get the daughter of a wealthy family with aristocratic ties off to a promising start on her art career then maybe just maybe get *mater* and *pater* to sort out the school's financial problems? Oh, that's clever."

"Or cynical." Penelope smiled. "Maybe there's more in that book of hers that we can't read."

Penelope and Richard both looked up at Amy at the same time. Amy inhaled and held it.

Gemma shook her head. "All the proof's right there, isn't it? She's just not that talented, and the painting tells us that much."

Amy breathed out. "I'm not supposed to go into the book case where the memoir is displayed. I signed a non-disclosure agreement, anyway, and the book will be available as soon as Mrs. Lewis disembarks."

"What's the harm?"

"The harm is to the art world, Richard," Gemma said. "You have dozens of millionaires, billionaires lined up and waiting to buy heretofore unseen Diane Westgrove Lewis original paintings. And the only reason they want them is to say they have something from this talented artist who had to work in secret her whole life."

"But the proceeds will go to charity," Penelope said.

"As nice as it is, if those same millionaires and billionaires went to their local galleries and just looked for a few moments, they'd find more talent there in a lesser-known artist than in anything Mrs. Lewis created." Drinks arrived. Gemma's Deep Blue Sea Martini seemed to rock back and forth with the ship. Penelope and Richard drank gin and tonics, while Amy stuck with what she'd binged on since arriving on the ship: iced tea with two packets of sugar. "Wouldn't that do something to make the world a better place?"

\*\*\*\*

After dinner, Amy rode the elevator down to her

room, but she didn't get off. She pushed the button for the floor that housed the library. In the dim halls, there were still people up and around. She walked past them. If anyone asked, she could tell them she'd left her sweater in the library, which she had. Amy passed her badge over the locked library door. Inside, the only light came from the moon through the windows and a small light flashing through the stacks.

Chapter Three

Amy turned on the overhead lights. Which, she realized afterward, just made her more visible to whoever was behind the oak bookcase with the leather-bound copies of the presidential biographies. She groaned at her own lack of sophistication at dealing with this. Her stomach tightened with the idea of calling security now. But what was done badly was done. Not for the first time on this leg of the trip. Wasn't that all part of the adventure, though? "Okay, you know I'm in here. Who's there?"

A squeak came from the case near the floor. Amy heard the flashlight click off then fall on the plush carpeting. Whoever it was either wasn't prepared for anyone else to enter or was probably not intent on hurting her. She took her chance and looked around the case. It wasn't like she hadn't done this before, that last sweep before closing time when she'd found seniors asleep in the armchairs or high school students making out where they thought no one could see them. That was their mistake. Someone could always see them.

In this case, what Amy found was a young woman on the floor surrounded by a half dozen Polish romances in mass market paperback. "Please," she said. "I'm not supposed to be in here."

"How did you get in here?"

"Someone left the door unlocked. Cleaning staff. It

happens from time to time." She held up a book. "The librarian before you, he would order books in Polish for us. There's not a lot to do in our downtime below deck, especially when you don't get much internet."

"And you thought you'd try tonight?"

"We take turns. One of us brings back what we'd all read, get more, that sort of thing. We'd hoped the previous librarian had told you about us." The young woman smiled. "He was so nice, he would buy us what he could."

If only Beatrice knew this about her perfect previous librarian. "No, he didn't, I'm sorry to say." Amy waved. "I'm Amy, the new librarian here. The cruise line hasn't given me a book budget yet, but, look, if y'all want more books, I'm happy to help."

"We can't check out books," she said. "I'm Zuzanna. I'm in housekeeping. My friends are also in housekeeping or they're valets, the ones who've been here longest. Some of us read Polish and some of us read Spanish or Portuguese. The library is stocked with Spanish books because of all the passengers. But we can't check out any of them. Books would be good."

"Yes, books would be good." Amy looked at the painting. If it were amateurish, how would she know? Maybe with access to her database, she could tell. Maybe with access to the internet, she could arrange for more books to be brought aboard in New York. "Wait, you said some of your friends are valets?"

"Yes," Zuzanna said. She was clutching a book on which a couple held hands and looked off toward a farm, complete with a farmhouse and a red barn. On such solid, unmovable land.

"Are any of your friends the valets for the

Westgroves? Diane Westgrove Lewis and her sister Wellie?"

Zuzanna let out a curt laugh. "That's Lucia."

"Not a good experience working with them?"

"Not at all."

"Do you think Lucia might talk to me? About the Westgrove sisters?"

Zuzanna was quiet for a moment. She looked down at the stack of books beside her. "You won't tell anyone I was here?"

Amy inhaled sharply. The smell of old books and leather, yes, but also something else—was it paint? "Look, you get Lucia to talk to me about the Westgroves, and I'll make sure there are more books on ship for below deck. Deal?"

"And if Lucia won't talk?"

"Just ask her," Amy said. "That's all I'm asking for. I'm not telling anyone regardless. This will be our secret." She looked around the stacks. "I'm a librarian. I'm the last person aboard this ship who'd stop anyone who wants to read books. So, deal?"

"Deal."

****

Amy had helped Zuzanna carry down a stack of a dozen novels, mostly in Polish and Spanish, to her room in the floor just below Amy's own. The upper staff deck was reserved for the entertainment and technical staff. Amy's room wasn't spacious, but she and her roommate Roisin had an ample stretch of gold carpeting between their beds, separate closets, and a good view out their large window. A writing desk and vanity finished off their suite, and they had cozy chairs in gold velvet that covered so much of the ship's public spaces. Between the chairs was a tufted gold storage ottoman, in which Roisin kept books of music. The cruise line reused the furniture from the guest suites in Amy's staff floor after *The Cullinan Diamond's* last style refresh. The furniture may have been slightly worn, but the chairs were still beautifully detailed with silk piping, and the vanity boasted crystal knobs that caught the light from the window.

Just about everyone on the top staff deck had roommates, except Beatrice, of course. And she'd arranged for Penelope and Richard to have a balcony suite among the passengers so that those who attended the lectures felt that the professors were more available to them. Amy hadn't been down to the lower staff deck—she hadn't needed to be—so the shock of the barrenness around her made her shudder. She nearly dropped the books she carried.

The cold that penetrated the ship on the upper floors seemed to blast straight through the hallways here. They were dimly lit, not in the warm light of the passenger areas, but in a stark industrial way, making the cold level seem even more inhospitable. "It's like winter down here, isn't it?"

"You get used to it," Zuzanna said. "At least they have a pool and a bar for us. Here's my room. I share with Miri, Agata, and Ania." She knocked a pattern with her foot. The pattern was answered and a young woman wrapped in a fleece opened the door. "Success."

"You brought company?"

"Amy's the new librarian," Zuzanna said. She handed the books to her roommate. "Amy, this is Miri."

Miri thanked Amy for the books. Two other young women, also wrapped in fleeces, waved from around a tablet. Amy said goodnight and excused herself.

It was getting late, and she tried not to wake her roommate, Roisin, who'd need to be up early for the first shift as ship's pianist for the day. Quietly, Amy went into the room. She got ready for bed and lay down for a while, but her mind was racing.

She looked out the window, which sat just above the water line. A deck above where she'd just been. She did have the key to the glass case, didn't she? Too much to think about. If she lay here any longer, she'd keep herself up all night with questions. Which was probably a factor in her divorce.

Amy slipped into the jeans and t-shirt she kept in her nightstand drawer, just in case they'd needed to evacuate the ship in the middle of the night. She grabbed her badge, her sweater, and the bag Angus had packed for her, which he'd said he'd made for her if she got homesick.

"Shouldn't I make one for you?" she'd offered. "You'll be off to college soon." Angus had already packed up his room, separating out what he'd take to his dorm at A&M and what he'd leave in the old barn. Stacey had said they could use it for storage while Amy was at sea. Amy had expected there to be more for her to store, but after Neil had taken what he needed for his new apartment much closer to Houston, and after she had sold, donated, and gave away what she didn't need or couldn't stand to hold onto, there hadn't been much left. Angus and Amy had spent an afternoon barely talking to each other as they loaded boxes into Rick's pickup. She didn't know whether it was sadness or just not knowing what to say to her son. Maybe it had been both.

\*\*\*\*

"I'll be less than an hour from home." He shoved a box all the way on the pickup bed until it bumped the liner under the back windshield. When had he gotten so big? "Or less than an hour from Dawville, anyway. Aunt Stacey said I can come back anytime."

"You be sure to come back when you need to," Amy said.

Angus shrugged. "I packed you a few things in a bag. Aunt Stacey has it."

"That's sweet of you, Angus."

"You'll probably get bored," he said. "I know how much you like listening to the BBC World Service overnight on KAMU." The station was the NPR affiliate housed at Texas A&M, where Angus would be soon, and it put a good signal into Dawville. Amy had stayed up listening on nights when she and Angus waited up for lunar eclipses, or, more often, when Neil stayed out late for work. "And in Birmingham, too, when you visited Gran and Aunt Kate. There's a shortwave radio with a decent antenna. Maybe it will work on the ship. Probably not. Too much interference from electrical devices. If it does work, you can listen to the BBC. I left you some information about how to hear them. Anyway, there's a bunch of other stuff in there too, like a photo book of all of us and an armadillo I 3D printed in the library's lab. And some survival rations and anti-nausea medicine."

"How did you get to be so practical?"

Angus shrugged again.

Rick laughed. "Got it from whatever makes Stacey so practical. Guess it just skipped you."

"Right," Amy said.

"You were never practical, Amy. Even in high school you were all ruffles and long skirts like you were out of some fairy tale, Stacey used to say." Rick laughed again. "Didn't believe it at first when Stacey said y'all were sisters."

"She said that, did she, that I looked like I was trying to be some fairy tale damsel?" Amy lifted another box into the truck bed. Books. She couldn't bear to lose all her books, but at the same time, she worried about what would happen to them in the old barn between the spring rains and the summer heat. And that wasn't counting anything that happened to blow up off the Gulf in the fall. "That's great coming from Princess Cowgirl herself."

Angus snorted. "You called Aunt Stacey that?"

"Not to her face," Amy said. "She wore these pink jeans. And she had her name on her belt. And a fancy belt buckle. And the pink lipstick and big hair. I don't think she was one to talk." She watched her son's face melt into a smirk. "These big gold barrettes with chains. She curled her hair every morning, and she must have used up a can of hairspray every two weeks. All that for school."

"Glory days, Mom?"

"Well, for me, that was college. And grad school." Which was true. Amy had been a romantic English major without much direction until one of her professors suggested she apply for a master's program in library science. "I hope college is good for you, too." She didn't finish her thought aloud. She didn't want to think about how she and Neil had drifted apart over the years, barely talking, until Neil asked for a separation and then a divorce. He wanted space. And if there wasn't enough space in the vast expanse of land here in Central Texas, then she didn't know where he'd ever find enough. But that was all in the past now.

"I think it will be."

**\*\*\*\***

Amy looked in the bag Angus gave her. She had tried not to look inside it before, since she wanted to wait until she really needed it. Which might have been after the disastrous party, or now that she had finally realized she should have been the one driving Angus to his dorm and helping him unload his boxes from Rick's pickup.

One thing, she told herself. Just one thing. She felt the box that must have been the anti-nausea medicine and moved her fingers past that.

There it was, the cool metal of the radio she and Neil had bought Angus for his twelfth birthday. A bit worn and replaced by more sophisticated models later on. But still in working order. By this time, she was on a deck that looked out over the west side of the ship. It was still busy with couples taking in the night air, but quieter than it was during the day.

She unwound the wire antenna as Angus had shown her how to do and clipped it to a low rail that jutted out above her. Amy turned on the radio. It cracked and hissed into the night, like the sound of the water through the speaker. She'd forgotten how to tune it, how to find what she was looking for. Wasn't that always the way. Amy blinked the heaviness from her eyes, took the antenna down and put the radio back in the bag. Tomorrow, when she had internet access again, she'd try to find the radio station that Angus said was out there.

\*\*\*\*

Beatrice stood at her waypoint with her clipboard in hand, the dim room in which she barked out orders for the day. It was hard for Amy to imagine that all the elegance of the ship's entertainment came from a room that was, essentially, a long, drab space with a few hard metal chairs and a desk repurposed from some other part of the ship. But it worked.

Standing by the elegant desk that looked as out of place as the well turned-out entertainment staff in the gray light, Beatrice chatted with the members of the midday string quartet. They were all dressed in their tuxedos, cases in hand, laughing. Something felt off about her days here, Amy realized, and she felt that more acutely here in the windowless room. The musicians waved their goodbyes to Beatrice. They filed out the door, the violist angling himself through the doorway behind the cellist. Amy could have sworn that they were about to go out into the evening, that they were on their way to play for the formal dinner guests at Le Bœuf du Duc, the most elite of the dining experiences aboard *The Cullinan Diamond*.

"Amy, did you even hear what I was asking you?" Beatrice pursed her almost plum lips and narrowed her darkly lined eyes. Evening makeup? "I'm sending you a tray. Report to the library, please."

"No, I'll be fine," Amy said. She smoothed out her burgundy blazer while trying to ignore the fact that the left leg of her tights had somehow twisted as she'd put them on this morning. The bunched heel pressed down on the top of her foot. She'd worn her brown velvet oxfords with the low heels, and the tongue of the right shoe had begun to migrate toward her arch. "I didn't sleep well last night."

"Do tell me something new, Amy," Beatrice said. "Perhaps I ought to send some of the musicians to converse with the Diamond-class guests at breakfast instead? That lovely violist, especially. I think he'd absolutely charm them."

"Then who'd play his shift?" Amy said without thinking.

Beatrice scowled. "Impertinence is not something we tolerate on *The Cullinan Diamond*, Ms. Morrison." She looked down at her clipboard. "The previous librarian was a stickler for manners, you know. And rules."

Amy nodded. She wanted to nod off, but that would have to wait for later that night.

The library was dark and, except for the dozen novels missing from a tucked-away lower shelf, undisturbed. Soon, passengers would take books out, but mostly, they would come to enjoy the light from the long windows and the ambiance as they read books they might not have otherwise chosen on land.

Amy sat down at her desk. She started up her laptop, which popped up a message: "You have exceeded your internet allowance for the day." Already? Was it time to admit defeat?

Amy sighed. Her twenty years as the de facto IT department for the Dawville Public Library should have given her more to go on here. Her decades of solving Neil's laptop problems left her with no inklings. She had no idea where to begin even troubleshooting her technical issues in a system this big and complex.

She pulled out the laminated contact sheet and ran her finger down the departments until she found what she was looking for: Information Technology. There were a few names of lower-down staff members, whom she skipped over.

There he was: Kevin Park, Head of Information Technology for *The Cullinan Diamond*. She couldn't email him, not without access to the internet. She could call him, however. Amy picked up the phone. She imagined this Mr. Park as yet another one of the Brits aboard the ship, there to make things sound as though they were running smoothly. Which was her job too, even if she was a Brit by marriage only. And a former one at that. Amy pressed the first two digits of his extension when she heard the knock at her door.

"Just a moment," she called out. Amy set the phone down and slid the contact sheet back into her desk drawer. She rushed to the door. Who would be here this early?

"Your tray?"

"Oh, thank you." Amy went to take the tray from the young woman who wasn't wearing a badge. Is that why she had to knock? "I can get it."

"Please, allow me," the woman said with a smiling edge to her voice. "It's my pleasure."

"Okay then." Amy opened the door and the woman crossed over to the desk. She set the tray down and removed the cover from the hot plate. Steam rose from the two biscuits with sausage gravy, scrambled eggs, bacon perfectly crisped. Next to this was a plate of strawberries sliced up into a bouquet. Coffee, good strong coffee, too, from the smell of it, with a tiny pitcher of cream. Orange juice that looked solidly orange. "Is this for me?"

"Don't tell Beatrice," the woman said. She set the

cover down again. "It's the breakfast we often take to our American elite guests. A taste of home on a long journey."

"It feels like the last couple days have been a long journey, yes," Amy admitted.

"Zuzanna said you wanted a word with me?"

"About the books?"

"About a certain set of sisters in the Grand Diamond Suite," Lucia said.

"Oh, yes." Lack of sleep joined with hunger to push Amy toward the biscuits and coffee, but she fought back. "The Westgrove sisters."

Lucia folded her arms. "There's not much I can say. We're not at liberty to say much about the guests we work with."

"How about this. Did you see the case that Raymond Entwhistle—that's Diane Westgrove Lewis's nephew—took from their suite the day before last? He was taking it here to have the painting put into place." Amy put her hands around the coffee mug. The warmth of it began to wake her from her grogginess.

"As I said, I can't say much, but I didn't see him in the suite that day." She picked at the cuff of her navy jacket. Through the professional set of her calm expression, Amy could just make out the hint of a scowl. "But I doubt either of the Ms. Westgroves would have seen him either. Particularly Mrs. Lewis."

"Why's that?"

"Look, I'm not at liberty to say anything to anyone else other than to ensure our guests have a wonderful time aboard ship." Lucia picked at her cuff again. In the dim light, Amy just made out a trace of something luminous on the edge of her jacket sleeve. Gravy, or maybe the color to paint a silver gown? "And anyway, I need to get going. I need to bring them their breakfasts shortly."

"I know you're not at liberty and all, but if you see anything strange, will you let me know?"

"I need to go. Thank you for the books."

"Thank you for breakfast."

Lucia slipped through the door and down the hallway. She looked as though there was more she wanted to say, but couldn't. Amy was sure of that.

The woman in the painting seemed to watch her eat. The biscuits had just the right crust and lightness to soak up the sausage gravy and still hold their structure. This was, as Lucia said, a taste of home. Amy's home. The eggs were the right balance of fluffy and creamy, and the bacon held its crispness until she'd taken the last bite of it. A *moreish* breakfast indeed, a word she'd picked up from Neil's family, even if they were moreish in a small town Texas sort of way. The strawberries were fresh and sweet, and the coffee brewed so that it was strong but not bitter. The orange juice was almost ambrosia. Amy looked down at the plate with some disappointment. Angus had been right in that she'd be homesick. She'd cleaned the plate, hadn't she? Amy looked around the rim of the plate and on the tray. Not a drip of gravy on it. Lucia probably wouldn't have dished up the food herself. Amy put the gray paint—if it was paint—on her sleeve away for later.

No one was in the library, and the hallway to it was empty as well. She wanted to run her hands over the silk on the walls, to feel the smoothness of the sapphire tiles. The library wasn't near enough for the musicians' live performances to be audible, but the well-hidden speakers played some string quartet piece that Amy was sure she had heard before but which she couldn't name. Why did everything have to be so close and yet so much out of her reach?

The ship held a number of gemstone and precious metal themed events, dances, and parties, culminating in the Gold and White Ball for the elite passengers and their guests later in the week. This morning was the Citrine Festival, and just about everyone on board wanted to be there. Those who were awake, that is.

Amy slid open the desk drawer to retrieve the contact sheet again and felt the cold metal of the key that opened the lock on the glass case. The internet could wait. And she could figure out the technical problem when the caffeine kicked in fully.

Amy slipped over to the case and opened it. She took the book from its velvet stand and lay it in her left hand. The book fell open. Amy turned to see it better in the sunlight. The table of contents began on the right side page, and on the left was the backside of the title page. In between them lay the remaining paper roots of multiple pages that had been torn out. Roughly, from the looks of the jagged edges.

The door shushed over the carpet behind her. Quickly, she closed the book and locked it back into the glass case. "Good morning," she said a bit too loudly to the passengers who'd come in, seeking a bit of quiet from all the festivities going on around the decks above and below them. They nodded, took out a couple volumes on naval history, and sat in the chairs that had held Ms. Westgrove and Mrs. Lewis two nights before.

Just as she returned to her place behind the heavy

librarian's desk, Brent Detweiler, scowling, walked into the library and directly over to her.

Chapter Four

"Good morning, Mr. Detweiler. Nice to see you here." Amy smiled, the couldn't-tell-it-from-a-genuine-smile sort of smile that she'd learned to put on over the years. Sometimes for patrons. But more often, for Neil. "How may I help you?" One of the passengers sitting by Mrs. Lewis's painting looked up with a pained expression. "Sorry," she said to the passenger, who went back to his book.

"Sorry is a good place to start."

"I'm sorry?"

"Yes," Brent said. "You should be." He lowered his voice. "Sorry about how the launch party went. My shareholders will be very sorry."

"But it was all very exciting, wasn't it? The glamour, the people, Venus just over the horizon, all that?"

"There's excitement, and then there's *excitement*, if you know what I mean."

Amy didn't, but she nodded anyway. "The painting is captivating, anyway. I've had a number of passengers commenting on how fascinating the woman emerging from the ocean is." That number, to be fair, was exactly one, an older gentleman who'd wandered into the library after a particularly happy hour. His wife apologized. "Anyway, it was hardly a launch party in the traditional sense, was it? There weren't any copies of the book on sale. And none to sign. So how could it be a failure?"

"Aside from the old bat's confusion about the painting, you mean."

Amy leaned toward him. This was her chance to press him on something that had bothered her. Brent Detweiler was exactly the sort of person she'd had no experience dealing with at the library. He was worldly in an aggressive sort of way. But when would she see Brent Detweiler again? And when would he want to talk with her again? The caffeine took over, and she wished both that she'd had a second cup and a breath mint. "Can I ask you an uncomfortable question, Mr. Detweiler?"

Brent leaned back. "I have the feeling you're quite good at asking uncomfortable questions," he said, his voice echoing off the metal ceiling panels above them. The passenger who'd looked up at Amy before stifled a laugh into a cough. His wife looked up from her book long enough to glare at him.

"Did you see the painting yourself before this trip?" she asked quietly.

"What do you mean?"

"I mean, you took on a multi-million dollar project in Mrs. Lewis's memoir. I doubt she or her sister or her nephew paid a dime for their trans-Atlantic journey, for instance. But you've invested an awful lot of money in this project, haven't you? I mean—"

He leaned toward her again, cutting her off. "If you think I'd pay a nickel to haul Raymond Entwhistle across a puddle, you'd be wrong. If I'd known Di was planning to bring him along, I would have—" He crossed his arms over himself.

"You'd what?"

"I would have been far more careful about this whole thing. He was the one in charge of hanging the picture, you know. At Di's request."

"I do know that, Mr. Detweiler."

"Good. I didn't find out until it was too late. And look, who hung the picture isn't important."

"It's not?"

"What's important here is that someone needs to talk to Diane Westgrove Lewis. Jog her memory a bit. Make her remember that the painting hanging up over there, the one she droned on and on about in the memoir, is the one that almost made her career as an artist." He pointed behind him with his thumb, as if he didn't want the couple next to the painting to notice him. How could they not? They looked at each other, then the wife pointed up at the painting. The husband made a sort of lewd face at the picture of the young woman in her clinging silver gown. The wife shook her head and glowered back down into her book. "The picture she painted so long ago that maybe she just forgot what it looked like."

Amy exhaled sharply. "Look, we've both been in the book business long enough to know that there are some writers who couldn't tell you what they wrote five days ago, much less five decades ago. And that some of them reread their old work and it's like someone else wrote it."

"My point exactly."

"But that's not exactly a comfortable place to be in, is it Mr. Detweiler?"

"It doesn't matter whether or not Di is comfortable. You're right in that she and her sister have cost my publishing company quite a lot in the deal. And the whole pile is going straight to Di's charities. We *have to* make that back. But how can we when Di goes into hiding after the shock of seeing her painting for the first time in fifty years?"

Amy resisted correcting him. Sixty years. "You think she's in hiding?"

"Have you seen her? I haven't. Your friends, the professors, they haven't. I even talked to that creepy ghostwriter, and she hasn't seen her either, which is an odd thing, indeed."

"Why would she see Mrs. Lewis? They're finished with their project together."

Brent Detweiler laughed. The couple both looked up at them again. He shook his head and whispered. "You'd think they were finished. You heard about the stolen necklace, didn't you? Nearly fired her, but Di herself went to bat for the wretched creature. Said she'd given the family heirloom to her after Wellie saw it on her and raised a stink. Di called her the only one of the many, many writers I sent her that she could actually work with. Dozens. Di and the creepy one finished the book together, so maybe I shouldn't complain."

"This is fascinating, Mr. Detweiler, but why are you telling me all this?"

He placed both hands on her desk. When had she begun to think of it as her desk? He had well-groomed nails, a wedding ring on his left hand and a class ring on his right. A black techie watch on his left wrist and a thick silver chain on his right. What was she looking for? "I'm telling you all this, Ms. Morrison, because *you* will go find Diane Westgrove Lewis and convince her that *that* painting is the real one. You'll do that for me to make up for the flop of a party you hosted, and you'll do it for this cruise line, my publishing company, and most of all, for Di."

"What makes you think I can do that?"

"You and all your uncomfortable questions." Using his ringed hands, he pushed himself up. Standing over her, he seemed imposing almost, even if some of his details didn't add up. "I wouldn't have come to you if I didn't think you had something to lose too."

"Look," Amy started. She did have something to lose, didn't she? Or had she already lost it? "I don't think I can just barge into her room, if, as you say, she's in hiding."

"Then find someone to lure her out for you. I don't care how you do it, just convince her that that painting is the one she did in art school."

"But what if I'm not sure that is her painting?" As soon as she said it, Amy regretted airing her doubts. "I'm not sure that it is a fake, either. I'm just putting that question out there. Uncomfortably."

"Quite. Just tell me you'll do it."

"Or?"

"You're aware that the parent company of this cruise line and my publishing company are, shall we say, in talks?"

"About?"

Brent Detweiler rolled his eyes. Amy's stomach dropped farther than it had gone on the night of the gala for the painting. "In talks. About them. Buying my company. It's time for me to go another direction."

"Oh, I see." She saw it, her one chance at adventure, crashing just as she'd begun it. "I can't promise anything, but I'll try."

"Good." He walked toward the library doors. Then paused there. "And tell those professor friends of yours that they're missing out on the chance of a lifetime if they don't go with my company on a travel memoir. Giving lectures around the world on a luxury cruise liner, who wouldn't want to read about that?"

"Especially when the publishers also owned a cruise line?" Amy asked. Uncomfortably, of course.

"I'd read it," the husband sitting by the painting chimed in.

"See?" Brent laughed. "One reader already."

He left, the door closing noisily behind him. But it wasn't noisy enough to drown out the wife's guffaw. "You wouldn't read that. You don't read anything that doesn't have a spy or a spaceship in it."

The husband shrugged.

\*\*\*\*

Two things bothered Amy about her conversation with Brent Detweiler.

First, the book had to be just as bad as everyone hinted at. Or if not bad, then boring. A boring book was worse than a bad book, because sometimes, a person read a bad book to the end just to see how bad it was in the end. But a boring book? A person would just put that down. And that person would tell everyone else how dull it is to warn them off. Not worth the time or money, right? But if Brent convinced Diane that the picture *was* the one she painted, and she could then claim that the sight of it shocked even her after all these years. What a lurid story that might make. And a lurid story would sell books, wouldn't it? Which is just what he needed to happen.

The second thing that bothered Amy was that he'd

called her Ms. Morrison. Which, technically, she still could call herself, even if she wasn't Mrs. Neil Morrison anymore. She could have changed her name back to Wullschlager, what it had been for the first twenty-five years of her life. But she'd been glad to switch from her hard-to-pronounce, hard-to-spell German last name to one that was easy on both accounts.

And, besides, she'd lose her tie to Angus who'd been slipping away from her for ages now. The physical distance hurt. He was all grown up, at least legally, but he was still her little boy, the piece of her heart that glowed warmest and brightest inside her. Awkward, shy, a bit pudgy, but deeply confident in himself and his abilities. She credited Stacey and Rick for much of that. They'd treated him as one of their own, pushing him when Amy hadn't. Angus tumbled with his lean, capable, tough cousins, and that did him some good too. And now he was away from her for good, out of the nest she'd sold after Neil left.

Her laptop dinged. An email from Angus had slipped through her internet access problem. It was mid-morning London time, which she was still on. Six hours earlier for him. But the email was timestamped from the night before. Angus was a night owl, partly his own nature, but also from his hobbies, which were amateur astronomy and shortwave radio.

Amy had encouraged him to study astronomy in college, but he'd resisted. He had wanted to pursue something practical, he'd said. Electrical engineering, which was nothing but practical. Neil had teased him about fixing the ever-shorting electrical lines in their house. Angus had waited until his father had left for work and wondered aloud whether he was really that daft as to think that an electrical engineer was the same thing as an electrician. "You know your dad," Amy had said in an attempt to defend her husband. "He's always trying to make a joke, isn't he? To sound more backwater than he is?" She wasn't sure that he was, and anyway, now, after Neil left, she wouldn't have tried so hard to defend him. Angus was what was important. Angus was a product of her marriage to Neil, but a long time ago, her son had transcended it. Amy saw that now, and she wished she'd seen it sooner.

Amy clicked on the message. The subject line left her with nothing: "Saw this and thought of you." The message opened on her screen. Where the image should have been was a box that indicated a broken image, or one that couldn't be downloaded, anyway. Apparently, data was not cheap here, and they had to provide quite a bit of it to the paying customers. She right-clicked on the image and selected "download," but nothing downloaded. The warning message popped up again, the one that indicated that she'd used up all her data for the day. Was someone sending her something that she didn't know about?

Her email client indicated that there was another message in her queue, one that couldn't be downloaded yet. Maybe tomorrow, Amy thought, and she clicked away from her personal email account.

The couple under the picture left their books on their chairs and nodded a goodbye. Others filed in and out again, some staying to read, others merely browsing what was on offer here. If she'd had control of this much of a budget back home, how differently she would have stocked her tiny community library. True, she hadn't worked at any major library, no big city main library or even a suburban branch. Not even a small university library.

But she had made the leap here. And she intended to stay, no matter what Brent Detweiler threatened her with.

All alone again in the library, Amy looked over at the painting. Why wouldn't Brent Detweiler have demanded that Mrs. Lewis show him the painting she wrote about—or the ghostwriter wrote about, anyway, before he made it the focus of the book's launch? Well, who hadn't heard about Diane Westgrove Lewis? Maybe Angus and his friends, but there was much he and they knew that she'd never even have an idea about.

The chime on her desk clock sounded. Noon. The library would close briefly for her lunch break. She put the painting, the torn book, and the publisher out of her thoughts for a bit.

Amy locked the laptop in her desk drawer then locked the door to the library. In the hallway, she ran her hand across the tops of the golden velvet armchairs, some in couples, some in quartets around small round tables. When she had first met Neil, she couldn't have known that her life wouldn't be the one he seemed to offer, could she? He was older, more established, a regional representative for a wine distributor who worked with the wine producers in Central Texas. As he moved up in his field, Amy had stayed in much the same place. It worked exactly as he'd planned, hadn't it?

When she'd asked him if she could join him for some evening reception for one winery or another, he'd always said the same thing: "But Amy, darling, you don't like wine." Which was true. Amy didn't like wine, but that was beside the point, wasn't it? She'd enjoyed a hard cider now and again, and she'd indulged in a margarita on rare evenings out with friends, but that didn't matter either. What mattered was that Amy was smart and sophisticated enough to spend the evening with her then husband's clients even if her taste in drinks didn't overlap with theirs. She was, after all, a librarian. She knew how to research and prepare herself for evenings like those Neil spent with wine critics, restaurateurs, sommeliers, and dedicated oenophiles who'd landed in the middle of Texas to taste the best vintages the Lone Star State had to offer.

What she figured out instead was that she was part of a life he didn't want the wine critics, restaurateurs, sommeliers, and dedicated oenophiles to know about. To them, Neil was a Brit, a sophisticated guide through some backwater that just happened to be a good place to grow grapes and to mash and ferment them into wine. To himself, though, he wasn't above the place. He wanted to be a part of it. Marrying Amy and moving to Dawville had been one part of that. Neil's passion for barbecue, for country music, for cowboy gear was genuine, and maybe his passion for her had been too, once upon a time. The more she pushed on Neil to include her in his work life, the more the boundaries between the Neil of his career and the Neil who just wanted to be a small-town Joe wavered.

So the end hadn't surprise her, really. One last time, she had asked to go along to an event, which was being held at a nearby vineyard. Amy already knew the owners, and Angus had gone to school with one of their kids. In fact, they'd asked if she'd be there, when they'd checked out a few novels at the library about a week before. "Look," Amy had pleaded. "It would be rude if I didn't go."

Neil had shaken his head. "But, Amy, darling, you don't like wine."

"But, Neil," she had said, looking at him flatly. "You don't like wine, either."

Something had cracked between the worlds he wanted to keep apart. A week later, Neil left her a rambling voice message, telling her that he'd found a place near Houston, and that it didn't matter to him one way or another what she wanted to do with the house.

****

Amy had walked the long interior corridors to get to the passenger decks. She wanted to be surrounded by the golden walls, the golden carpets, the soft warmth of the light from brown glass sconces. It was the longer way to get to where she was going, but, she reasoned, sometimes it's better to take the more interesting path to wherever one was going to end up anyway.

Penelope and Richard's suite did not disappoint Amy. The furniture in the sitting area echoed the design in her own, but it was sleeker, more modern. More elegant. And the orange striped feline who approached Amy sauntered over as if he owned the entirety of it.

The cat bumped his head against Amy's leg over and over, marking her shin, or at least the fabric of her tights that covered it, as his very own and to ward off any other feline competitors for her affection. Not that there were any others aboard the ship.

"Oh, Carrington," Penelope cooed at him. "You don't need to pester Amy for her lunch. See? I ordered

54

you a tuna fish on white bread right here." The rather hefty orange and white tabby shifted from Amy's leg to follow the plate Penelope had set on the bathroom floor for him. The sound of his smacking echoed off the tiles.

"I think the old boy is quite fond of Amy, sandwich or no," Richard said. They were seated at a small table beside the balcony's sliding glass door. A light rain had begun to fall. "Besides, he's glad of a body here that isn't ours. Or Edyta. We're tipping her quite well to keep our little secret."

"Don't you think that would make a charming story?" Amy said between bites of the chicken salad sandwich she was trying not to eat too quickly. Keeping her mouth full, she figured, would keep her from saying too much before she figured out whether there was anything to say. And besides, the chicken salad was almost as good as the version her grandma used to make when she'd host their church's ladies' committee each June. "You know, if you ever wrote about your time on the ship after you've settled back on land?"

"Ah, someone has put you up to convincing us to write our travel memoirs." Richard straightened his shirt where a tie would have been had he been wearing one. "The retired professors aboard the world's most expensive luxury cruise liner, *The Cullinan Diamond*, giving groundbreaking lectures on astronomy and history to the rapt audiences of affluent passengers." He and Penelope laughed.

"I wish they were groundbreaking," Penelope said, wiping a crumb from her cheek. "But no, they're pretty standard university fare."

"But quite good, mind you," Richard added. "Especially that historian chap. I've heard he's quite a dashing figure up at the lectern. He even keeps it to himself about the ship's rather unfortunate name."

"Not nearly as fascinating as the astronomer and her talks about ancient monuments lining up with the first days of summer and winter." As if on cue, Carrington waddled over and leaped up into his mistress's lap. "She agrees with the historian chap about the ship's name, by the way."

"Well, it's settled, then. The cat prefers astronomy, doesn't he?" Amy poked at a slice of honeydew that was far too big for her to eat as it was. "Why is he called Carrington?"

"He sort of came crashing into our lives about five years ago, while we were still at the university," Penelope said. "Everyone in my department thought I'd named him after Richard Carrington, who'd studied sunspots. But no, I named him after the 1859 geomagnetic event that was named after Carrington."

"She means the big solar storm that took out the telegraph lines and caused auroras way down south," Richard added. Amy couldn't quite place his accent. British of course, a contrast to Penelope's almost Canadian accent.

"I know that one," Amy said. "Benefits of being a librarian."

"Speaking of the library," Penelope began. She cut her honeydew into thin slices and gracefully slipped one into her mouth. "Hmm, have you gotten anywhere with the painting?"

"The painting?"

Richard nodded. "Pen and I have a suspicion that someone isn't telling all, if you know what we mean."

"I think I do," Amy said. "Strangely enough, Brent

Detweiler just paid me a visit this morning. And he wanted me to convince Diane Westgrove Lewis that the painting was the one she did at school."

"Aha! I was right about Mr. Detweiler's attempts to convince us to write the travel memoir." Richard gave Penelope a knowing look.

"And I was right about the painting not being an original Diane Westgrove," Penelope added.

"You don't think she painted that one?" Amy said with a mouth half-full of melon.

"Well, if Mr. Detweiler asked you to convince Mrs. Lewis, then something must be off." Penelope said.

The sound of the rain against the balcony window shook Amy from her plate and the conversation. Carrington let out a long sigh. "I suppose that it wouldn't matter to Brent Detweiler whether the painting was original or not, as long as it sold copies of her book."

Penelope scratched the cat behind his ear. "That's the painting they have, so that's the one they'll need to use to market the book, won't they?"

"But why replace the original?"

"What if the original can't be found?"

Amy set her fork down on her plate. "Okay, you're asking me to solve a puzzle. Worse, you're asking a librarian for information. You're trying to get me to look into the possibility of art fraud, aren't you?"

Richard smiled. "We're curious too. We've never solved a mystery like this before, not without archives and star charts, anyway. It's more adventure for us. And it's your library after all."

"It's the ship's library." Amy looked around and found all too easily what she wanted: paper and a pen.

The cruise line spared no expense on the creamy white cotton writing paper with its logo in navy blue at the top. And the pens, matching blue ink that just caressed the page. She grabbed a few sheets of writing paper and the pen and sat down. "Let's start at the beginning," she said. "Who would be interested in either discrediting Diane Westgrove Lewis or hiding the original painting?"

"Brent Detweiler, you've already mentioned," Penelope said. The cat curled up in her lap. Carrington's purrs were loud enough to be heard even over the rain.

"I think we ought to cast a wider net than that." Amy wrote down a number one and his name.

Richard pointed a finger toward the window. "That nephew, Raymond Entwhistle. He was supposed to be a chancy character, if the chatter at the party was anywhere near true." Amy listed him beneath Brent Detweiler.

"Oh," Amy said. A sudden thought disturbed her. Two of them, really.

"You don't think he's a suspect?" Richard asked.

"Raymond, yes, definitely. He's the one who was with the staff who hung up the painting in the library. I wasn't even allowed in there. What if the original had been damaged?" Amy tried to push the other two suspects out of her mind.

"Or," Penelope said, "What if he has it hidden somewhere, perhaps to get into Mrs. Lewis's will? Rumors, as your said, Richard, were making their way around the party."

"Quite possible," Amy said. She turned to look at the gray rain pounding against the window.

Richard put his hand on hers. "Amy, dear, you look frightened. Is it the weather? We can close the curtains."

Amy laughed. "This? Oh, the rain out there is nothing compared to some of the storms we'd get in springtime. It's not that."

Richard gave her hand a squeeze then let it go.

"Something's disturbed you, Amy." Penelope smoothed out the cat's short fur. "Do tell."

Amy looked back at the list of suspects. "All right, I should say the two others I'm thinking about. Lucia, one of the housekeeping staff, brought me breakfast this morning after Beatrice shooed me away from the restaurant for looking too exhausted to mingle with the elites. I don't know how she knew, but she surmised that I'm a little homesick, and she brought me biscuits and gravy of all things. Anyway, Lucia told me, well, not much, but she said that the Westgrove sisters were not exactly treating her well. And—" She paused.

"So Lucia is perceptive," Penelope concluded. "And?"

Would Lucia have risked her job just to get back at her haughty clients? "And there was gray paint on her jacket sleeve. Or gray something."

"Gray something?" Penelope asked. "That's not much to go on."

"No, it isn't."

Richard took the paper and pen from Amy and wrote down Lucia. "You said two others. Who else?"

Amy shook her head. "It's impossible."

Penelope gasped softly. Carrington stirred and put his head back down. "You're not thinking Gemma, are you?"

"Well," Amy started. "Well, it's just that she had collected all this art that was making its debut on this journey, and who shows up to steal her thunder but Diane Westgrove Lewis. It's possible that she could have painted the replacement picture. And it's more likely that she could have done so than anyone else we've mentioned, right?"

"Not right," Richard said. "She told Pen and me that while her boyfriend Keene is a light artist, she herself doesn't have the gift for making art."

"Having the gift and having just enough skill are two different things, Richard," Penelope said. "And he's not just her boyfriend. You've seen that necklace? She holds it to her heart when she talks about him." She smiled and lifted her coffee cup.

Richard, shaking his head, added her to the list. "One more," he said. "Curtis Jenkins. Art collector."

"I'm going to see his collection of early Diane Westgrove paintings this evening, in fact," Amy admitted.

"Ah, so she is curious," Richard said to Penelope.

"Of course, she is."

"All right then," Amy said. "Tonight, I'll snoop. As much as I can. But there's one other thing I need to figure out if I'm going to snoop properly. Which I need your help with."

"Anything, my dear." Carrington peeked his head over the table. Nap taken care of, he nosed at the crumbs left on Penelope's plate.

"How do I get to Mrs. Lewis herself? I don't think I can just knock on her door, can I?"

"No," Penelope said. "How about if you snoop around the art collector's suite tonight, then we'll figure out some way for you to get to Mrs. Lewis. Sound like a good plan to you, Amy?"

Amy looked at her watch. The rain came down in gray sheets, which meant more people would be inside. Many would be watching the rain in the piano lounge, while others would take in a lecture or tour the luxury shops that lined the ship's commerce deck. But, Amy knew from past storms, others still would come to the library.

She hurried back. Of course, she knew the great pleasure of reading while the winds and rains knocked at the window. All the better still with a cup of tea. Her library would be full this afternoon.

But who of those aboard would come by to see the painting?

Chapter Five

Amy passed a busy afternoon in the library, doing what she loved most: connecting readers with books. She never went back to the glass case to confirm what she'd seen, that someone had torn out what looked to be the acknowledgments section of Diane Westgrove Lewis's memoir. Few people would have known what was in there, or few people were supposed to know what they contained. Brent, certainly, but if she asked him, he'd know she'd snooped in the case. The ghostwriter, too, though she might well run off and tell Brent what Amy had done. There was Mrs. Lewis, of course, but Amy didn't want to unsettle her any more than she'd already been unsettled by the painting.

Day slipped into night as swiftly as the ship slipped forward, on to New York City, leaving London behind it. Amy had spent so much of her day trying not to think about the torn pages that she had forgotten her dinner with Curtis. She trudged back to her room. Roisin was already in their room, in flannel pajamas, stretched out beneath the blankets on her bed and nearly asleep. Amy tried not to disturb her, but she woke up. "It's okay, you can turn the light on."

"Thanks. Just need the closet light." Amy opened her closet. Three long dresses which ranged from sky blue to royal blue to cobalt blue hung at the end of all her librarian suits. The cobalt blue one she'd worn on the night of Mrs. Lewis's reception. The royal blue one clung far too much for her to be comfortable in. She pulled the sky blue one out. It looked vaguely Edwardian with its stand-up collar, long billowing sleeves, and full skirt.

It looked like a dress she would wear when she definitely did not want to signal interest in her dinner companion.

Her daytime makeup would have to do. She'd take a darker lipstick and the pair of earrings that Stacey and their mother helped her pick out online before she left for London.

As directed by her (now former) sister-in-law, Kate, who worked for the Regal Diamond cruise line as an associate vice president of entertainment in their corporate office, Amy had photographed all her outfits and sent Kate a copy so that Amy could shop in Texas before she left. Kate had sent a quick email back telling her that her daytime outfits were fine, all the "professional librarian" jacket and skirt suits Amy had bought after she'd been contacted by *The Cullinan Diamond's* entertainment director about landing the job. But, Kate added, Amy had needed at least three evening-appropriate dresses, preferably floor-length gowns along with a wrap and shoes that would match them all.

****

She could have shopped the bridal stores in nearby Madisonville or Huntsville a bit farther away, but the thought of slogging through formals alongside all those young and happy brides made her even more miserable than she'd been thinking about her divorce. Instead, she wrangled Stacey and her daughter, Addie, who wanted to go dress shopping in the mall, into coming along on the hour's drive there.

Stacey parked herself on the bench in front of the trifold mirror outside the dressing room. She just shrugged when Amy came out in each candidate dress. Addie made supportive noises at the first round until she wandered over to the juniors section to find more interesting things than the stuffy dresses her aunt was trying on and scowling at

"What do you think?" Amy held out her arms, and the beaded cap sleeves draped over them heavily.

Stacey squinted at the dress. "It's decorative? I don't know. I'm either in flannel over a t-shirt swatting mosquitoes or scratching at my pantyhose in church. Last time I wore a long pretty dress like that, well, never mind." The princess cowboy get-up had long since been tossed aside once Stacey had actually begun to work on a farm.

"You were going to say you last wore a dress like this at my wedding." Amy stared at herself in the mirror. Maybe she should have put her hair up or done her makeup before they'd left, but she hadn't had the energy to between sorting out the house and getting Angus everything he needed for college. A sallow face stared back at her. When had her jawline gone so soft and saggy? Her pecan shell brown hair, as had Neil liked to call it, caught in the beads at the neckline.

"Nicest bridesmaid dress I ever wore," Stacey said. "Though it wasn't as heavy as that thing looks. You're slouching in it."

"You're supposed to be helping me."

"You *are* slouching, Amy," Stacey said. "Which might be the ten pounds of beads or it might be something else." Her sigh echoed off the trifold mirror. "I'm not good at this. Why didn't you bring Tiffany?"

"Because she had to work today." Amy twirled in the gown. Or she tried to. The beads on the bottom of the dress kept the skirt from going much of anywhere. It was heavy and cumbersome. She went back into the dressing room, the dress clacking around her, and crossed it off her list. "The library is still open on the weekends, and someone has to be there. It was Tiffany's weekend."

****

Tiffany—could she get access to the art database and search for Diane Westgrove's early work?

"That one," Roisin said from her bed. "That one will work."

"Tiffany?" Amy said aloud, catching herself mid-word.

"Hmm, I wouldn't call it Tiffany blue, but it's a nice blue. Wear that one," she directed.

"This one it is," Amy said.

"Where are you off to?" Roisin's voice was slow and heavy with sleep.

Amy took the sky blue dress off the hanger. "Meeting with a passenger for dinner. Purely professional."

"A formal dinner?"

"His idea," Amy said. A bad one, she had a feeling, but it was too late to turn back now if she wanted to figure out the puzzle of *Venus Rising*.

She changed in the semi-darkness of the bathroom, hoping that the lipstick she put on didn't stray too far from the lines of her lips, and charged on through the hallway to see for herself what Curtis Jenkins had in his collection.

The butler met Amy at the door of Curtis's suite. "Ms. Morrison? Mr. Jenkins is waiting on the balcony for you."

Beyond the butler, the second most luxurious suite in the ship—after the one in which the Westgrove sisters were staying—boasted a number of fixtures and features that were modeled on the Crown Jewels of the UK and those owned and worn by British royalty. Such nods toward royal riches were found throughout the ocean liner, and many were pointed out to her by Beatrice during her first days aboard ship. She could still hear Beatrice's prim voice telling her that even the wallpaper in this suite was patterned in gold and white after the Girls of Great Britain and Ireland Tiara, a piece in gold and diamonds that had graced Queen Elizabeth II on a number of occasions.

Amy nodded and stepped through. She was glad now that she'd remembered her wrap, the navy blue one that added a nice layer over the not-quite-Tiffany-blue of her undulating dress. The suite was chilly with the evening wind off the water.

Something else, though, was cold about the suite. Everything about the rooms was exactly as it had been when she toured them not long after she'd been hired on. Beautiful, with a crystal chandelier above the sitting area, the sapphire pillows aligned just so on the long cream sofa, the waves in the drapes perfectly straight. As if no one had moved anything. As if no one had sat down. The doors to the bedrooms were closed, though, and the hum of cheering filled the silences between the notes of the string quartet music that came from the balcony.

"A vision in aquamarine," Curtis said as the butler led Amy through the doors out to the table.

The afternoon rain had cleared up; low clouds still hung in the sky, illuminated by moonlight. A trio of candles flickered on the table where champagne and appetizers were already laid out. From the speaker system, state-of-the-art and apparently waterproof, a string quartet trilled just above the crash of the waves against the side of the ship. Somewhere in the sky, Venus had already begun to sink toward the sea, a last message to them in the darkness of the evening before she sunk into mysteries of her own.

The whole thing might be ever so slightly romantic if Amy hadn't been caught up thinking about Neil living near the mall where she bought the dress. And if Curtis hadn't been, well, Curtis. Older, balding, a bit portly, but there was a patina of charm over that. Amy tried to see in the flickering light what it was that made her think the latter, that there was something to be found in the slightly pasty, slightly sagging face, but she couldn't. "Champagne for my lovely companion?"

"I don't drink," she said. Tonight anyway. And never champagne, even though she'd tried it several times at Neil's insistence. She had to keep her head about her to find out what she could about Diane Westgrove's early works, and to work out what Curtis Jenkins's motivation to forge her most famous unseen work might be. So, no alcohol tonight. Tomorrow, who knew? "I appreciate the offer, though."

A breeze wrapped around the ship and grasped at her wrap. Amy was glad she'd left her hair up, secure from the wind. She thought she smelled something acrid in it, exhaust perhaps, along with the salt from the ocean water. Mostly, though, she smelled the canapés arranged before her. Figs stuffed with goat cheese, herbed tartlets, and small toasts with what might have been *pâté*, though Amy had no real idea what that would look like.

"Just as well, Ms. Morrison. Better vintages to be had on shore." He raised his glass toward her and drank. "You'll have a canapé, then."

"Saving my appetite for the main course, I'm afraid." Though the canapés looked tempting, the dress, which had been just the tiniest bit loose on her in the fitting room, now hugged her a bit too tightly around the waist. Breakfast, when she could manage to convince Beatrice that she was up to entertaining the elite passengers, was proving to be her downfall. A beautifully flaky, crispy, scrumptious downfall. Fortunately, a wide belt tied in the back of her dress covered this up.

The butler approached quietly from behind her and offered her another beverage.

"Sparkling water would be lovely, thank you." She watched the water rushing into her glass, the tiny bubbles catching the light. At least her eyes were adapting to the dimness. Not totally dark out here, at least, not with the lights from the ship, but close. "It's dried up since this morning, hasn't it?"

"Why do you talk about the weather when there's art to discuss?" Curtis gestured to the butler. "But first, dinner."

"The culinary arts," Amy said. "Of course." Which was half the reason that she'd said yes to his invitation. The food aboard this ship more than justified the exorbitant fares customers paid to journey on it. And food eaten under the light of the moon over the ocean, well, it was all a bit dizzying. Part of an adventure.

Amy told herself to forget about the dress and the lights and why Neil had never treated her to something even a quarter as romantic as this after the first few dizzying months of dating. It wasn't the expense she was after. It was the attention to detail. And Curtis Jenkins paid attention to details, didn't he? Details in painting as much as in business and anything else he was after. "And then the visual arts."

"No, no, no. The culinary arts are just as concerned with the visual elements as anything else. I've ordered us a tasting menu, one that plays on Chef Fournier's particularly playful and yet contemplative eye. So I disagree with you there, Ms. Morrison." Another belch of exhaust blew across Amy. She pulled her wrap more tightly and shuddered.

"Amy, please." From the entryway, the sounds of voices, clattering trays, and underneath it, the sound of an audience, like at a football game. Had she not noticed that before, that the cheering must have been part of some game? A staff member wheeled a tray to the balcony, which the butler smoothly ushered over the threshold.

"There's something you're not comfortable with about me calling you, Ms. Morrison?"

"Well, when you're so recently divorced," she began. Amy knew that she'd need a line out to pull him into her confidence. "It's a matter of identity, I suppose."

"One of the many benefits of being a man, I'll say."

"Are you married, Mr. Jenkins?"

"Curtis, please. If you're Amy, then it's only right." The butler laid out two plates in front of them. Curtis was right about the visual presentation. Whirls and lattices and pirouettes of vegetables and sauces caught her attention.

She looked up at Curtis, though, trying not to miss anything, any gesture he might make. He picked up his fork and pointed it at her first, then the plate. "You're right." He held up his left hand, on which there was a gold ring. "I am happily married. This time. Wife number three is the keeper. Lily, my darling Lily."

"She's not with you on this voyage?" Amy speared an asparagus that seemed to be angled backward with either pleasure or anxiety. At least the thing didn't have eyes to tell her which it was. "Seems like a romantic thing to miss."

"Her work keeps her busy this time of year," he said. "And, of course, she trusts me."

"That's nice," Amy said. "Of course."

"You don't believe me. No one does," he said. He looked out over the ocean and laughed. The clouds were clearing, and the sound of the water mixed with the cheering and the string quartet reminded her of sitting with Angus at night while he tried to pull in some weak and distant station on one of his radios. Something sought but never clearly identified. "You sensed there wasn't anything to worry about once you came into my suite. You're right there. I have a bit of a reputation, one I've cultivated. You have to, you know, to keep up appearances in the C-Suite. There's a reason Mr. Hughes and his fine staff are clattering about in my living room." He was quiet for a moment, then bit into an heirloom tomato. "My dear, there are layers of flavor in this fruit that most people would never sense."

"There are layers, and there are *layers*, aren't there?"

"Astute observation, Amy."

After the consommé and the main course of three slight pieces of roasted meat, Curtis requested his tablet from Mr. Hughes. The butler set the tablet, something new and expensive, on the table between them. "As promised, the early art of Diane Westgrove."

Amy cocked her head. The wind succeeded in grabbing one errant strand of hair from her chignon and tugged at it. "You said the pieces were in your suite, Mr. Jenkins. You could have shown me your tablet in the library just as easily as brought me here for dinner." As she pushed the hair back into place, Amy saw a motion in the darkness that seemed to come from the side of the ship. There were other balconies that were on the same level as this one. Maybe other parties in other suites.

"I wanted company," he said and shrugged. "And there's my reputation as a womanizer. You're attractive in a commonplace way and within a reasonable age for me to show some interest. Now, let's look at the art."

Amy saw piece after piece of early art, which Diane Westgrove must have painted at college or slightly before. The paintings, or what she could see of them in the tiny pixelated renderings on screen, were somewhat akin to the one in the library, but not quite. "These are before *Venus Rising*?"

"Yes," Curtis said. "And better, I think. Don't you?" Amy reached for the tablet, but Curtis shook his head and turned it off.

"I'm no gallery goer," Amy said with a forced

smile, "but I do think there's something to these paintings. Are they all self-portraits? Some of the women look almost like Diane Westgrove, but not quite."

"Most of them are. Some are of Wellie, when she was a dancer." Curtis laughed again. "I hear tell that Diane was somewhat jealous of her darling little sister, the prettier of the two with that lithe dancer's body." Curtis made some guttural sound as if he were still enjoying the chef's offerings.

"I've seen pictures of her when she was younger, and Diane Westgrove was beautiful herself. Why would she be jealous when she wasn't by any means plain?"

Curtis shrugged again. "I'm no judge of women's affairs."

"Dad, I need your tablet." A young man, perhaps the same age as Angus, padded out onto the balcony in a t-shirt and athletic shorts, his feet in poolside slides. If there was any familial resemblance, it was hard for Amy to see in the darkness. They did share the same petulant undertone in their voices, so there was that.

"Cole, manners, young man."

"Father, if it pleases you, might I have use of your tablet for an hour?"

"Ms. Morrison, may I present my son, Cole. Product of marriage number two, if you're wondering. He's on a gap year, sailing the high seas with his father while he 'finds himself,' as he says." Curtis handed over the tablet. "Cole, meet the ship's librarian, Ms. Morrison. I'm certain that if you find yourself in need of entertainment, she might be able to find you something more educational to do with your time that doesn't involve betting on sports."

"*Mrs*. Morrison? Dad, it's bad enough you're cheating on Lily, but with a married woman? Ugh." Cole pushed the tablet's screen with frenetic fingertips. "I'm going to need another thousand, by the way. Two if you want me to keep quiet about whatever this is."

"Ms.," Amy tried to correct him, though she really wanted to correct any notion that she was remotely interested in having an affair with Curtis Jenkins.

Curtis nodded and the boy—was he still a boy?—stomped back through the doorway, nearly crashing into what Amy had hoped was the dessert cart. She was exhausted. "Gap year? I thought most eighteen-year-olds would be clamoring to get out of their parents' company. Mine was."

"We had some academic difficulties, we'll call them. And an ethics violation. He's making up credits aboard ship for a while, then, I do so fervently hope, he will be off to college." He signaled to Mr. Hughes, who brought over the dessert and coffee. "Chef does not disappoint."

Twelve tiny bites of pastries lay in front of them: chocolate tarts, dots of meringue, raspberries floating in what looked like glass, something lemony dotted with lavender flowers. Amy wanted to grab them all, but wary as she was, her dress as tight as it was, she shook her head and declined coffee. Tomorrow would be an early morning, especially if she'd hope to catch Penelope and Richard to tell them about what she'd found out tonight.

"Really, nothing?" Another motion caught Amy's eye. She could just barely make it out, something large and flat flying out to sea. Another party, too much alcohol, and inevitably, this was what they'd do with their pizza boxes? Suddenly, she felt sick for being in this decadent space.

"Would Cole enjoy them?" She asked. Angus certainly would, even more so than she would. She thought of him, a farm kid raised on fresh vegetables and free-range eggs thanks to Stacey and Rick, slogging through his dorm cafeteria meals. "It would be awful if they went to waste."

"To Cole they'll go. To be honest, I'm not usually such a glutton myself." Curtis waved a refill to his champagne glass. He'd finished off most of the bottle on his own. "But how can I resist?" To Amy's horror, Curtis stroked her wrist where the dress's lace sleeve ended. "Tell me, how can I resist?"

"Thank you for dinner and for letting me see your art collection, Mr. Jenkins." She stood as quickly as she could, weighed down with fabric and anxiety. "You'll have to tell me sometime how you managed to procure the early works. Good night."

She thanked Mr. Hughes and waved an appreciation to the two staff members clearing up the coffee service and the untouched desserts.

"Wait, I'm sorry," Curtis called out to her. He said something else, but she didn't want to stop and hear it. "Sorry," he shouted again.

We both are, Amy thought.

She'd misread people before. She'd come away with so little now, when she should have asked to see the paintings on the ship. She'd failed before. Why did she think this would be any different?

Chapter Six

The screech of Amy's alarm hit her head hard the next morning. She'd come in late the night before, but even without touching the champagne Curtis downed, she still felt groggy. Not a hangover feeling, really, but that she hadn't slept well, if at all. Her mind had done that before, worrying about Angus at school or Neil who had wanted her to not to worry about his travel for work. But there it was. Fortunately, her roommate Roisin had gone already and was off playing piano for the morning crowds at the gilded cafes. Unfortunately, Amy herself was late for breakfast, if she could get anything. Even after eating as little as she had eaten last night, she felt empty, but not hungry.

She dressed quickly and put her hair up in her usual librarian bun at the nape of her neck. She put on a spare round of makeup, just mascara and the bold lip color from last night that was still out on her nightstand, and she hoped no one would notice the dark circles beneath her eyes.

Penelope met her at the library door. Amy had come rushing down the hallway, and she nearly knocked into her friend. "I come bearing breakfast," Penelope said. "Since you weren't there, and Beatrice said she hadn't seen you yet. I told her you'd had quite a night."

"What did you tell her about last night?" She

imagined the horrified look on Beatrice's face coupled with her lecture on how the previous librarian would have behaved. Amy fumbled with her keys to open the heavy wooden entry doors. Morning light from the other side of the ship still made its way into the library somehow. She turned on the soft overhead lights hoping they'd mitigate the brightness that maybe only she saw. "Did you tell her I was with, you know?"

"I said that you were entertaining one of the ship's more esteemed guests with your literary knowledge." Penelope floated in after her and set the bag on the desk. "Orange juice, coffee, cream, and a lovely egg tart with spinach and *Gruyère*. And one of Chef's brown sugar cinnamon muffins. There's orange and grapefruit marmalade for that in there too."

"Who all are you feeding?" Amy grabbed for the bag and pulled out the egg tart. Even before reaching her desk, she bit into the tart. Crisp crust followed by the warmth of the egg and cheese—this one bite was more filling than all that she had eaten or thought she had eaten last night. She took another bite.

"You, apparently. Sit. Are you still having internet issues?"

Amy powered up her laptop with one hand while the other still clung to the egg tart. "I must be. Says here I have twenty-four emails waiting for download. But I can't get anything to download. And I can't search the web to figure out what's going on."

"You should see the IT department for that, dear. It's what they're here for. Get it? Get IT?"

Amy groaned. "Is that one of Richard's jokes?" It might well have been one Angus would tell.

"I don't tell it as well as he does, I'm afraid,"

Penelope said. She laid out the rest of Amy's breakfast for her. "Of course, I'm here for all the gossip. What do you have for me?"

Between bites of egg tart then brown sugar cinnamon muffin on which she'd smeared more marmalade than she'd intended, Amy told Penelope what she'd found out last night, little of it as there was.

"Fascinating," Penelope said.

"What is?" Amy gulped down her orange juice. She told herself to at least savor the coffee.

"Here we were thinking of Diane Westgrove as a self-portraitist, but you said she'd painted her sister, too."

"She's family," Amy said. "And their faces are so alike, I'd imagine that made things easier for Diane, didn't it?"

"I'm no painter, but it is interesting."

"It doesn't give us anything about the puzzle at hand, though, does it?"

"I'm sure you're right."

"Look, Penelope, if there's anything else you can look up about Curtis, I'd think it would be useful. Married three times, at least one kid. I met him. Cole. If you're not having internet issues, can you look him up for me?" Even in the softness of the indirect morning light, the edges of the library stood out to her, all corners and shadows from the tall bookcases and the heavy drapes lining the window. Wasn't that where they needed to look for clues? In all the corners and shadows?

"I'd be glad to," Penelope said. "But for now, I have preparations to make for my afternoon lecture. Seems there's no end to the fascination with

Stonehenge, is there?"

"I'd think not, judging by how often our book on the place was checked out back home."

"Oh, there's an idea. Bring the lad a book."

Amy took a sip of her coffee. "He's not the naval history kind, I don't think."

"Maybe not, but if there's a cache of Polish romances here, I'm sure you can find something along those lines to entertain a bored young man." Penelope waved a quick goodbye as a group of older women filed through the doors. Amy almost didn't recognize the last among them, who was near the other women but not with them. Wellie Westgrove strode past them and up to the librarian's desk. Amy quickly brushed the crumbs off her blouse and inhaled deeply. Just the woman she wanted to see, in real life and in a portrait.

"Ms. Westgrove, what an honor to have you here." Amy stood up to walk around the desk, but Wellie Westgrove held up a hand to stop her. It was a strange and affecting motion, which seemed slower than it must have been. She had been a dancer, hadn't she, back when Diane was at art school honing her craft. "What can I do for you?"

"See me to the chair, first. Then we'll talk books." Only then did Amy notice the cane that had been supporting the older woman's stride. How did she walk with the cane while looking like she didn't? Another dancer's trick?

"Absolutely. Which chair? There's a wonderful reading nook beside the naval histories over here. With fresh roses this morning." Amy gestured to a pair of plush armchairs behind a row of books. Between them, in an inset shelf, stood a vase that contained two dozen pink roses, that medium pink between shocking and blush. Beatrice had told her yesterday that the ship's florist would set up a fresh bouquet of Princess Margaret roses before the library opened. Another thing that happened here without her notice. What had they replaced with the roses?

Again, a hand cut her off. Wellie turned in the direction of the chair she wanted to sit in, the chair Diane had sat in the night of the party. "Better light by the window. Come along, then."

The younger Westgrove sister took Amy's arm, and they walked together to the window. Amy placed her in the chair, and she took the one Wellie had been in the night of the party. The painting hung between them. "Shall I bring you a book? Are you looking for anything in particular?"

Wellie nodded. "Something on dance in and of the 1960s."

"I don't think we have anything on that subject," Amy said. "But I can look it up. Any particular kind of dance?"

"The dance," Wellie said with some exasperation. "Contemporary dance of the 1960s."

"I'll look that up," Amy said with her best customer service smile. Fortunately, she could look that up, since accessing the ship's library catalog didn't require web access. If she'd had internet access, then maybe she could look up Wellie Westgrove in the 1960s, but that would have to wait. If she was as famous in the dance world as Amy was gathering she'd been, then there must be a trove of information online about her. Amy found a few books on ballet and a series of guides to popular social dances, but nothing about modern dance.

"Well?"

"Nothing in the library, I'm afraid. Is there anything else I could look up for you? We have a wonderful selection of histories from the 1960s, particularly political and naval histories." Amy paused. Wellie's eyes closed as if she were falling asleep. "Ms. Westgrove?"

"Everything is politics, isn't it?" She breathed in deeply, then let it out, her hands over her stomach. "I'm sure you'll have some wretched novel by some doubly wretched old man, something that's a must read for the season? Something by an old literary stalwart who thinks he knows the world from his smoke-filled den in better ways than you could from living in it. Hmm, I could tell you a story or two about some of those wretched old men when they were young and ambitious but still just as full of themselves as they are now." Wellie laughed. Amy ached to know some of these first-hand stories, even if they were dubious. Half of what people thought they knew about famous writers turned out to be if not outright false then at least unverifiable. But here was a source who knew firsthand. "I could, but I don't think I will. Not yet."

"Of course," Amy said. "It's a nice morning just to sit in here with the light coming in after yesterday's storm."

Wellie waved a hand. "What does the weather matter? Or astronomical alignments? None of it means anything. You look for symbols, but there's nothing in them. Nothing behind the images."

"You're right."

"Of course, I'm right." Wellie opened her eyes

again and looked at Amy. Scrutinized her, it seemed. "You have spinach in your teeth. You ought to take care of that before someone more important comes in."

"Thank you, Ms. Westgrove. I had no idea."

"You'd be astonished at what people have no idea about," Wellie said. She shifted her leg—was it the bad one?—and leaned toward Amy. "Take, for instance, what my sister has no idea about regarding her purported nephew."

"Mr. Entwhistle?"

"The same," she said. The older woman's eyes opened wider, and Amy noticed for the first time the brilliant blue that must have taken men aback, especially if she'd had the same auburn hair as Diane had in the painting that hung between them. "You're one to appreciate a bit of research, aren't you, Ms. Morrison? As a librarian?"

"It's one of the things I love best about my job, to be frank."

"Then you ought to look up the disaster of a gallery he opened with my sister's money last year," Wellie said. "A non-profit, of course, but you can only lose so much capital before the whole thing goes under. Without, let's say, looking suspicious."

"You think he took the money?"

"I'll let you do the research, Ms. Morrison."

"I'll add that to my list of things to look up when I can."

"You have a list?"

"I do," Amy said. "Quite a long one, in fact. Though it would be simpler if my internet access weren't blocked."

"That's a shame," Wellie said. "I don't know

anything about that. It is easier to ask people directly, you know. If they're available."

"You're right, and they are."

Wellie smiled. "Am I on your list?"

"Well, you could answer me this," Amy said. "You go by Ms. Westgrove. That seems a bit, well, progressive for a woman of your generation, isn't it?"

"I am, yes. We both were, my sister and I, and we still are, in our way. Diane, you know, was engaged by the time she'd begun her last year at art school. She sold a few pieces as Diane Westgrove, and once you've made a name for yourself, you're stuck with it, I'd say. The world knew her as Diane Lewis, but she wanted to reclaim some of what she'd been as Diane Westgrove. And me, well, I married and divorced so often that it seemed hardly worth the effort to go back and forth. So Diane did as her little sister did, for once."

"For once? She paved the way, then?"

"Oh, not for me." Wellie looked at the painting between them. "Diane did her thing, and I did mine. Neither of us ended up with the career we were meant for, though, so maybe it didn't matter in the long run. She'd like to give the illusion that she was successful, and she was. But as a philanthropist, not as a painter. Not as the artist she'd hoped to be."

"That must have been a disappointment, then?"

"For her, yes," Wellie said. "By the time she'd begun art school after taking a gap year, I'd already become an apprentice to the dance troupe. And the year she painted this, well, I'd danced for royalty twice, hadn't I?"

"That must have been exciting."

"It was, it was. Diane never achieved anything

close to that, did she?"

"But still, you're sisters, and that's something, isn't it?"

"Diane wanted me along on this trip. Said she needed me now since I wasn't there years ago. Not that we've ever been close, not after we married and went our separate ways. It was a different life she wanted. And she got it." Wellie closed her eyes. Amy examined the woman, how frail she looked and how strong she must have been under that frailness. There was her style, of course. The steel gray bob that flattered the angles of her face. The white linen pants and the sage green blouse. Ballet neck, of course. And the gems, too. A cocktail ring and a pearl and sapphire brooch, both in an art deco style.

"Did you get the life you wanted?"

Wellie opened her eyes and laughed. Light caught the pearls in her brooch. "I'm still living it, dear. While Diane is dwelling on her past, her glory days and might-have-beens, I'm the one focused on the here and now. Do you happen to know who my dinner partner was last night? Or the night before?" Wellie's blue eyes widened. "If that Curtis Jenkins fellow happens to ask you if you're interested in his collection of my sister's early paintings, turn that man down. And whatever you do, don't entangle yourself with that horrid son of his either. Like father like son, let me tell you."

"I've been tasked with finding educational materials for the younger Jenkins, I'm afraid."

"You must have a book on etiquette in here somewhere. Or, I'll say it more plainly. Manners, you must have a book on manners."

"I'll see what I can find, Ms. Westgrove."

"Ah, do call me Wellie, please. Only my staff and the media call me Ms. Westgrove."

"Wellie it is, then. Thank you."

"I'll take the liberty of calling you, Amy."

"Of course," Amy said. "May I ask another question?"

"Certainly. I am, as they say, an open book."

"I don't think I've ever met another Wellie. It's certainly posh, isn't it?"

"Posh or an old rain boot, take your pick." Wellie laughed that deep laugh of her whole being, as if her laughter too was a dance she undertook with her entire body. "Diane was still quite young when I was born. She couldn't say Jacqueline, you see, so she called me Wellie. And she was quite taken with me, being fond of baby dolls as she was. Wellie this, Wellie that. The nickname stuck, and here it is, I'm Wellie Westgrove. How do you like that?"

"Would you prefer to go by Jacqueline?"

"Where's the uniqueness in that? If I were just another debutante, just another wealthy wife and mother, just another has-been crone, then Jacqueline would suit me fine. But I'm none of those things, never was. It may have been ridiculous in its way, but it's what my sister gave me, and there it is." Some sadness crossed her face for a moment, but then it passed. She raised her beautifully drawn-in eyebrows.

"Speaking of your sister, would it be possible for me to come see her? I do want to make sure all is well with her after the night of the party, and the difficulties it resulted in."

Wellie's face tightened. She turned away from Amy, toward the window, toward the roiling ocean just outside. "No, you cannot."

"Oh, but I do just want to see her, just for a moment. I could bring her something to read, though I don't think we have much on art that would be of interest to her." Amy pushed back the urge to get between Wellie and the window, to see the expression on the older woman's face. "Just for a few minutes."

"Diane, I'm afraid, is unwell. She has been for some time. I told you she wanted me on this voyage, and I think it's because her memory is failing her. You saw her the other night. She didn't remember the painting that was the apex of her artistic training." Wellie lowered her voice. "Her children weren't able to come, and her husband died five years ago. So it's just me."

"And Raymond Entwhistle."

"And him." Wellie turned back toward Amy. "But the difference, my dear, is that I don't want anything from my sister, do I? I'm here out of a sense of duty, to ensure her well-being. I'm afraid her scene the other night proves my worries about her dementia."

"May I have some flowers sent to her, then? Something to thank her for being aboard this ship to begin with? And for having her party in the ship's library?" Amy bit her lip.

"Your library, you mean? My dear, you did look as though you were in your element as hostess of the event, even if it didn't turn out as expected."

"I'm honored. This was my first event of this magnitude," Amy admitted. "I wanted to work at a larger library, but I was happy in my role at my small-town place. And I got to live near my parents and my sister and her family."

"Older or younger?"

"She's older than I am by two years."

"Ah, the right distance for sibling rivalry."

Amy shook her head. "No, it wasn't like that for us. We were so, I don't know, different when we were younger. She was sensible where I was a dreamer. I suppose we're still different like that. There was never any competition, just a sense of bewilderment at how we both came from the same parents." Amy wondered for a moment whether Angus had called his Aunt Stacey, especially after she hadn't replied to his email that hadn't fully downloaded.

"Come now," Wellie said. "All sisters compete on some level."

"Well, we'd both had the same teachers, of course," Amy said. "Once, I overheard our history teacher telling the math teacher that I was just like Stacey, except it was like someone had stuck me in a book, like a pressed flower, and had forgotten about me."

"It was that bad?"

"No," Amy laughed. "Not at all. Stacey has always had her head on her shoulders. Married her high school sweetheart. They went off to college together, took over his parents' farm when they retired, and they had four kids. She always knew she wanted to work in agriculture. She got lucky, married a farmer's son who wanted to stay on the farm more than anything. It's all worked out for her just as she's planned. Which is nice, I think." Though Amy and Stacey had never discussed it, Amy watched her sister tick off all the items on her wish list, one she'd started when she must have been eleven or twelve. Amy, on the other hand, didn't, not out of lack of trying. It was that Amy never had a list. There were too many possibilities, too many dreams to write down, to confine to a list.

"How perfect for her," Wellie said. "And how perfectly dull. Look at you, Amy. You're here on this ship, traveling the world, talking to famous people. Wearing gemstones and evening gowns. When was the last time your sister even put on a dress?"

"Sundays, she does." Amy felt a bit defensive, but she stopped herself from pointing out that Stacey's transformation from farmer to church-goer always impressed her. The up-swept hair, the pearl earrings, the pumps that matched her Sunday handbag.

"Well, that's different. That's not glamour. You, my dear, are capable of glamour. Don't forget that."

"I won't, Wellie. Thank you."

"Of course." Wellie looked up at the slightly graying man who'd just entered the library. He moved in much the same was Wellie did, consciously taking up space between them. "Ah, my lunch date is here. Amy Morrison, have you met Rafael Alvez? He teaches the ballroom dance classes aboard ship. How I wish I could waltz."

"Ah, well, I'll leave you to your lunch date, then."

Wellie laughed again. "Amy, you think too much of me. I'm meeting Rafael and his lovely wife Milena to talk about our shared art. They specialize in Argentine tango. You ought to see them perform."

"I will, soon, I hope."

Rafael extended a hand toward her and shook it warmly. "Lovely to meet you. Wellie?" He helped the older woman to her feet. She took his offered arm and they started toward the door.

"Wellie, if I can't see your sister or send her a book, I'll have roses sent this afternoon. What color does she prefer?"

Wellie turned back to look at her. Amy couldn't read the expression in the low light of the entryway, but she could hear the sharp note in her voice. "Not pink. Yellow carnations, perhaps."

Amy made a mental note to call and ask the florist what could be arranged. In the meantime, she went straight to the biographies section and pulled the one on a son who managed to overcome the shadow his father had cast over his life. She'd have to hurry, but if she skipped lunch, she could get the book to Curtis Jenkins's suite and swing by the office of Kevin Park, head of IT, so she could finally get access to the internet to download and reply to her message from Angus and to look up Raymond Entwhistle's failed gallery and Wellie Westgrove's failed career while she was at it.

Going to IT for help meant she'd been unsuccessful at solving one puzzle, of course, but maybe admitting her defeat now would help her solve the larger puzzle at hand.

Amy called Lionel, the florist, but he was out. As she hung up the phone, the clock chimed noon. She stood, keys in one hand, book for Cole in the other, ready to dash out to the elevator banks up to Curtis Jenkins's suite, which, conveniently, neighbored that of the Westgrove sisters. And there was the matter of catching Kevin Park, unless he too was on lunch. She'd take that chance.

"Hello?" A wildly over-lipsticked woman in a shorts suit bright enough to match her makeup stuck her head in the doorway. "Would you be a dear and let me and my friends just grab a few books to read while our ingrate children party through the lunch hour?"

Her friend held a compact mirror in front of her face in one hand and swept her hair back with the other. "Patsy, that's an awful thing to say."

"Well, it's true, Belinda." The woman's two friends, equally garishly dressed, pushed into the doorway. "We need something to take our minds off our terrible children."

Amy smiled her best customer service smile, but she didn't put down the keys or the book. "What can I get you?"

"Oh, I don't know. Anita, what do you think?"

"Romance. But only sweet romance. None of that bodice ripping stuff." Anita was the one with starfish printed on her shorts suit. Belinda's was covered in sunglasses. On closer inspection, Patsy's was festooned with flip flops, the same deep magenta as her lipstick, earrings, bangles, and, of course, her gem-stone adorned kitten heel flip flops.

"How can you read that?" Belinda pushed past Anita. "If it weren't for the hanky-panky, I'd die of boredom. Give me a good tell-all biography any day of the week."

"You have no imagination, Belinda," Patsy whined. "And you're a prude, Anita." The smell of umbrella-laden drinks hit Amy as the women passed the librarian's desk. "You're just as bad as your children. What I need is a psychological thriller. Preferably with a younger, well-built spy. Preferably with a French accent."

Before either of Patsy's friends could retort, Amy

stepped in. "If you're wanting to relax, the music in the Crown Jewels Lounge is particularly soothing."

"We don't want to be soothed," Anita snapped.

"Oh," Amy said. "Then I suppose the spa is out, then."

"You're right, the spa is most definitely out," Belinda nearly shouted.

Anita waved her hands at her friends. "Maybe for you, Belinda."

"Have you tried the massage services?" The book nearly slipped out of Amy's hand. Ten after noon. Still time to make it to both suites and to Information Technology.

"Massage? Isn't that rather," Anita lowered her voice to a stage whisper. "Rather prurient?"

"Oh, not at all," Amy insisted. The keys bit into her palm. "In fact, you can request your masseuse or masseur based on your preferences." Amy directed her smile toward Anita. "There's the nice foot rub package, fully clothed, totally decent. Belinda, you should ask for Cindy. She's a complete gossip. And you, Patsy, ask for Marceau. He does the best shoulder massage, and he has the most charming French accent…" While Amy hadn't been to the spa herself, she had received the full run-down on its staff from Beatrice during her training.

The three friends nearly collided with each other, commending each other on what a fantastic idea they'd had going to the Massage Services Spa. Amy waited until their voices echoed in the hallway, then she locked the door and ran to the service elevator. Faster that way. She waved her badge over the request for elevator pad, then, once it had opened, waved it again to request the suite level. She nearly cursed when the elevator stopped halfway up.

"Amy, how are you?" Lucia rolled a cart filled with petit fours and tea onto the elevator.

Amy laughed. "Rushing. And you?"

"I am, but the trick is to never look like you're in a hurry. Just, focused, direct. You know?"

"I wish I did know." Amy remembered the box flying off the balcony next to Curtis Jenkins's. "May I ask what will be a, well, questionable question?"

Lucia nodded.

"Does the ship's food services deliver pizza in boxes?"

"Boxes?" Lucia mocked an affronted posture. "We serve our artisan baked pizza on silver trays, I'll have you know." She laughed. "Part of the ship's green initiative, which I applaud them for, but honestly, the passengers like it better when it comes under a dome."

"Everything is better served under a dome, isn't it?"

The elevator stopped for Lucia's destination. "Where did you see a pizza box, out of curiosity? Either someone must have brought it aboard in London, or there's one dedicated delivery driver out there in the middle of the Atlantic."

"I'm not positive that it was a pizza box. It was flying off a balcony."

"Hmm," Lucia said. "Sometimes the passengers leave towels out on their balconies. Especially the ones in the elite suites with the personal hot tubs. It happens."

"You're right, maybe it was nothing. I'm sorry for keeping you."

"No, it's good to see you, Amy," Lucia said as she

rolled the cart out. Amy looked at the sleeve of Lucia's jacket, but it was spotless, as anyone might have expected from a head valet. "I have a couple requests if you can get them from bookstores in New York. Poetry. I'm from Spain, but my real love is for South American poets. I'll get you a list?"

"Any time, Lucia. Just let me know, and I'll have them delivered to the ship."

The doors closed, and the elevator lurched up to the suites level. The lack of pizza boxes on board the ship complicated matters. But Amy didn't have time to think about what thin white square might have fallen from the ship, if it even had been anything at all.

Chapter Seven

Amy stopped to catch her breath outside Curtis Jenkins's suite. She smoothed her suit, pushed a stray hair from her forehead, and strode up to the door. Her knock sounded hollower than it had the night before. A woman answered the door. She glanced down at Amy's badge. "Good afternoon. Is Mr. Jenkins expecting you?"

"No," Amy said. "And I'm not here for him. I came to deliver this to his son."

The woman emerged from the doorway to take the book. "I'm afraid Mr. Jenkins and his son are both out at the moment. I'll be happy to leave this for him, if you'd like." Her own badge jingled against the book as Amy started to hand it over.

"You know what, he's not expecting this. Cole, the son, I mean. May I come in to jot down a note? I don't have any paper on me," Amy said.

The woman shrugged. "Fine by me. You'll have to excuse me, though. They must have had quite a morning, and I need to straighten up before they get back from lunch." Amy entered the suite. Whereas the night before, the living room had contained all the finery of an exquisite meal served by dedicated staff, now, it was reduced to a mess. The coffee table had been upturned, and beneath it was a dark brown stain. Throw pillows had been thrown on the floor. A chair leaned out the French doors to the balcony. In the incoming breeze, pieces of the ship's stationery fluttered across the carpet. "Oh, the writing desk is out for repair. You can leave a note in the sitting room. It's in there. Paper and pen are, well," she waved her hands, "you see."

Amy grabbed a still-flat piece of paper and a pen that had rolled into the divot of the plush carpet where the desk had been. She went into the sitting room and wrote a brief note. Something caught her eye behind the two armchairs that were still aligned in front of a television. Amy looked out at the housekeeper, who was still dabbing at the stain on the wallpaper.

Beside the chair, leaning against the wall, was a case that looked similar to the one that Raymond Entwhistle had clutched when they first met. Ostensibly, it contained Diane Westgrove's painting, but Amy wasn't so sure of that now. It was, however, marked with the same sharp-beaked sea bird as the one Raymond carried. She opened the case and saw a small, square canvas, not the shape or size of the painting in the library, but definitely the same large, looping signature in the bottom right corner. Wellie stood at the ballet barre, her face almost in profile, looking into the mirror. Could she see what the viewer saw? What looked back at her, Amy couldn't make out before she snapped the case shut.

"You have a visitor, Mr. Jenkins," the housekeeper called out loudly. Amy added more books to the tally she'd have to pick up in New York.

Curtis came in, with his son, Cole, looking both defiant and rather hangdog, shuffling in behind him. "What a lovely surprise, Ms. Morrison."

"And here I thought I'd miss you. Both. I was just leaving a note for Cole, here. I brought him a book that he might enjoy." Amy held up the book. Curtis frowned.

"You might have seen our upended living room, Ms. Morrison. Terrible thing. Sea bird flew right in through the balcony door this morning, just as we were enjoying coffee. We had a time chasing it back out again, as you'll see. Nasty old thing, wasn't it, Cole?" Curtis looked back at his son.

Cole began to speak, but his father cut him off.

"Cole, thank Ms. Morrison for thinking of you," he said.

"Thank you, Ms. Morrison," he said, then skulked off to his room, leaving the book on the sitting room table.

"It's my pleasure to be of assistance," Amy said. She stepped back toward the door, which Curtis had blocked. "But I'm afraid I must get back to the library. I just popped up for a moment. I'm off to grab lunch. If you'll excuse me."

Curtis stared at her for a long minute, his face moving from doubt to desire back to doubt again. "I do appreciate you bringing Cole the book. You might as well take it back to the library. The lad doesn't read much."

"If it's all the same to you, Mr. Jenkins, I'll leave it. Children have ways of surprising us, don't they? Mine does."

Curtis stepped out of the doorway, and Amy rushed through. She felt some relief once the door had closed behind her, and two voices, deep and masculine, argued behind it. Well, let them argue. It would distract them from anything she could have seen or thought while she was inside their suite.

Amy rounded the corner. The Westgrove sisters' suite lay next to Curtis's. She hung back a bit, watching the hallway. The slight shape of a woman dressed in dove gray leaned against the wall across from the suite's entryway. Amy took a moment before she recognized her: the ghostwriter. Amy wished she'd left the library even earlier, for at least then she'd have a more plausible excuse for lingering in the hallway.

A housekeeper passed the ghostwriter, who was startled out of her reverie. What had she been looking for there? The rattling cart must have shaken the young woman, who turned, looked at her hand, and then dropped to her knees. Frantically, she patted the floor. Even in the hallways surrounding the elite suites, the carpet was plush and easy to lose something in.

Amy stepped forward. Light from the silver shape showed the object's outline: a sea shell. Filigree, worked in silver, pearls, and diamonds. Where had she seen that before? She held her breath and watched the ghostwriter, who seemed even paler and thinner than she had in her gown the night of the party. Amy had been so occupied during the event that she hadn't introduced herself to the young woman. Nor, oddly enough, had Brent Detweiler, who had brought Diane and the ghostwriter together, introduced her to Amy.

"Where did it go? Where did it go?" the young woman whispered, loud enough for Amy to register over the cart's receding rattle. She patted the carpet, working her thin fingers through the carpet's fibers. If she were at the wrong angle, the brooch would be impossible for her to see. Like something lost under dark water. At last, the ghostwriter turned her head and saw it. She grabbed it up and looked at it, precious thing it was in its metal and gems, but it must have meant something more to her too. Amy slipped back into a shadow.

Trembling, the ghostwriter knocked on the Westgroves' suite. No one answered. After a few moments, she took a key card from her pocket and slipped it into the door. A few heartbeats later—fast ones for Amy, at least—the young woman slipped back out of the suite and closed the door softly behind her. She looked around and rushed away.

Amy looked down at her watch. Twenty minutes until she'd need to be back at the library. She filed as much of the incident as she could to memory and once again ran to the service elevators.

Amy stood outside the Information Technology office suite, her heart pounding. She should have eaten something. She should have stopped the ghostwriter to ask about the brooch. She should have confronted Curtis Jenkins about the portrait of Wellie at the barre and given him what for after he lied to her about the sea bird in his suite. But she hadn't done any of that. And now, slightly disheveled and distracted by her stomach's warbles and her heart's insistence that something strange had happened and that something strange was probably still happening, Amy opened the suite's gold-handled door.

The receptionist, a prim young woman with auburn hair pinned back much the same as Amy's was, looked up at her. "May I help you?" Her accent could have been the Queen's.

Amy's stomach bubbled. "Is Kevin Park

available?"

"This is his lunch hour, unfortunately," the young woman said. Was she giving Amy the customer service smile? "If you'll wait a moment, Kit will see you shortly. Or Montague, if he returns from lunch on time."

"You make it sound like that's not his routine," Amy said.

"I'm not at liberty to speak about human resources matters," she said with a sigh. "If you'll have a seat, Kit will see you as soon as she gets back from a router maintenance call." The young woman pointed Amy toward the plush gold chair near the door through which she'd entered.

Her own lunch break was ticking away. Behind the young woman sat a pitcher of iced tea with glasses and packets of sugar. Maybe she'd still have time to grab something at the staff canteen, if she hurried. If she could get to Kevin Park. "I would love to be able to wait," Amy said. "But I need to be back at my desk in fifteen minutes."

"You're staff?"

"Yes," Amy said. She fished out her lanyard, which had lodged between her blouse and her suit jacket. "Librarian, in fact."

"Is this an issue with the library's technology or a personal problem?"

"It's personal," Amy admitted. "But it's kind of bigger than me. Kind of a lot bigger. There's a puzzle I'm working on."

The young woman picked up a clipboard from which a pen swung on a chain. "All staff must fill out form 990B to report any personal technical issues."

"No," Amy said. "It's urgent."

The young woman sighed again. Amy had just been dumped in with Montague in the receptionist's opinion, hadn't she? "Form 990B. A technician will contact you within seven days."

"I can't wait seven days," Amy said. "They'll all be off the ship by then." The receptionist shrugged and returned the clipboard to a filing cabinet, next to a book. The title caught Amy's eye. "Oh," she said. "I love that series. That's the latest book isn't it? We have that in the ship's library."

The receptionist beamed. "It's wonderful. This is the latest in the series in paperback, and I just finished it. I can't wait to read the next one, but I have to. The hardback came out last week, but on my salary, I can't go around buying hardbacks, can I?"

"Look." Amy leaned toward the receptionist's desk. Half buried under a pile of clipboards sat a memo holder with a name engraved on it. Amy could make out the first name, "Regina." She put on her customer service smile and said in a low between-you-and-me voice, "I know staff can't technically check out books, but what if I acquired a copy of the next book in the series when we get to New York? You get to read it first, if—"

"If?"

"If I get five minutes to chat with your boss," Amy said.

The receptionist, Regina, looked down at the book then back up at her. "He's the last office on the right." Her voice was flat, quiet, and obviously American.

Amy knocked on Kevin Park's door.

"Yes? It's open."

"I need to talk to you," Amy sputtered. "It's about my internet access. Or lack thereof, really."

"You'll need to talk to one of my assistants. Though Kit's out on a call, and good luck finding Montague," he said. His office was dimly lit, like all the offices aboard the ship. "She can help you. Her office is just around the corner."

"No, I'm not a passenger," Amy tried again. "You don't understand."

"Kit can help staff too," Kevin said. His back was turned to her, and he was typing something into a laptop that was on a corner of his desk outside the area lit by golden lamplight. "She'll take care of you."

Amy breathed in and tried again. Something in his voice caught her, but she had to keep focus on her problem and the fact that she had about five minutes to convince him to do something about it. "No, look, my name is Amy Morrison. I'm the librarian. Usually, I'm brilliant at fixing technical things. Really brilliant. But apparently, I'm also good at failing spectacularly at things on this ship, and I need your help."

"You? Hold on. You're the librarian?" Kevin swung his chair into the light. "You should have said so. Weird stuff going on down there, pulling down a lot of data at random times. At least your account is capped, so no real damage done."

"So you've seen this happening?" Amy felt her stomach jump, though whether it was out of hunger or from hearing this news, she wasn't sure. Or something else. "Does this mean you have some idea who is taking up all my data? Can you tell me who it is? And why I can't fix it on my own?"

"Wait, Montague hasn't contacted you yet? He was

supposed to do that yesterday morning."

"Did he send me an email?"

Kevin sighed. "Okay, I should handle this one myself. And to answer your question, no, we don't know who it is. The plan was for Montague to contact you first to see whether you were instigating the suspicious downloads."

"There was a plan, then. Well, that's something." Amy's eyes landed on the gold ring on his right hand. "Is that a Texas A&M ring?"

"Yes, it is. MBA, class of '94." On the bookshelf behind him was a picture of two small children smiling in a field of bluebonnets. "History degree there before that, with a minor in computer science. Don't tell me you're an Aggie?"

"My son is," Amy said. "As of a week ago." She stopped herself from asking about the children in the picture, about his time at College Station, about how much of a coincidence it was meeting another Texan on this very British ship. "I'd like to talk A&M, but I have to get back to the library as soon as I can. I'm on duty in four minutes. I can't access the internet, and I have no idea why."

"Have you changed your password since the problem began?" He looked at her matter-of-factly, which is exactly what she would have done, and had done herself, diagnosing computer problems back home at her library in Dawville. "Or have you forgotten your password?"

"Neither one of those," Amy said. "Okay, I'll try that. Changing the password. Not forgetting it." She giggled. Maybe it was hunger or the episodes inside Curtis's suite and outside the Westgroves' that had her light-headed.

"What's so funny?"

"If only I had time to tell you." Amy's stomach gurgled.

"You haven't eaten?"

"My lunch break has been full," she admitted.

"Seriously, though, change your password. It's just good practice anyway when something unexpected happens."

"I will," Amy said. "Next time, I'll do so sooner. Thank you. It's almost one."

"I'll check in with you later today," Kevin said. "And maybe go eat something."

"That is definitely the plan."

\*\*\*\*

Amy giggled again on her way down the service elevator to the floor on which the library lay. Something was suspicious in the downloads, but she felt too light-headed to think about it. She ducked into the staff canteen, grabbed a sandwich, and ate it as she dashed toward the library. An older couple waited at the door for her.

"So sorry for making you wait," Amy said as she brushed the crumbs from her jacket. "I let my lunchtime errands run away from me."

"As breathless as you sound, you must have given it a good chase," the woman said. "And we're in no hurry. Such a nice warm afternoon, we thought we'd be the only ones in the library. We've wanted to come by to take a look at the Diane Lewis painting. Or I should say, Diane *Westgrove.*"

"Were you at the unveiling?" Amy opened the door for the couple. They clasped hands, both reaching for the other without words, the way Amy had wished Neil had done all those years they'd been together. Water under the bridge now. A whole ocean full. "At the celebration?"

"Oh, no," the woman said. "We don't know her personally. Just by reputation."

"From her philanthropic work?" Amy followed behind the couple. The woman approached the painting and looked closely at Venus's face. At Diane's face.

"How else would we know her?" the woman said. "Even for someone famous for her wealth and beauty, she wasn't all that interesting a figure outside of it." She ran her free hand through her short hair. Paused, one elbow crooked at the side of her head, her feet planted beneath her shoulders. She looked every bit the woman Diane must have been trying to paint. She stood, almost moving, her linen pants swaying around her, the gold of her bracelets hinting at falling toward her shoulder. Almost like a dancer? "Not a spot on her record, even when she was young."

"The more she did, the more she stepped out of the spotlight for doing so," the man said. "I worked with an organization she'd supported about ten years ago, an arts program for underprivileged youth. Painting lessons, museum trips, that sort of thing. I found the space for their headquarters and arranged the setup of the gallery space, offices, classrooms. It's a wonderful place. Thriving. But when the organization asked if they could name a gallery after her, she graciously declined. And then bought all the work on exhibit in that gallery."

Amy nodded, though neither faced her. "She seemed subdued at the party."

"Strange that she'd write a tell-all book," the woman said, moving her arm back down to her side. "Seems more like something her sister would do."

"Wellie?" Amy asked.

The woman turned and exhaled sharply. She dropped her husband's hand. "The stories I heard." She shook her head and laughed.

"My wife is a dance teacher."

"Retired, now, but yes," she said. "Modern dance, which was Wellie's genre. No doubt she could have made a name for herself as a dancer, and really, she had in the dance world as someone incredibly gifted, but then she made her name for herself as a party-goer too. And then, there was the accident."

"The accident?"

"The, as in, the one that ended her career," the woman said. "You didn't know this? Maybe it's faded from popular memory. It was all over dance circles and even made the national news. Jacqueline Westgrove, known as Wellie, daughter of a jewelry design heiress and an English aristocrat, drank too much one night, which wasn't unusual. But then she'd had one too many and tripped on the top of a wooden staircase."

"It's surprising that she survived the fall, but with luck, she didn't land in such a way that was fatal." The husband looked closely at the painting, then sat in the chair.

"Not to her, but fatal to her career, definitely. She spent several weeks in the hospital, and never danced again." The woman shook her head again. "It's a shame, in a way. She could have contributed to the dance world even if she couldn't dance. Like her sister did supporting the visual arts after she decided not to pursue a career as a painter. No one ever saw her at performances, and she always turned down requests for her to speak."

"Maybe it was too painful for her?" Amy ventured.

"True," the woman said. "But how many talented dancers' careers end too soon because of an injury? We're better than we used to be about taking care of our bodies, but still, you can't control everything. Maybe if it were a dance injury, it would be different."

"It was something she had a measure of control over," the husband added.

"Or maybe it was something she couldn't control, Harold."

The couple thanked her and left. The warm afternoon was too tempting, and they were, after all, on the trip of a lifetime on a trans-Atlantic cruise. Amy watched them walk out of the library together, once again hand-in-hand. There was something reassuring about that.

As much as she'd had to refine her customer service smile, she reminded herself that for the vast number of library patrons—back home in Dawville and here on the ship—her interactions with them were a pleasure to her. She'd gained a reputation as an undergrad as a sort of literary match maker, one with an uncanny ability to recommend a book to a friend or acquaintance if not a whole genre. She'd introduced Stacey to the fascinating worlds of Agatha Christie and Sir Arthur Conan Doyle. Rick, boots ever firmly planted in the mud, she introduced to space opera. Her Sigma Tau Delta honor society adviser heard about her ability to connect books to ultimately satisfied readers and suggested she pursue a degree in library science.

She had imagined working at the main branch of a big city library or at an academic library in a vibrant small college town. What a joy and a pleasure to have spent her career doing something she'd loved, even if it was in the small town she'd grown up in. How that must have felt to be denied that for both Diane and Wellie. Neither of the women needed to work, really, inheriting as much as they did. And they both found other ways to fulfillment.

Maybe it all worked out.

And sometimes, it didn't. Happy as she was in her career, Amy felt a pang of disappointment every time she thought of Neil. They'd met while she was at grad school, at the master's program in library science at Texas Woman's University in Denton, just north of Dallas. Her friend, Tiffany, had talked their circle into going south to the Byron Nelson Golf Tournament. "I didn't know you were into golf," Amy had said to Tiffany. "Oh, not at all," her friend replied. "It's just prime people watching."

And it had been. While Tiffany, Nicole, and Heather flirted madly all afternoon, Amy hung back, trying to figure out the layers of people watching people watching people watch golf. Neil had been watching her, though, and had offered to buy her a drink.

"Sure," Amy had said. She had been caught off guard by him, slightly older, confident, dashing. Dashing was exactly the word she would used to describe him on the way back to Denton, slightly sunburnt and her heart fluttering a bit at the memory of his accent. Not the strong Birmingham accent of his youth, the one his sister still held on to, but the

Received Pronunciation of BBC presenters, the educated set.

She'd given him her phone number, and he'd given her his business card. She'd also, along the line, given him the mistaken belief that she was a farm girl, a Texan through and through, one who wanted to cling to her roots. Not that she'd done much to disabuse him of this idea. But when he realized that the girl who fit his dreams of a country girl, one who'd be the real-life companion to his fantasy of life in the west, they both began to unravel a bit. Eventually, they'd both had enough. She wasn't a country girl after all. And he wasn't her dashing English prince.

She'd wanted a life of adventure. And here she was. Focus on that, she told herself.

And she did.

Amy turned on her laptop and opened her staff tools menu. All right, so she hadn't picked the strongest password, had she? At least it wasn't her son's name. Or her ex-husband's. Neil took the dog, so her name was out too. After working as a librarian for as long as she had, she knew better than to choose a password that was easy to guess. Amy clicked the "Change Password" button and the menu popped up. The program created a password for her, one that was quite strong and safe. But it was a string of random letters, numbers, and punctuation, and she knew she couldn't remember all that. So she thought for a moment. A memory of running after Angus, a stout five-year-old, as he ran toward his Aunt Stacey and his cousins and their grandparents in the darkness. Christmas Eve, they'd always celebrated at Stacey and Rick's. His parents were often gone over the holidays, visiting Rick's older brother, who had moved away as soon as he could. So, it was Amy and Stacey's mom and dad and all their grandchildren. There was the big tree in the living room and presents for everyone to open that night, which made the children anxious to finish their dinners. Of course, for Angus, the stockings and the presents from Momma and Daddy and from Gran and Aunt Kate and her family and from Santa would have to wait until the morning, but this made it easier to wait until then.

Angus hadn't been used to being out after dark. Amy had almost caught up with him when he stopped in the middle of the gravel driveway and looked up. Though the colorful Christmas lights around him blinked, he just stared into the sky. "How big is the world?" he had asked. "You mean, how big is planet Earth?" she'd asked in return. "No, Momma, how big is the world? The one with Earth and the moon and all the stars?" "Almost as big as how much I love you," she'd said, and she kissed his head right in the middle of his curly red hair.

Amy caught her breath again and she entered the password she couldn't forget first into the "Password" field and then again in the "Confirm Password" field. Then she clicked "Save," as if she could save that moment forever too.

Tomorrow, if all went as planned, she could download the rest of the picture that her darling boy had sent her from college. That and the rest of the messages that he and everyone else had sent her. It would work. She was sure of it.

Chapter Eight

Buoyed by the couple's information about the Westgrove sisters, Amy spent the afternoon pleasantly steering other library visitors toward the painting. Truth be told, she wanted to get a better look at it in the light of what she now knew about Diane and Wellie, particularly with an eye toward what she'd seen in Curtis's suite. Something about the picture seemed even more off than it had before to her, though she didn't know how to put it.

Amy locked the door at closing time, but she didn't leave. She approached the painting, standing in front of it, with the spotlight still shining down on it. Had she known what she was looking for, this would have been easier. The painting in Curtis's suite was smaller than this, square, but richly detailed even if it wasn't large. Wellie's face had been turned toward the painter, but not fully so, as if she'd been torn between looking at the painter and the mirror in front of her. At herself? What had Diane meant by putting her sister in front of the mirror? It seemed like a pretty standard ballet image to Amy, but there were images in the mirror she hadn't seen. She could try to get back into his suite, but her instinct told her not to go back there.

A knock on the library door startled Amy from her thoughts. She turned and saw Gemma standing just outside, waving at her. Amy opened the door for her.

Gemma looked every bit the artist herself, even if she claimed just to be a critic and curator. Her searching eyes, the t-shirt from a band Amy couldn't have heard of, the pencil skirt above black tights and military-style pink boots. And yet, there was also the diamond and sapphire necklace that she kept twirling around her finger.

"Glad I caught you," Gemma said, her London accent echoing down the hallway. "Pen and Rich are joining me in the staff canteen in about an hour. Lucia's coming too. She mentioned she'd talked to you. Books and whatnot."

"How did you meet Lucia?"

Gemma stayed just outside the door, as if she didn't want to enter the library. "Did you know the staff on ship are considering a strike in New York if they don't get a pay rise? Conditions as they are down there, well, you know." She dropped her pendant and put her hand on her chin. "Or maybe you don't know. They've got you on plush accommodations with the entertainment, don't they?"

"It's not like I'm on the passenger deck like you and Penelope and Richard are. But I can't complain," Amy admitted. "It's tight quarters, but good company."

"Nice. Anyway, I've put together some shows featuring artists examining the theme of labor relations, workers' rights, yeah? And I asked around about the conditions aboard ship and found out about Lucia. She's the one organizing the walkout." Gemma laughed. "Oh, that'll leave management in a bad place, everyone abandoning ship so to speak once we're in harbor in New York. That'll teach them. And they need to learn a lesson or two about messing with the help."

"Come in," Amy said. "Can you tell me more about this?" She gestured toward *Venus Rising*. "I'm afraid I don't know much about the visual arts."

Gemma leaned back toward the hallway, hesitated, and then stomped into the room with her big boots. "How about I tell you more about the labor situation?"

"That too." Amy pointed to the chairs in front of the painting. "But let's wait until Lucia can fill me in at dinner. I need to know something about this painting. And you're the expert." Gemma shook her head at the painting. "Or you could tell me how you got into art. And labor relations."

"That? Well, my dad is about as working class as they come. So you can say it's in my blood. My mum's family is from Jamaica. You heard about the Windrush affair?" Gemma sat down in the chair Wellie had occupied on the night of the party. "Word probably didn't make it to the States."

"No, I did hear about it," Amy said. "My husband—*ex-husband*, I mean—is from Birmingham. And I listen to the BBC whenever I can."

"Well, some of my extended family were caught up in that," Gemma said. "When I figured out that what I wanted to do most in the world was write about and think about and be around art, I figured I had to make that into something that mattered. Something larger than just in the art world."

"Like Diane Westgrove Lewis's philanthropy?"

"Not like Diane Westgrove Lewis's philanthropy, thank you very much." Gemma laughed. "I just told you I grew up working class, didn't I? Well, maybe I benefited from something along the lines of her philanthropic efforts. The British Museum is free, as is the National Gallery. Dad, Mum, my brothers, and I would go at the weekend. Part of my parents' grand plan to educate their children out of the working class, even if my dad was proud to be a part of it. They had us taking drawing and painting classes, but I wasn't as interested in what I was doing as thinking about what others had done. Even if I was a bit of a dab hand at painting." She looked up at the painting. "You've probably been to the National Gallery yourself, your husband being a Brit."

"No," Amy admitted. "It was always fly into London, catch the next train to Birmingham, and stay there with family until it was time to take the train back to Heathrow or Gatwick."

"No way." Gemma gasped. "When you and I are in London at the same time, I am taking you on the grand tour, got it? Top of the list is the British Library. We'll have tea there and everything." She looked back at Amy. "Your husband, a Brit, and he never took you to see the sights in London?"

"We barely saw the sights in Birmingham. I'm afraid he didn't like the historical parts. Or the art." Amy sighed. She didn't want to think about Neil. She especially didn't want to think of Neil when she possibly had a puzzle in front of her along with the woman who could be the key to solving it. "He wasn't the handsome prince I had hoped he'd be. But, to be fair, I wasn't the farm girl he wanted me to be either."

"You're looking up at the painting," Gemma said. "Again. All right. I give up. What do you want to know?"

"Oh, everything. But let's start with this. What do you think about it?"

"Easy." Gemma stood up. "Look, the perspective is off, for one. She's not looking at anything in particular. Venus was supposed to be the goddess of love. She pursued it, you know? There's technique in the brushwork and colors, but nothing innovative. Nothing particularly interesting about it. It might be a passable student work, but it's not a piece that was going to make anyone's career."

"Do you know any of her other work?"

"Why would I?" Gemma motioned toward the door. "A few of her paintings were sold before she gave up, probably because of her family's fame. But those were never widely shown, as far as I know. And everything on sale in New York is under lock and key. Probably for the same reason no one has seen a review copy of her book. There's just not much to get excited about, is there?"

Amy started to follow but stopped for one last look at the painting. "Do you think there's any possibility that this is a fake? Maybe someone trying to cause a scandal to drum up interest in her book?" She turned and followed Gemma out the door, which Amy locked.

Gemma shrugged. "I think people are always trying to find a story where there isn't one, you know? It's intriguing, I'll give her that. A talented young painter, on the brink of making her career in art suddenly gives up painting publicly because she doesn't think people can separate her fame from her work. And now she's back. But it doesn't make her art any good, judging from *Venus* back in there."

"What makes art good, then?" Amy looked past the gold silk wallpaper and sapphire tiles around her, out to the corridor that would take them away from the glamour of the ship toward the staff canteen and its harsh white walls.

"Hmm, well, first, it has to cause something visceral in the viewer. If it doesn't touch you in some way, then what's it doing?"

Amy nodded. While *Venus Rising* didn't do much for her, the painting in Curtis's suite did. And if they were painted around the same time, and the one with Wellie was so much more striking, then why wasn't that one singled out as her masterpiece? Gemma once again took her from her thoughts. "You and me, soon, we'll tour the ship. I'll show you what real art can do for you, what it can make you feel. What genuine art is. What it can be."

"I'd like that," Amy said. "I'd like that quite a lot."

\*\*\*\*

When they arrived at the staff canteen, Penelope and Richard were already seated with Lucia. The industrial feel of this place was so in contrast with the elegance of the passengers' dining halls that it didn't feel like they were still aboard the golden ship. Even waving their staff badges over the white plastic scanner at the entrance felt like it couldn't be part of that same world. Amy grabbed a tray and followed Gemma through the buffet line. Lasagna, to Amy's relief, was the feature of the evening's offerings. Warm, hearty, and difficult to truly get wrong, which happened more often than not at the staff canteen. After not eating much for lunch, though, Amy wasn't in a position to complain. She served herself a larger helping than she might have otherwise, along with green beans that were falling apart in the steel tray in which they sat warming and a slice of bread that was slathered in what she

114

hoped was garlic butter. At the dessert station, she grabbed what looked like a slice of white sheet cake.

She set down her tray and went to the drinks station. Iced tea, two packets of sugar. She looked down at her drink and grabbed another packet, just in case.

"Amy, dear," Penelope said. "Do sit now. Lucia was just telling us something about a certain set of sisters. You'll want to hear what she has to say about them."

Lucia shook her head. "Oh, I don't know about that. The older one just seems dazed all the time and tells me to go away and leave her alone. And the younger one snaps at me for the smallest things. For pink roses instead of yellow roses, the first night. And for the balcony doors being so complicated. As if I could do anything about that." She took a bite of her lasagna and looked thoughtful for a moment. "But I must have explained it well enough. She had the balcony doors open just about every time I came in."

"What do they call you in for?" Amy tried to pace herself, but something about the meal tasted like the microwave lasagna she'd made for Angus and herself on nights Neil would be away back when Angus was little. His favorite, a meal of microwave lasagna, a can of green beans, and a fruit cocktail cup with animal crackers for dessert. "If they don't want anything?"

"It's part of the job," Lucia said. "I get to know them. For the most part, it's nice, you know? A lot of these passengers, especially the ones in the elite suites, are taking the trip of a lifetime. Or they're celebrating something big, like a milestone birthday or anniversary. And they loop me in on that, because, as their valet, I'm a big part of it. I figure out what they want fast, and I make sure they have the experience of a lifetime. And really, they're happy with the service, because they know I'm excellent at what I do. For them and for the ship. But when things go bad, especially when we're fighting for better conditions, it makes everything worse. And the Westgrove sisters are about as bad as it gets."

"Hmm." Penelope laid her fork on her empty plate. "Could it be that they don't want you in their suite for some reason? I remember the news about Wellie's fall. I was pretty young then, but I remember watching the news and seeing these beautiful people in their beautiful house and wondering how something bad could happen to them. But it did. They tried to keep it private, and the media were much more willing to keep things out of the news than they are now, but the media has always loved a sensational story, hasn't it?"

"Bet the Beeb never covered it." Gemma pointed at Richard with her fork. "You don't have any childhood memories of that story, do you, Rich?"

Richard laughed. "Ah, no," he said. "But I have been doing a bit of digging, as you might say the media does."

"Not the BBC," Penelope added. "Far too dignified to dig."

"Through my digging," Richard said in his best BBC presenter voice, "I have found out that there is to be a second auction in New York, after the first, of early Diane Westgrove paintings. Care to guess who's selling off his work? And whether or not this one will be for charitable causes?"

"I think I can guess," Gemma said. "In an elite suite with his entitled prat of a son?"

"Precisely," Richard said. "One Cole Jenkins, who was dismissed from his fancy preparatory school for let's call them ethical violations. Graduated—just barely—from another school his father paid off to take the boy. A father whose business is not quite as profitable as it once was. A father whose messy and rather expensive divorce is on the horizon. And here's the best part." He dramatically took a bite of his garlic bread.

"Oh, don't keep us in suspense, Richard," Lucia said. "The staff have stories about that lot. Supposedly a sea bird came in and wrecked their suite. A sea bird with a taste for old bourbon."

Amy tried not to giggle.

Richard chuckled. "Cole is slated this fall to attend a rather forgiving university that is, shall we say, on hard times financially. Coincidentally, the ceremonial shovel show is also slated for this fall for the new Curtis Jenkins Student Center. State of the art place, from what I've read." He took another bite of bread.

Gemma smiled. "So you think he's taking advantage of this trip and Diane Westgrove's sale to make his art sale more profitable? If so, I don't think he's going to get much for his collection."

"Why is that, Gemma?"

"Well, Pen, first off, if you've seen the painting in the library, you'd know that no amount of her work would total the millions he'd need for that building."

"But," Amy said before she could stop herself, "what if that painting isn't really *Venus Rising*? I mean, it might be for the sake of the trip, but what if it isn't really what Diane Westgrove painted all those decades ago in art school?"

"Clever, Amy" Richard said. "He swaps out the painting to make the ones in his collection look all the better."

"Here's her masterpiece, but look how much more interesting her other early work was?" Penelope's brows edged toward each other. "Not much of a plan, is it?"

"No," Amy said. She'd finished off the cake faster than she'd planned to, though it was just about as flavorful as the third packet of sugar she was contemplating adding to the iced tea, a disappointing concoction that had perhaps seen a tea leaf or two during the "tea concentrate syrup" manufacturing process. Amy picked up the remaining crumbs of cake with the tips of her fork tines. "I don't think that's it. I think, and this might be reaching, that he might have taken the original. Think about it. You get the story of the forgery, the artist claiming that the painting wasn't hers, and then, oh, hey, look at that, it was in his collection all along. He gets to sell the painting at a higher price and take care of the matter of Cole's education, student center and all."

Lucia waved her hands. Amy caught herself looking for gray paint again, but nothing showed up on her shirt sleeves, just as nothing had been on her jacket earlier in the day. "What, does he think he can get away with saying that he bought the painting somewhere along the line? Is he going to have papers that prove the sale?"

Amy paused. If this were the case, then her theory wasn't much of a theory. "Well, how did he get her early work in the first place? I know the art school she attended has always suffered financially, taking on students who can't pay tuition, room, or board, much less for their supplies. Maybe she gave them to the school to sell?"

"Can you contact someone at the school?" Penelope wondered.

"Alas, not, my dear. The art school closed about twenty years ago. The buildings were sold, and the school couldn't find a new space to rent." Richard put his finger to his chin. "But all universities have newspapers, don't they?"

"Would an experimental art school have a school newspaper?" Lucia asked.

"If not that, then an archive, surely," Gemma said. "But I don't think this is a forgery."

"Why not?" Amy asked.

"None of this makes sense to me," Gemma said. "The figures, the techniques, they're all out of the time and place Diane Westgrove was painting in. Almost clichéd versions of them. And this is the piece she singled out as her best work. Why would she give it away to be sold? It's not like her family couldn't swoop in with an endowment and solve the matters of their financial problems."

"All right, then," Amy said. "Curtis just outright stole the painting and forged the sale documents. He didn't think through all the implications because he's under a lot of stress from Cole's doings and from his business tanking. But that doesn't mean he wouldn't try something this underhanded, would he? Something that violates ethics, if not the laws?"

"Like father like son?" Lucia ventured. "Or the other way around?"

Gemma shook her head. "Just wait for the auction.

It'll be canvas after canvas of technically decent but uninspired work. People will buy it because she's Diane Westgrove Lewis, and she's famous. But no one will buy this unseen work for its artistic merit."

Amy was skeptical, but she kept that to herself. They all said their goodnights and went to their separate accommodations. Gemma's room was near Penelope and Richard's. They walked off together, and much as Amy wanted them all to be in agreement about Curtis's possible guilt, Gemma's refusal to believe that the painting was a forgery bothered her. Why should it? Amy lay in bed that night trying to convince herself that Gemma was right, that the painting wasn't a forgery. But all signs in Amy's mind pointed to the fact that it must be.

Why couldn't Gemma see that? She was upset about the painting upstaging her debut collection aboard the ship, so there was that. And she didn't believe Curtis Jenkins had it in him to steal a painting. So what? She could be upset and doubtful and still be right.

But she was the only one aboard ship who could paint such a portrait. And she had access to all the materials to do so as well. Which led Amy to the one conclusion she didn't want to reach, that Gemma may have painted the forgery and hidden away the real painting to get back at the very cruise line that had hired her to curate a collection of art from up-and-coming artists on the topics she chose.

Art that, because of Diane Westgrove Lewis, no one was paying much attention to.

Amy tried to put it out of her thoughts and sleep, but she didn't have much luck. What if shining some doubt on Gemma was part of the plan? A red herring, maybe, but if Gemma didn't buy the other Diane Westgrove paintings for *The Cullinan Diamond* or for any of the other cruise line's ships, then she'd be discredited all the same, wouldn't she?

Amy decided she'd have to ask Gemma again to try to figure this all out.

Amy must have slept in spite of all her thoughts, since she woke up refreshed. Beatrice waved her off, however, when she asked whether she'd be needed at the elites table this morning an hour before she was to be at the library. Just as well, Amy thought. More time to spend in the library before the passengers came in. More time to spend online, downloading messages from Angus and whoever else sent her an email. She thought of Tiffany, too, what she needed her friend back home to look up for her. But that was later.

After she'd grabbed a staff canteen coffee and a dry muffin that was labeled "blueberry" but offered no hint of fruit, Amy went up the elevator to the floor on which the library was located, but she didn't go in straight away. Instead, she walked on the deck to take in the morning air, drinking her coffee, and watching the passengers around her do much the same. Midway through their journey, they were at a beautiful point in which the novel energy of the cruise had settled into a calm enjoyment. And they weren't near enough to the end of the cruise to eagerly try to do everything all at once. Amy wasn't either. She needed time, but she didn't feel pressed by its lack. She had enough time to puzzle this all out, didn't she?

What she wanted now was a distraction, really. She set her coffee and muffin down on a little table that would be in demand once the sun had warmed the deck but was almost too cold this morning. From her bag, she pulled the little shortwave radio Angus had given her. She pulled out the telescoping antenna to its full length and turned it on. What was she looking for? Or listening for, really. She wished she'd committed to memory all the little details that Angus filed neatly in that pragmatic brain of his. Meters and kilohertz and Universal Coordinated Time. Things like that.

Hadn't her brain been like that once too? When she'd had the chance to study something, to really look at it. But after twenty years in the same place, she wondered if she was capable of that anymore. Dawville had changed, of course. More people, the expansion of the interstate, the expansion of the stores around it. That had happened just about everywhere, either one way or the other.

What Amy wanted was something to see, something to hold on to. This job aboard this glittering golden ship was supposed to be it. This was supposed to make up for her years of small-town life with a husband who thought she'd love small town life as much as he had thought he would. Turned out, neither of them did, which was a shame. Maybe Angus would have been fine if they'd moved to one of the outer suburbs of Houston. Or if they'd moved to Huntsville, which was a couple hours north of Houston, not that far from what the big city offered.

Amy fiddled the wheel on the side of the radio, but all she heard was static. She tuned in the few stations she remembered that would most likely have something at any time of day—Angus had given her a list—but nothing came up over the static she heard from its speaker.

The morning was getting away from her anyway. She put the radio back in her bag and finished her coffee and muffin. At least the rest of the morning would be better, she reassured herself.

Inside, the library felt cold, as if she couldn't shake the breeze from the deck. Amy wrapped her scarf around herself more tightly, opened her laptop, and turned it on. The laptop went through its usual round of loading up what it needed to load up. And, at last, her email client sprang open on her screen. There was another email from Angus, along with several the email client indicated that it failed to download. Amy clicked "get new email" several times with the same error message as a result each time. She wanted more coffee. She wanted the library to feel warmer this morning. She wanted to know if Angus had started college in a good way, that his transition from his Aunt Stacey and Uncle Rick's had gone as smoothly as it would have gone if it had been from their home. His childhood home.

And then there was the pop-up that indicated that she'd reached her data limit for the day. So much for that. She'd have to break her technologically adept image and ask Penelope and Richard if she could use their internet to check her email. Even if she had to show them that she hadn't been as competent as she'd first presented herself to be.

The door to the library opened slowly. Through the entryway came the person she'd least expected to see in the library again: Raymond Entwhistle.

Chapter Nine

Raymond looked uncomfortable and slightly nauseated, as he had at the party for his aunt. Amy stood up and greeted him quietly from behind her desk. "Good morning, Mr. Entwhistle."

"Bit drafty in here this morning, isn't it?" He walked toward the painting then paused before reaching it. "Strange how the light changes things."

"The painting?"

Raymond bit off a laugh. "The painting and all else around it. My aunt's behavior of a few nights ago, I do apologize. I don't know what came over her."

"No need to apologize," Amy said. "Is she quite well?"

"I wouldn't know. Wellie won't let me see her." He folded his arms over his pudgy middle. If Amy had to contrive a sycophantic nephew type, it would not be Raymond. Dressed in a drab green sweater that had seen better days—years, really, judging from the worn spots—over a yellow polo shirt and slightly wrinkled gray trousers, he looked more like a man ready for a day out in the woods. He just needed binoculars and a guide, and he'd be the image of a fussy bird watcher. He unfolded his arms as if he didn't know what to do with them, then ran his hand through what remained of his hair. No wedding ring, no jewelry of any type. If Raymond Entwhistle was after Diane Westgrove

Lewis's money, he certainly wasn't spending any of his in anticipation of receiving hers. "Wellie also harangued me quite thoroughly for hanging the picture in such a way that her sister didn't remember it. As if I had any say over how or where it was put. I was just the errand boy she sent with the case."

"She? Wellie Westgrove sent you?" A couple wandered into the library, smartly dressed and beaming, the utter opposite of Raymond. And they seemed happy enough to float through without needing any assistance. Amy turned her attention back to Raymond. "Not Diane?"

"No," Raymond said, his arms back around his middle. "Which was strange, because Diane had asked me to come sit with her the afternoon before the event. We do that, you know. Maybe it's odd, but she'll have me over for tea, and we talk about nothing, about my work, about her life as a child. Before she'd been put out into the world, as she calls it. When I went to her suite for tea, Wellie told me that Diane changed her mind, and that she wanted me to take the painting here without seeing Diane first." Amy had not known what to make of his accent either, the middle-class accent that had, on occasion, plummy notes. That didn't fit with his sweater, either.

The couple picked books and sat in the nook with the Princess Margaret roses, which seemed to glow pink under the lights above it. "Had she changed her mind before?"

"So abruptly? No. Diane knows her own mind," he said, still searching the painting. For what, Amy wanted to ask, but she didn't want to scare him away. Why did she think she would? Was he as nervous as some bird he might watch in the woods? "And she's gracious, in the sense that she'd call me herself. Not just dismiss me like a servant."

"Does Wellie think of you as a servant? Beneath her?"

"Wellie thinks I am after her sister's money," he said, his voice flat over his chill, or whatever it was that was causing him to tremble slightly. "I'm not. I am her nephew of sorts, the son of her sister-in-law's first husband. They divorced. My father wasn't good at marriage." He bit off another laugh. "Anyway, we weren't wealthy, by any means, but I'm not in any need. Who needs money when you have a title, even if it is a minor one. And unlike Diane and Wellie's father, mine held on to his and the meager estate that went with it. For whatever that's worth."

Amy wanted to ask about that childhood split into his parents' marriages and divorces. And she really wanted to ask about this title of his. But her phone rang. Hoping it was Kevin Park, she excused herself to answer it.

"Ah, I caught you, Amy," Lionel said. The florist. "I missed you yesterday."

"Didn't we both?" Amy kept her eye on Raymond as best as she could from the librarian's desk. "Look, I have a favor to ask of you. Can you arrange for a specific type of flower in an elite suite? If I know of a passenger's preference?"

"Of course," Lionel said. "It's what we do."

"Wonderful." Raymond stood closer to the painting and leaned in toward the signature. "Could you do a bouquet of carnations for Diane Westgrove Lewis. Maybe yellow?"

Lionel laughed. "Oh, no. We don't do carnations on this ship. Especially not yellow ones. Did someone in the luxury suites tear up a book? Or a hundred?"

"Nothing like that at all." Amy made a mental note to read up on flowers, particularly which ones were gauche. "Roses, then? Yellow or cream, maybe?"

"Roses are always a safe choice. I could do that, but I'd have thought she'd want pink."

"Pink?" Amy recalled Wellie's directive: not pink. "Why?"

Lionel excused himself for a moment to answer one of his staff's questions. She kept the muffled exchange pressed to her ear while leaning a bit to see where Raymond had gone. "Sorry about that," Lionel said. "I would have assumed she'd want a pink rose because of the Diane Westgrove Lewis hybrid."

"She has a rose named after her?"

"Reluctantly, so I heard, but yes. Medium to light pink double. I couldn't source any for the leg Mrs. Lewis would be on, so I did the best I could. Her hybrid is a descendant of the Queen Elizabeth rose, also pink, as you'd imagine. None of those are available either, but I got the next best thing, the Princess Margarets. They're also a descendant of the Queen's rose." Lionel excused himself again.

When he returned, Amy thanked him for the information and left it at that. While checking on the couple in the nook, she peeked over at the painting. Raymond was behind it, looking up at what she imagined must be the hardware used to hang the wire from which the painting seemed to float. He produced an embarrassed smile when he caught Amy watching him. "Fascinating stuff, how they hang these things up.

I'm not much for art, I'm sorry to say."

"Well, as much as I think I ought to be, I'm not either," Amy said. She looked behind the painting too. Stamped on one of the top strips of wood over which the canvas was stretched was a sharp-beaked bird in flight. "I've gone to woefully few art museums myself. So I'm at a loss, too, Mr. Entwhistle."

He laughed to himself. "I'm not much for art, but I am one for communities, you could say. I did assist my aunt in an endeavor to set up a gallery on a charming island off the coast of Scotland last year. One of those places with more sheep than people. We talked the gallery's director into moving the space onto the mainland. Not much of a tourist draw for the island, and the locals' art got more views in the new space." Raymond shrugged. "Failure in one way, I suppose, but a lot more sales for the artists. Success is in how you look at a thing, isn't it, Ms. Morrison?"

"Oh, I don't know. Some failures are just that," Amy said. "Just failures. But your art gallery sounds like a success after all."

"Are you thinking of the party here?" Raymond looked at her intently. Amy suddenly felt very much like a bird in the center of the sights of a very powerful set of binoculars. "I wouldn't call that a failure. Not yours anyway. How were you to know how Diane would react? Besides, whether something is a success or a failure or not depends on where you leave off on the project, I'm sure you'll find."

The library door opened. In through it stormed Brent Detweiler, who aimed his stride toward Raymond Entwhistle. "Ah, I thought I might find you here," he said. "Looking at the painting. You haven't been anywhere else as far as I've gathered."

Amy stepped between them. "Of course, you can always find me here during the library open hours. What can I do for you, Mr. Detweiler?" She smiled. The couple in the nook set their books in their laps.

"What you can do for me is let me have a word with Mr. Entwhistle." Brent motioned with his head for Amy to move, but she stayed where she was.

"We're just admiring the job the staff did hanging the painting. What do you think, Mr. Detweiler?" Amy motioned up toward the ceiling. "It's as if the image were floating, don't you agree?"

"I don't care about what's back there," he said. "Except for you, Raymond. Come out from back there. You look like you're hiding from me."

"Well, what if I am?" Raymond said. "This is an entirely undignified display, Mr. Detweiler, and I'd be mortified if I happened to be caught up in it." He shook his head at the publisher, and though he was at least a head shorter than Brent, he managed to look as if he were looking down on the taller man. "If you'll excuse me."

"I will not excuse you," Brent said loudly. The couple in the reading nook left their books on the table between them and left. "I will not leave here until you explain to me why Diane Westgrove Lewis believes a painting that you were entrusted with is not the one she painted."

Raymond inhaled deeply. He spoke slowly, his voice deep, clear, and definitely more upper class than it had been. "There's your error, Mr. Detweiler. I was entrusted with a case that was presumed to contain the proper painting. I was not entrusted with the painting itself, inasmuch as I was not allowed to look at the contents of the case before accompanying the ship's staff into the library to install its contents here. I must be going now."

"You will not be going anywhere," Brent said. He paused for a moment and looked up at the painting. "Are you telling me that Diane didn't let you see the painting?"

"It's not as if she let you see it either, now did she, Mr. Detweiler?" Raymond sniffed.

"Diane is not letting me see her for that matter," Brent said. "You must have done something to upset her. Further, that is. You have to talk to her. Tell her I need to see her. Now. You're the one who started this mess, so you need to fix it."

Amy stepped back. The couple that she'd thought had left were, in fact, hanging out in the doorway with a half-dozen other passengers. "This isn't the time or the place to untangle the facts of the puzzle," she said. She was as curious as any of them, but she couldn't let the quarreling take over her library. "Please, let me remind you that there are business offices to which you have access that would provide a more private place to speak about this matter."

"Puzzle, did you say, Ms. Morrison?" Raymond pursed his lips. "I agree, Mr. Detweiler, that we ought not to be arguing here. Or anywhere, for that matter." He turned and left. The crowd parted and let him through the doorway.

Brent ran his hand through his still dark, still full hair. He'd been bested by the sniveling little man, and the hurt showed through the way he watched Raymond exiting through a crowd who seemed to be on his side.

"All right then, Amy," Brent said in a more subdued tone. "Puzzle. Explain." The crowd filtered in through the stacks, hanging back just enough to not obviously show that they were trying to listen in on the remnants of the conversation.

"I just meant why Mrs. Lewis wasn't seeing you," Amy said. "Or why neither of you saw the painting before the event." Not the puzzle of why this forgery was hanging in her library, and why no one knew what the original looked like except the artist who refused to see anyone.

"That's not new," Brent said. "I don't suppose you've talked with Diane?"

Amy shook her head.

He recovered his former posture and turned to leave her. But he didn't go far. In a voice loud enough for all to hear, he said, "You ought to watch out for Raymond Entwhistle. Did you ask him about what he does for a living? Or did?"

"That hasn't come up in our brief conversations, Mr. Detweiler," Amy said. She returned to the desk on which her useless laptop sat glowing at her.

"You should," Brent said, pointing at her computer. "Look him up. And after you've finally seen Diane, you tell those academics Richard and Penelope I'm waiting for an answer to my proposal. Their travelogue would make for compelling reading."

****

Amy settled back into the routine of the library. Reshelving those exquisite leather-bound classics, replacing the high-end magazines in their racks, assisting passengers with finding just the right read for the moment. She couldn't shake the image of Raymond

Entwhistle as something other than what he'd presented himself as. She tried not to think about Neil, but hadn't he done the same to her? At least a bit? Or had she overlaid a fantasy on him, obscuring what was there? He'd done that with her. One day, she'd get enough courage to ask Angus about all this, whether, as a child, he'd been able to see through what neither of his parents ever managed to—but that was a conversation for later. For now, there was the puzzle of the forged painting, of Raymond, and of Brent's insistence that she be the one to talk Diane out of her suite.

At noon, Amy closed the library for lunch. She'd arranged to meet Penelope in her suite for lunch, sandwiches again, with Carrington butting at her ankles. She'd had cats as a child, but never as an adult. Neil had been dangerously allergic. Amy had heard that childhood exposure to animals provided some protection against allergies, so when Angus was three, she'd asked Stacey if she and Angus could come play with the barn cats at the farm.

"Anytime," Stacey had said. "You should bring one home."

"But you know Neil is allergic," Amy said for the thousandth time.

"Sometimes, you have to make sacrifices for your kids," Stacey had said with a shrug.

At the time, Amy had thought that her sister had meant that Amy would have to spend her free Sunday afternoons chasing Angus who chased after the docile, well-fed barn cats, all of whom had been named after dinosaurs by Stacey's oldest son. Ankylosaurus, the grandmother to the lot who'd been fixed after she'd brought her second litter to Stacey and Rick's barn, hissed at Angus's approach. The child didn't cry as he did with so many other small and frightening things. Instead, he sat down and watched her. He hadn't approached her after that, but he hadn't ignored her or shied away from her either.

He had soon learned which cats were interested in him—mostly Velociraptor and Pterodactyl—and which ones preferred he keep his distance. Angus proved to be methodical in his cat-watching, in ways that he had not been with just about everything else at that age. And who wouldn't be?

Amy looked out at the waves far from the ship. She was too far inside looking out over a deck to see anything up close. Well, here she was, anyway, finally seeing Angus. It hurt her, but it also gave her some comfort. Away from home, maybe Angus was finally seeing himself too.

For a moment, Amy wondered if she'd ever tire of the gold around her. She closed her eyes, breathed out, then opened them again. One of the many things Angus had taught her was to look at things. To look really closely. She paused for a moment. Already, Amy had a decent mental map of the ship: the elite suites at the front of the ship to the observation decks at the rear with their glittering pools. Grand staircases linking everything between, the chandeliers hanging over them with their signature pear-shaped crystals meant to honor the Cullinan I stone in the Sovereign's Scepter, and the swirling gold handrails guiding passengers up and down between decks in imitation of the scepter's handle. Amy wanted to learn this ship as well as she'd learned her own home. But how well had she done that?

It all came back to home, didn't it? Home. And

family.

Amy wandered back inward toward Penelope and Richard's suite. She was greeted at the door by Zuzanna, who seemed to be expecting her. "The professor is waiting at the table on the balcony," she said. "I'm just leaving."

"No, stay," Amy said. "Just for a minute."

"I'm expected in the next suite in ten minutes. Edyta normally works this floor, but she's not feeling well today. So I'm working this one too." She tapped the railing of her cart. "You're asking about the books back?"

"Oh, no," Amy said. "Keep them as long as you'd like. We haven't had any requests for them. In fact, if you want more, I have a rather extravagant budget, so I'm happy to pick up more in New York once we've docked. Sadly, I could pick up a whole series of paperbacks for the cost of one of those leather-bound histories everyone wants to be seen reading."

Something in Zuzanna's expression softened. "Well, there is a series. I'll leave a note for you?"

"Perfect," Amy said. She paused and caught her breath. Carrington bumped her ankle tenderly. "Why are you not out with Penelope?"

"The professors, they don't want anyone to know that he's here. He has a rather loud meow, doesn't he?"

"But I'm sure the staff knows. Doesn't word get around?" Amy leaned down to scratch Carrington behind his ears. The tabby slumped over and purred.

Zuzanna stifled a laugh. "We know, but we don't say what we know. Professionalism. A cat here, a dog or a bird there, as long as it's kept quiet. We clean up messes, and we keep quiet."

Amy stood up again. "Professionalism, definitely. But the cruise line, do they treat you like professionals?"

The young woman bit her lip. She looked up at the ceiling in a practiced manner, as if she knew how to control her feelings. "Things could be, well…better."

"Better?"

"The pay for our hours, it could be better." Zuzanna breathed carefully. "Our hours could be better, for that matter. If they hired more staff, well. I mean, I'm happy with my three roommates, but it gets to be too much after a while, I suppose." She took a deep breath and straightened the belt of her uniform, a navy blue polyester dress that made Amy's arms itch at the thought of having to wear it. "No, I shouldn't say more."

"I was talking to Lucia last night," Amy said. "If I can be of any help?"

At Lucia's name, Zuzanna brightened. "Lucia is an amazing organizer. She even painted signs for us after we walk out in New York. Gray like the ship. I know the ship is supposed to be silver, but gray is all we could manage here."

"Sounds like y'all have everything under control, then." Amy looked closely at the wallpaper. Not something she'd ever done at home once she'd realized that the twining purple iris print in the kitchen turned her off from the flower soon after Neil had it installed. Cream and ivory birds flew in complex shapes on the wall behind Zuzanna. Amy gasped. "No, I'm sorry, did you say birds? As in birds on the ship?"

Zuzanna laughed. Amy was relieved that she was in better spirits again. "Are you asking about a specific bird that happened to fly into an elite-level suite?"

"Do you know about that one?"

Zuzanna nodded. "We keep quiet from the management, but we do talk among ourselves. You're asking about the Jenkins suite?"

"That's the one," Amy admitted. Carrington bumped her ankle again.

Zuzanna looked down at her watch. "I need to go, but yes. Jagoda said she was cleaning the bathroom when the son started to argue with the father about a woman. Something about being obsessed with this woman, but Jagoda couldn't make out a name. Something too about art, the father was yelling about having to sell his art collection. About how it was all aboard the ship and why that was a problem. One of the paintings in particular. That one, that one, the father kept yelling. I'm sorry, but that's all she heard. Then Jagoda goes out, they realize she's there, and then they tell her they were chasing a sea bird." Zuzanna shrugged.

"Thank you, Zuzanna, you've been very helpful."

The young woman nodded and rolled her cart out into the hallway.

"All right, you," Amy said to Carrington. "I'll bring you in some tuna salad, deal?"

Carrington meowed while still purring. Amy took that as an agreement.

Chapter Ten

"Amy, sit," Penelope motioned as Amy came through the balcony doorway. This side of the ship was shaded, and the coolness of the breeze belied the fact that it was late August. Still summer, but so far north and on the ocean, still quite cool. Far out on the surface of the water, the waves hinted at the presence of the sun somewhere in the sky. "You were chatting with Zuzanna for a while."

"About books, I'm afraid. You can take the librarian away from the books, but you can't take the books away from the librarian, or something like that," Amy said. "Mostly, though, we were talking about clues."

"A half-eaten sandwich is evidence that, alas, I have not waited for you," Penelope said. "I'm not a very gracious host when I'm hungry."

"Neither am I," Amy said. "I do apologize for making you wait—or not—but Zuzanna just took Lucia off our list of suspects."

"I didn't think she should have been on it." Penelope raised her glass of iced tea.

"I saw gray paint on her jacket sleeve," Amy said. "And I jumped to conclusions because it was pretty similar to the gray in Venus's dress." Penelope passed her the tray of sandwiches. She nearly took the tuna fish but remembered the hungry tabby inside and chose the club sandwich instead. "I didn't seriously think she could have anything to do with the forgery. I just felt like something was amiss. Anyway, Zuzanna explained the gray paint. Protest signs. So there's that."

"Indeed," Penelope said. "I'm glad, anyway. Lucia is too much of a professional for that sort of business, I'd think."

Amy took a bite of the sandwich. In spite of being out in the damp air, the bread was still softly toasted, and the bacon and lettuce crisp. "I have another confession to make, Penelope."

"You committed the forgery?"

Amy laughed. "No, then that would answer one major question. Actually, I'm having trouble with my internet access. I went to see the head of IT, and he just told me to change my password, which I did. But still no access."

"You want to use ours, then?"

"If you don't mind," Amy said. She speared a strawberry with her fork and held it to her nose for a moment before biting into it. The smell of summer. The smell of those long summers growing tomatoes and peppers in the backyard with strawberries just outside the back porch in those strange pots they seemed to like. Angus had liked the dirt, and to be honest, so did Amy. "I'm not the technical whiz I made myself out to be, am I?"

"Or maybe someone is sabotaging you?"

Amy shook her head. "I hadn't thought of that. Why would someone do that?"

"If there was a forgery in the library, a crime, then wouldn't the perpetrator want to cut access to the internet for the person who had the most direct access to the painting?"

"Makes sense," Amy said. "But who? I'll puzzle that one out later. So, the laptop?"

"I'm afraid Richard has ours for the afternoon. He's giving a talk on the history of naval battles in the north Atlantic." Penelope laughed. "Terribly boring stuff to me, but he can go on about it, and moreover, the passengers love it. Or enough of them do so that the cruise line has kept us on this long."

"All right, then," Amy said. "Let's change the subject. If you're not into naval history, then how did you get into archeoastronomy?"

"Sideways," Penelope said. "I grew up in New York, but my father's parents had an apple farm upstate. In the summers we'd go out there, my sisters and I with my mother and father. He was something of an amateur astronomer. Found a comet, even. The stars got me out there, I suppose. The dark night sky, it was something I wanted to be a part of."

"Like a goddess?" Amy said. "Venus rising?"

"More like an explorer. Maybe that's why the idea of cruising the ocean appealed to me so much. This was all my idea, you know." Penelope set her head in her hand. "Richard is just a good sport. About a lot of things."

"That must be wonderful," Amy said.

Penelope shook her head. "You say that as if Neil wasn't?"

"Oh," Amy said. "Maybe not. He was wonderful in his own way. He was a good dad to Angus, even if the two of them baffled each other. Neil never withheld himself from Angus. Or me, either. For most things. It was just that he didn't stop to think about whether we'd want what he gave us."

Amy told Penelope about the house in Dawville, the one he'd bought not too far from where she'd grown up. It had been a surprise, as had been the fact that he'd spent a small fortune on repairing the house and having an addition built after he'd bought and torn down the two neighboring houses. Amy had just finished grad school and was sending out resumes to urban branches and larger suburban libraries around Houston, where Neil's employer was based. They could afford the house and its necessaries, or at least he could. Neil made sure of that.

When she'd graduated having none of her calls from the interviews returned, Stacey said glibly one afternoon that she should try the local library. "Jewell, the librarian, just retired, so there's a position open there. Two actually, since they never filled her junior's position, either." Amy did, and she balanced the major duties between herself and her grad school friend who'd interviewed not long after she did. Tiffany took to small town life like she'd grown up there, not in some wealthy suburb of Austin, as she had done.

"So, controlling, then?" Penelope wrapped up the tuna sandwich in a napkin and motioned for Amy to join her inside. In spite of the sun, the cool breeze overwhelmed her, and she was glad to get out of it. Or maybe it was just thinking about her home, that now wasn't.

"Not quite that, either," Amy said. "How am I supposed to figure this art forgery thing out if I can't figure out my own marriage?" She laughed. Carrington hopped off the chair he'd been lounging in, having had no luck finding a sunny spot. With each step, his purr was punctuated by a chirp, as if he were asking her a question he already knew the answer to.

Penelope laid the tuna fish sandwich on a plate on the bathroom floor for him. "Marriage is, let's say, difficult to puzzle out. You're too close into it when you're there, but then once you're out of any relationship, how can you trust that you remember things as they were?" The cat's smacking up the insides of the sandwich echoed in the bathroom. "And it gets more complicated once you add children into the equation."

"Well, you and Richard have succeeded, haven't you?" Amy peeked inside the bathroom with its pearl white tile, the crystal light fixtures, the gold accents along the shower and vanity, and a slice of bread disposed of on the floor. "Five girls, I can't imagine how you managed."

"In our way." Penelope told Amy that Richard had been married before, and his three daughters were the product of his first marriage. His wife passed away when his daughters were teenagers, a complicated time without the heartbreak of losing a parent on top of it. Penelope, well settled into her career, used a fertility clinic to fulfill her longing to be a mother. After her twins were born, her parents moved in with their daughter and granddaughters, while Penelope kept on with her career. Only after a heated debate in a faculty senate meeting five years later did the widowed Richard meet with Penelope. "It wasn't a long engagement, you could say. Richard's daughters were mostly grown by the time we were married, and it took some work, but we all meshed together. So not simple, but it can be done."

"I don't know," Amy admitted. "I look at my sister. She knew since junior high that she wanted to live the farm life, work on the land. Everything she did was in service to that dream. She even met her future husband in the Future Farmers of America club freshman year of high school. They got married right after they graduated, went off to college together, came back and took over his parents' farm. Four kids, a solid marriage, a thriving farm, and no doubts at all."

"I can't think she's never doubted any of it," Penelope said. Carrington finished his tuna, then buried the bread under the plate. He poked his head out of the bathroom and chirped. "No, that's all for you, darling boy. Come up here for a clean and a scratch." She patted her lap, and the cat waddled over to her and leaped up to the sofa. He took his time cleaning his whiskers and his paws before settling into Penelope's lap for a scratch behind the ears.

"That's definitely what it looked like from the outside," Amy said. "But we aren't ones to talk about deeper things like that. I can talk with Tiffany, because she's so open about how she feels about everything. It's hard not to be open back, you know? I've tried to tell Stacey how much it means that she practically raised Angus while I was at work and while Neil was away on business."

"Why haven't you told her?"

"You're right, I should tell her. She just doesn't seem like someone who'd need to be told these things, though."

"Sisterhood is complicated, too, Amy," Penelope said. "But it's worth investing in."

"You're right. Sisterhood is complicated, but it

shouldn't be." Amy reached over to pet the sleeping cat, who was now drooling on the sofa cushion. "Better wipe that up so we'll stay in the housekeeping staff's good graces."

"Of course," Penelope said. "Otherwise, I'll be on the hook for buying books, too."

Amy sighed. "New subject. Here's an odd one," Amy ventured. "Have you seen Diane Westgrove Lewis since the night of the party? Brent Detweiler has asked me twice now to go talk to her. He thinks Raymond Entwhistle turned her against him, but I don't quite know why. Maybe hiding his tracks from messing things up with the wrong painting?"

"I haven't crossed paths with her, though Richard and I have invited her for tea and conversation and to be the guest of honor at our lectures on this leg. Just a politely worded 'no' back from her every time on the ship's stationery, I'm afraid. Wellie is, from what I've heard, part of the late night crowd with the dance instructors and the ship's astronomer," Penelope said. "She doesn't act the part of the older woman, that's for sure. Diane seems more grounded, more present. Why are you so insecure about seeing her?"

"Because she's the kind of philanthropist I wanted to work with at some main library. I used to think about gala fundraising nights for literacy programs or having big name talents in from New York or London, and I was too scared to act on that dream. I thought I wanted what Neil seemed to want from me. Plus, it was simple, wasn't it? To be the small town librarian with the son playing in the backyard and the husband who worked out of town. I didn't have to push myself, I didn't have any challenges, did I?" Amy grabbed a tissue from the box and dabbed first at Carrington's mouth and then at the ivory upholstery of the sofa. "Neil left me about a year ago, so that wasn't my doing. And Angus, well, he needed to leave me, didn't he? It was his time to go off to college, spread his wings. So I left because everyone else had."

"Your sister and her family didn't," Penelope pointed out. "And your parents are still there."

"They are," Amy said. "But I was the dreamer. And at some point, a long time ago, I stopped dreaming."

"You're here, aren't you?"

"Because my sister-in-law, or formerly so, pretty much talked me into it," Amy admitted. "I don't think I would have made this leap on my own. Not this far."

"Well, you're here now," Penelope said. "And this seeing Diane Westgrove Lewis business, that's part of your job. You're a good librarian, Amy. I've seen you at work with the passengers. You know what people want."

"Everyone except myself, right?"

"Go find out what Diane wants. See her and ask her. Preferably without the oversight of her sister or her nephew. Just her." Carrington sighed deeply in his sleep, snorted, and then turned over onto his back. "Ask her why she thought the painting in the library isn't her original work."

"You're right, Penelope. Thank you." Amy looked at her watch. She had ten minutes to get to the library before she'd need to open for passengers again. "You're right."

Penelope was right. Amy faced her nerves all afternoon, the painting staring down at her. Something *was* wrong with it—Amy was convinced of this by now. This was her library and the event had been hers to host, to steer toward success. She'd failed in the first place by not showing who she was, how capable a host she could be. She couldn't fail again, even if it meant facing her fears of inadequacy. Her fear of failure for lack of trying.

Amy locked up the library at 5 p.m., her usual closing time. Dinner would begin in an hour, a formal affair for most, which meant most of the passengers would be back in their staterooms, preparing themselves, or, for the later diners, amusing themselves with a drink or an appetizer in one of the cafes before dressing in their finest for an unforgettable meal beneath one of the crystal chandeliers the cruise line was known for. Everything glittered aboard this ship. It was supposed to. It was what the passengers wanted, and, to be honest, it was what Amy herself wanted. To be a part of that glamour. She'd probably grab something at the staff canteen and eat in her small room, trying to keep warm, while reading if she could manage it. If the lights weren't too bright for her roommate, who needed to sleep early and wake early.

They all kept different cycles, but that kept the ship running smoothly.

Or looking like it, at least.

Before she did that, Amy decided to go back to the Westgrove sisters' suite. If she happened to run into Curtis and Cole, then she'd face that challenge if she needed to. Right now, she needed to focus on talking to Diane. She'd done it before, and Diane had proven to be as gracious and elegant a person as her reputation purported. All she needed to do was repeat that here.

Under Wellie's watch. Or, worse, the complicated watch of Raymond. When they'd first met, Diane Westgrove Lewis seemed brighter, more attentive than she had at the party. Was it the fatigue of the party? Or knowing the long journey ahead of her, one with an uncertain end in New York? The paintings would sell. Diane Westgrove was, after all, the philanthropist Diane Westgrove Lewis, and the charities she chose to support were always sound. Someone that invested— literally—in people couldn't be that much of a misanthrope, could she?

Besides, Amy remembered what Wellie had said about her, that she was capable of glamour. Wellie's words buoyed her. If Amy was capable of glamour, then she was capable of the grace she needed to get to Diane Westgrove Lewis.

Amy thought better of coming empty handed. She had no time to visit Lionel at the florists' atelier, so she went back inside and silently thanked the IT staff for making the library catalog a database she didn't need internet access to search. There wasn't much on dance, unfortunately, but there were a number of books on twentieth century art, including one on the art scene in the 1960s. It wasn't much, but maybe Amy could use a book to make a connection with Mrs. Lewis. It wasn't the first time she'd done so, and she reminded herself that a book often eased a conversation in the way so many other things could not.

Throughout her walk to the elite suites, Amy sensed the increasing excitement in the passengers. For the most elite and most loyal of passengers, there was to be a Gold and White Ball after dinner at the fanciest restaurant. Maybe Wellie would be there, or maybe not.

Why would Wellie take an interest in the dance instructor if she had eschewed dance herself for so long? Maybe Wellie would be dressing for dinner. Amy could see her in a long white satin gown trimmed with gold, looking every bit the aristocrat her father's family had been back in England. That Raymond's was as well, if Amy remembered the connections correctly. Already, some of the passengers had begun to emerge from their staterooms, women in long gowns, some white, some gold, some both, and men in white tie with top hats. Tiaras sparkled even in the muted lights of the passageways. Diamonds shimmered around wrists and fingers and above decolletage.

It was all just over the top, and there was something wonderful about it. It all suggested that someone royal—or at least titled—was aboard the ship. Raymond? She couldn't see him in white tie, dancing the night away. Amy knew far more about these things than she ever admitted to anyone, especially Neil. She'd read the *Debrett's Handbook* forward and back. Ages ago, she'd procured a copy for the reference section of her hometown library. Tiffany had laughed about it, had called her Lady Amy for weeks. Occasionally, someone would open the book, gaze at it for a while, and Amy felt the intensity of the daydreams it made possible. How often would anyone from a small town in Texas use proper British form in their day-to-day lives? She couldn't even manage it, married to a Brit as she was. Well, a Brit who pretended to be something of a cowboy, even if Stacey and Rick didn't own horses— too expensive to maintain—or cattle—they were farmers, not ranchers after all.

Amy arrived on the elite floor. She exited the

elevator and turned into the passageway that led to both Curtis Jenkins's suite and the Westgrove sisters'. The slight movement of a spectral figure in the shadow outside the Westgrove's suite stopped her. The ghostwriter, again, stood looking at their door. After a few moments, the young woman approached and knocked. No one answered. She hung back in the shadow again, then balled up her fists. Knocking loudly this time, she called out, "Diane, it's me. Can you come to the door, please? I'm worried about you. I haven't seen you for days."

The door opened. Wellie was even more resplendent than Amy had imagined. She wore a white gown with cap sleeves and long white gloves. Over these were at least four gold rings set with large, white stones. A tiara sat atop her angled gray bob. The impression was striking, even more so after she emerged completely from her suite. In the soft light of the hallway, gold palmettes in a Roman style glowed on the hem of her dress. The motif appeared in a more muted pattern on the bodice, giving Wellie the appearance of a temple in herself. A golden court shoe peeked from beneath her hem. "What do you want?"

"Ms. Westgrove, I do apologize, but I'm looking for Diane. Is she there?"

Wellie straightened, marble-like in her posture. "If I recall, she said she had a luncheon planned with you and the publisher, what's his name, Rottweiler, I think. I saw her off late this morning, and I haven't seen her since."

"You haven't seen her either?"

"I'm not her secretary, now am I?" Wellie moved back into her suite, the gown rustling around her. "If I see her, I'll be good enough to report your concern to her. Now, as you see, I am about to meet some darling young dancers for dinner and entertainment after at the Gold and White. Good night. I can't imagine you'd received an invitation."

"Thank you all the same," the ghostwriter said.

"Oh, and the pin on the clasp of the brooch you borrowed from Diane is bent," Wellie half-shouted from behind an almost-closed door. "I'll send you a repair bill once we're back on land."

The ghostwriter stepped backward across the hallway. She leaned back against the flocked wallpaper behind her. She turned her head up, as if she were looking at the ceiling. Amy stepped forward toward her. "Diane's missing?"

"I don't know about that," the young woman said. Her eyes were glassy and she kept looking up at the figure work on the ceiling, or so it seemed. "If you'll excuse me."

"No, wait, I'd like to talk to you about the book," Amy said.

The ghostwriter shook her head and walked quickly toward the stairway. She opened the door and vanished inside.

Chapter Eleven

Amy looked down at the book in her hands, the burgundy leather cover of which was now marked with a bit of moisture from her palms. No matter, she'd take care of that later. After a deep breath, she knocked on the Westgrove sisters' door. "I told you, I don't know where my sister is. Now, please leave me alone."

"I'm sorry," Amy shouted. "It's Amy Morrison. From the library. You don't know where Diane is?"

After several moments, Wellie opened the door again. This time, her mascara had begun to run a bit and her posture had drooped. "I don't," she said. "The valet laid out her gown and shoes. We were supposed to have dinner together. It's the night of the Gold and White Ball. I suppose you wouldn't know about that. Which is a shame, someone as elegant as you are."

"Maybe not as much as you'd know about these events, Ms. Westgrove. It all sounds lovely." Amy tried not to lose focus on Diane for all the glamour Wellie offered her. Later, she told herself. Maybe she'd have a chance to know that glamour later.

"You should know, too. I mean that." Wellie led her into the suite. "Look in there," she said as she pointed toward what must have been Diane's bedroom. On a mobile rack hung Diane's gown. Shoes, stockings, gloves, jewelry, and tiara all lay waiting for her at their different stations around the room. "Lucy or whatever her name is came in and steamed it for her." Diane's gown was not as florid as Wellie's. The long gold satin dress trimmed in white ribbon and modest in its boat neck and cap sleeves had an almost austere quality next to that of her sister's. Her shoes were low-heeled, and even her tiara was less showy than Wellie's. But the overall effect was one of grandeur, elegance.

"It's so beautiful," Amy said in spite of herself.

"Of course, it's beautiful," Wellie said. "That's the least Diane could do." She took a ragged breath in. "I apologize, Amy. I'm so worried about my sister. What could have happened to her?"

"Let's call the ship's security, first," Amy said. She picked up the phone and dialed the ship's emergency number. Amy reported what Wellie had said as closely as she could. "They'll be here shortly," she said as she hung up the phone.

Something in Wellie's face shifted. "Good," she said. "They'll take care of things."

"I do hope so," Amy said. "Does Diane spend much of the day out on ship?"

"I do," Wellie said. "And my sister isn't forthcoming with her plans. If she even remembers what her plans are. She did say before we departed that she had a celebratory luncheon planned with the publisher and the ghostwriter at Le Bœuf du Duc today, and that she couldn't miss it. I tried to remind her, but you've seen her memory deficits."

"Mrs. Lewis seemed better before departure," Amy said. "Has she been unwell on the trip?"

"Who's to say?" Wellie walked over to the vanity and leaned toward the mirror. "I must seem a horrid old thing to you and all the younger set here. I'm not, really. I've always been brash as a matter of covering over old wounds, you see, and that comes off as, well, uncaring. Diane should be here. This isn't the first time she's abandoned me, though. I'm worried."

"I believe you, Ms. Westgrove."

A knock on the door stopped whatever Wellie was about to say. "Will you get that? I want to fix my eyes before anyone else sees me."

"Of course," Amy said. She went to the main door of the suite and let the two security officers in. They were dressed in gray, and they seemed to belong more to the cold world of the lower decks than to the gloss and glow of the passenger levels of the ship. And yet, they blended in somehow, in the room, with its rich woods and damasks. Much like the phone that Amy found as soon as she needed it, they were there. The two men introduced themselves, showed Amy their lanyards, and asked for Wellie.

The heiress met them in the sitting room of the suite as only a grand hostess could, with grace and charm, even through her worry. Her eyes were fixed, smoothly lined in a color that made their blue compelling as topaz, and no mascara showed beneath them.

Did that mean that she was adept at recovering from bouts of tears? Through practice? Amy suddenly felt sorry for the old woman whose youthful dream of a career on stage had been cut short by her own recklessness. It was all quite pitiful, really. Could Wellie Westgrove not see the gifts she still had, the wealth, the beauty, the privilege? Diane had seen it, and she'd shaped her life around the fact of her fame as best as she could. Which was quite well, really. Amy's sadness for Wellie shifted to pity. What else could she feel for her?

The security officers were thorough if brief. They would first alert all staff to be on the lookout for Diane Westgrove Lewis, and her actions would be tracked through her room card. As an elite guest, she wouldn't have been asked to wear a wristband. If there was no sign of her, then they'd do a more thorough search of the suite. "Oh, thank you," Wellie said, the relief in her voice a bit too much as she showed them out. "I'll be worried, but at least I can go to the Gold and White now, after being a bit late for dinner. My companions won't mind. They'll be waiting for me." She wrapped herself in a white fur capelet with a golden ribbon. Her tiny bejeweled handbag swung on its golden chain beneath. Gloves adjusted, Wellie paused at the door. Amy had followed her. She'd left the book on Diane's nightstand. "Hmm, I suppose you don't have an invitation to the Gold and White either. It's a shame. I have a gown that might suit you."

"That's generous, but you're right, I don't have an invitation." She closed the door. The lock whirred and clicked its reassurance. "And I'm not white tie material, am I?"

Wellie laughed. "You underestimate yourself, dear."

Amy walked Wellie to the elevator. "I hope you have a good night," she said as the elevator going down to the restaurant opened its doors to Wellie.

"You're not coming?"

"No," Amy said. "I think I'll take the stairs. I need to see someone a couple floors down."

"Very well, then," Wellie said. "Good night."

\*\*\*\*

After the glitter of Wellie's gown and jewels, the hallway to the IT office was dark and hopeless. On the off chance one of the IT staff was still at a desk on a late shift, she'd gone by seeking help. The password change had done her no good. And she wanted to have access in the morning, if for no other reason than to be able to send a message to Angus. Kevin Park's office door was locked, but she could see in through its window by the light of a lamp on his desk. She looked at the two children laughing in the field of bluebonnets and smiled. How old was Angus when he stopped letting her take such pictures? "Good night, Kevin Park," Amy whispered, and she made her way back to her room.

A sudden wave of shame overwhelmed her. She'd laughed while she was at his office not because of the absurdity of the situation or out of lightheadedness she felt from skipping lunch. No, she'd laughed to keep herself from crying.

Maybe she should have told him that.

Amy fell asleep early, and she slept well, in spite of her worries about Diane. The whereabouts of the philanthropist no longer fell to her to find. For the first time in days, Beatrice pointed her up to the elites' breakfast table, even if she'd done so after shaking her head at Amy. She would have to do something to get back in the entertainment director's good graces, but until she had figured out the puzzle of the art forgery, Amy couldn't focus on anything else. She'd let security find the artist.

"So no one has heard anything from her?" Curtis asked. He'd dressed in a business suit, tie, and all for this breakfast, whereas the rest were elegantly casual. Another conversation had formed at the other end of the table, which was interrupted by his question. "I find that hard to believe."

"Why is that, Mr. Jenkins?" Brent asked. He waved his fork over his plate of fried eggs, bacon, sausage, and white bread toast. His coffee cup had been refilled twice already. "An old, entitled woman running away after her party doesn't go as it should. I find that easy to believe. You don't know how many divas I've dealt with in my line of work. In my many lines of work, all of which have been successful, I'll add."

The ghostwriter looked up. She was working her way through a croissant slowly, her bowl of strawberries left yet untouched. Her hands were wrapped around her coffee cup as tightly as her shawl was around her shoulders. "She's not a diva," the young woman said softly. Brent and Curtis sparred noisily, but Amy kept her attention on the woman. She was, if Amy had to guess, in her mid-to-late thirties, quite plain with her round face beneath large glasses. Her hair fell long and straight somewhere past her shoulders, and she kept tucking one errant strand behind her ear. "She's never been anything but gracious to me."

Amy nodded. "And to me, when I've been able to talk to her," she said. "She's always been lovely to talk with."

The ghostwriter turned toward Amy. She tucked her hair back, revealing an earring that must have been designed by the Westgrove sisters' grandfather. Or a knockoff that certainly looked like one, with its long strands of silver coming together in an Art Deco motif at the nadir. "I think it's because I've always been honest with her."

"Honest?" Brent knocked his knuckles on the table. "Honest is what you should have been with me. Honest is what you should have been with the editors before you and Diane came up with this—" He shook his head and drank the rest of his coffee in a single swallow. "Exceedingly dull book."

"What could possibly be dull about Mrs. Lewis's life?" Penelope smiled at Brent. "Richard here has told me that you were practically following him like a puppy trying to get us to sign a book deal with you. Without agency representation, I might add." She took a long sip of her coffee then set the cup down slowly. "I suppose it would be good to know what kind of story you find dull so that, on the off chance we take you up on your offer after acquiring representation, we'll know what you find exceedingly dull and try to avoid that."

"I'll tell you what could be dull about Mrs. Lewis's life," Curtis said. "No affairs, no celebrity divorces, no disowned children. Not a single scandal. But there is this one thing," he paused to look at everyone at the table who were now all focused on him, "And this one thing is that she took all of the energy that most of us with her wealth would have turned into champagne-fueled public screaming matches at our spouses and luxury clothes buying binges and marrying someone half our age, and she turned that into her art. That's where her fire is. In her paintings."

Amy wondered for a moment just how old the soon-to-be former Lily Jenkins was.

"That's all very well and good," Brent countered. "But it doesn't make for a very interesting read." He picked up a slice of bacon and examined it, as if it were defective. As if the food aboard ship and at the elites' table especially could be anything but exquisite.

"It might be dull," the young woman said, her voice shaking slightly, "and I might be part of the reason that you think the story is dull, but you wanted a story arc and I got you that. All the first three ghostwriters managed to do was assemble a pile of unrelated facts. Would you rather have had that?"

"Ah, a pile of unrelated facts," Brent laughed to himself. "As a mid-list author of literary fiction, you'd know quite a lot about that, wouldn't you?"

"Are you bringing this up again?" The ghostwriter stood up and excused herself from the table. Her croissant was half-eaten and her strawberries heaped in the bowl.

Amy called after her. "Don't let the wait staff take my plate, I'll be right back," she told Richard before dashing off to catch up with the one person who had earned Diane's trust.

She made her way out to the long golden hallway outside the restaurant. Everything was gold and plush, and, if she was honest, easy to get lost in. At least for her, it was. Beneath her, plush golden carpet which had been cut in a flowing pattern seemed to grab at her feet. She looked around for the ghostwriter in all the golden haze. Amy needed more coffee or more sleep. She didn't know which.

Someone knocked into her, or she knocked into him, a large man caught up in his own dream of the ship, looking down at a program for the evening's entertainment offerings. Amy apologized. She ran in the direction that offered the most solitude, at the end of which was the library.

Catching glimpses of her long hair and gray wrap, Amy followed as best as she could until her hunch was proven right: the young woman leaned against the wall just before the library's doorway. She looked up at Amy and apologized. "I know you don't open for another half-hour."

"No, it's fine," Amy said. She was hungry for the half-eaten eggs, fruit, brioche, and coffee waiting for her on her plate, but that would have to wait for later. "Let's go in."

The young woman nodded, and Amy unlocked the door. She steered the ghostwriter to the nook beneath the Princess Margaret roses. Someone from the florists' atelier must have tended to them while she was gone, for a drop of water held its shape on the back of the chair. "You saw me," the ghostwriter said. "Both times, outside Diane's suite. I wasn't sure if I should have said anything to you, but I think something is going on."

"Something?" Amy paused. "Hold on, I know you're the ghostwriter, but no one introduced us."

"I'm not surprised. I'm Erin Dunn," she said. She extended a hand, which Amy took. "Though my name is nowhere on the book."

"Erin," Amy said. "Please, you said you think something is going on?"

She took a deep breath in and looked up at the deep pink blooms above them. "Diane has a pink rose, too. A little lighter than that. She won't say it, but she's very proud of them. The Diane Westgrove Lewis hybrid. Pride of place in her garden, by the gazebo she brings her grandchildren to for ice cream when they visit her in the summer."

"You must know her pretty well, after writing the

book together," Amy ventured. She wanted to steer Erin over to the painting, but not yet. "And she let you borrow the brooch for the night of the party."

The ghostwriter paled. "I'm afraid I did bend the clasp a little. I didn't know I was holding it so tightly when I went in to replace it. Diane gave me a copy of her key, you see. And she said it was okay for me to come and go if I wanted. She knows I'm in an interior room, which is all Brent would book for me, since he didn't want me along on this trip really, and that I like seeing the outside, especially when I'm nervous."

"That's very kind of her," Amy said.

"Oh, Diane is very kind," Erin said. "And not in the arms-length sort of way a lot of philanthropists and elegant hostesses are. Or are supposed to be. Diane was quite forthcoming with me, though it took a while for us to break the ice. Brent was desperate for someone to come in and fix the piles of unrelated facts the other celebrity ghostwriters had amassed. I share an agent with the last one. They weren't getting anywhere."

Amy shifted in the plush chair. "So Diane saw you as a novelist, not just someone trying to get her story to write a sensational story?"

"I'm not a tabloid journalist, if that's what you mean. Unlike the others," she said. "Anyway, my novels were about to get dropped from my publisher's catalog, so I asked my agent if she could pitch me, since I know how to tell a story, even if my stories don't sell as well as celebrity tell-all's. Brent took a chance on me. I'd read the notes from the other writers, and I was honest with Diane at our first meeting. I told her that the book wasn't working because no one had found the story yet." She paused and laughed as she pushed her hair behind her ear again. "She told me that the book wasn't working because the other writers weren't satisfied with the facts she gave them. We spent three months together shaping what we could, and there's the book. Brent thinks it's dull because, as Curtis said, Diane lived a scandal-free life."

"Did you talk to Wellie? Truth be told, Wellie makes me a bit nervous too, even if she seems to be a good spirit." Amy resisted looking over at the painting. "She's just so, I don't know, grand."

"No, Diane didn't have much to say about her beyond their childhood," Erin said. "And, no, it's not Wellie that made me nervous when I went into their suite."

Amy leaned forward. "Raymond Entwhistle, then?"

Erin laughed. "Oh, he's a big puppy, really. Granted, he's a grand champion fancy breed, but a puppy nonetheless." She bit her nail. "I take it he's feeling some combination of seasick and sorry for botching his job transporting the painting. Don't tell him I said that to you, about him being grandly affable. He likes to keep his shaggy and off-putting appearance. Anyway, he wasn't there either. Wellie kept him out of their suite, as far as I could tell."

"I promise, I won't reveal Raymond's true nature." Amy watched the light change. She couldn't see the long sunrise from this side of the ship, of course, but something reflecting off the water made the library glow. She'd have to open soon. No time for another coffee between now and then. "What made you nervous? Something in the suite bothered you, didn't it?"

"I have to ask you not to tell anyone what I'm about to say, once again."

"Of course, but if someone is in danger—"

"I don't know about that," the ghostwriter said. She looked around, as if anyone else were with them. "Look, no one else besides Diane was supposed to see *Venus Rising* before its debut here, right? Part of the mystery. But Diane showed me the painting."

"That one?" Amy pointed to the painting hanging in the gallery. Outside, she could hear conversations, passengers waiting to come inside and escape into a book for a while.

Erin shook her head. "That's not the painting she showed me. It's nice, that one, but it isn't the one she painted at art school. That one was, I don't know, visceral and engaging. This one is just pretty."

"You think someone switched the paintings?"

"I don't know," Erin said. The voices outside grew in number. "Diane does forget things from time to time. But it's little things, like what time her appointments are or the name of an actress on a TV show she likes to watch. Something like this, she wouldn't forget. I don't know why someone would want to make it look like she did."

A polite knock interrupted them. Amy looked at her watch. She was five minutes late opening. "I'm sorry, I should open before we get complaints."

"No, please go," Erin said. "I understand."

Amy asked her to wait there until she let the passengers in. There were quite a few, none of whom would have attended the Gold and White Ball the night before, or at least not without foregoing sleep. She guided passengers to their sections of interest, looked up books, and made small talk with those who were still enchanted by the previous evening's show of tiaras and top hats. When the crowd settled into their reading nooks or filtered out with their finds, Amy went back to the corner where she'd left the ghostwriter.

Except the ghostwriter was gone.

Chapter Twelve

Something about the Gold and White Ball had set off quite the interest in the histories of such events, and there was a rush to the library as the day went on among those who wanted to know more. Good for the library, in that passengers who might not have registered it was there were now clamoring to use it. Good for Amy in that the cruise line had prepared her well by stocking histories of balls, etiquette books, and memoirs of those who had danced at such events. The rush kept Amy busy for the duration of the morning.

"Ah, look," a woman said to her companions. They were dressed in tiaras—plastic ones, but still sparkling in the pendant lights of the library—and summer dresses, as if they almost wanted to play the roles of the people in the hallways the night before. "It's the painting I told you about. You heard about the dancer? The famous one? Her sister painted this. Her *older* sister."

"I saw her on the grand staircase," said one of the group. "On the arm of the ballroom dance teacher. I've never seen so many diamonds on the same person at the same time."

"The painting is pretty," another one of her friends remarked.

"She is pretty," the other one said. "But must they display this painting of a woman practically slithering in that wet dress? It's not decent, is it? Good thing the children's activities are on the other side of the ship."

They shook their heads, stones in their tiaras sparkling, and moved off to the section featuring biographies of British aristocracy. The dancer, they said. Something had gone on last night at the ball, but who would know? Maybe she could catch Lucia and ask around.

Or Penelope and Richard? She'd ask them later. They were having lunch with a few of the elite passengers today, so no chance to talk to them until after their afternoon lectures. She would come back to that later.

As the restaurants began their lunch services, the crowds cleared out of the library. Amy locked the door and sat down at her desk. She changed her password again, just in case, but the same message popped up as the days before: internet access blocked. Data usage reached.

She grabbed her keys. Kevin Park, or one of his assistants, would be available. She closed and locked the door behind her, then thought better of going without evidence. Amy unplugged the laptop from its charger and took it with her. Maybe she should have done this the last time.

The hallways were still buzzing. Even the piped-in music in the ship, ever present and which she'd stopped registering a few days into her first leg, seemed more regal, more elegant, more ambitious. Amy couldn't quite say why. She'd sung in the school choir for a year in sixth grade, then decided she'd had enough music for a while. No one in their family had much musical talent, so no one much cared whether she kept singing.

But still, now, she'd wished she knew just enough to tell her why the music above her had changed.

Or why her attention to it had, at any rate, changed.

\*\*\*\*

The receptionist in the Information Technology suite smiled and waved Amy toward the staff offices. Kevin was closing his office door just as Amy rounded the corner. The assistants were elsewhere, either at lunch or out on calls to help with internet issues. The same thing she was seeking help for now. It was rather frustrating, that she wasn't able to solve this one on her own.

"Amy, hello," he said. "You've just missed Montague and Kit. He's on lunch, but she should be back soon. Something's amiss with one of the routers in the Boeuf."

"And you're leaving for lunch," Amy said.

"And I am leaving for lunch."

Amy looked down at her laptop. "I'm sorry, it's just that I changed my password twice and I'm still getting the same error message. I'm usually pretty good at resolving these things. But I can't, and I'm trying to download a message from my son at college, which I'll admit is personal, and I need to look something up about a dancer and a painting. Both of which are definitely not personal."

"Slow down, one thing at a time," he said. Kevin looked down at his keys then opened his door. "Come in. Sit down."

Amy did. She sat in one of the two chairs facing his desk, and he sat in the other. She opened the laptop and attempted to log in to her email, which brought up the error message. "This is as far as I can get," she admitted.

"May I?"

She nodded and slid the laptop toward him. He logged her out and logged himself in to an administrative account. After a few minutes of opening and closing things and typing on the command line, sat back in his chair. "So Montague still never got back to you, did he?"

Amy shook her head. "Can you fix it?"

"Just did," he said. "Something downloading lots of nonsense files, early in the morning. Got rid of that and all the files it had downloaded. Mostly pictures of nightgowns. Long frilly things with straps. Old fashioned, some of them."

"Nightgowns?"

"I didn't look at them all, but that's what the filenames indicated," he said. "Cameo satin. Bubble-gum cotton. Vintage coral. Any of those names mean anything to you?"

Amy shook her head. "Not at all."

"I hate to ask this."

"But?"

"But have you done any online shopping on your laptop? That's prohibited, you know. Personal shopping on the cruise line's property." Amy wasn't sure whether she was more embarrassed by his look of concern or the amusement in his voice.

"I do know that," Amy said. "Do you think I'd be careless enough to first of all go shopping for what sounds like lingerie on the cruise line's laptop, and second of all manage to download a virus on top of that? It's not like I haven't been single-handedly maintaining my library's computer systems for the past twenty years, okay? I know better than that, thank you."

"Okay then," Kevin said. "Next uncomfortable question. Do you leave the laptop out at all?'

"No, I don't. It's locked in the desk unless I'm actively using it," she said. "I'm aware of security protocols. I practically wrote them for my previous library."

"Then does someone have access to the desk lock? I'm assuming it's locked through your badge and keys like the doors are." He logged out and slid the laptop back toward her.

"No, I keep it locked unless I'm looking something up," she said. "Or someone needs to scan something with it." Then the realization hit her like a hard wave against the side of the ship. At the party the night of the departure, the scanner one of the staff had brought had malfunctioned. The scanner that she'd fixed. And she'd left her laptop with the staffer, thinking that nothing would happen. Except something had happened. She gasped and felt the blood rushing from her face and hands, leaving her cold. "This is my fault."

"Okay, step back a bit," Kevin said.

Amy related the events the night of the party. "I doubt it would have been the staffer, since he was scanning badges and keeping an eye on the door the whole time. And Beatrice Taylor was keeping an eye on him. But I wasn't watching the whole time. And when the party ended, badly, I might add, the staffer handed me my laptop from beneath his chair."

"Which he wasn't watching the whole time?"

"It seems not, unfortunately, "Amy said. "This is my fault. And I can't fix it."

"This is your fault, then. But maybe we can fix it."

Kevin tapped his Texas A&M ring on the edge of his desk. "Aside from downloading a bunch of nonsense files, no damage was done. And we haven't seen anything like this on any other account."

"So not bad for the ship," Amy said. She took in a deep breath. "But bad for me."

Kevin shook his head. "Since no damage was done, and since you fixed something Monty should have on the night of the party, I'll let you off with a warning. This time. But, Amy, that was pretty careless of you."

"Which I should have known better, I know." Amy rested her elbows on the desk and pushed her face into her hands. "That whole night was more of a failure than I'd thought."

"Maybe. For now, we just need to figure out which of the many, many guests and staffers at the party had access to your laptop, who had a bit of technical savvy and a reason to download this many nightgowns onto your laptop."

"No, we don't," Amy said. She looked up. "We need to figure out who was worried I'd figure out the puzzle of Diane Westgrove Lewis's fake painting enough to block my internet access."

"Sounds like you already have a suspect."

"Suspects, really." She looked over at the clock on his wall. Twenty past noon. "Can I get you lunch? As a way of thanking you? Maybe the Boeuf du Duc?"

"A bribe for my silence, is it?" Kevin shook his head. "No thanks. I'm not missing barbecue brisket day at the staff canteen."

"Barbecue brisket day? That sounds, I don't know, risky?"

Kevin laughed. "Let's say I have a morbid

curiosity about what this very British cruise line considers barbecue. It would be nice to have company for lunch. Shall we?"

"Are you going to make fun of me for my carelessness the whole time?" Amy met Kevin's smile. "Especially after I've basically bragged about my technical skills?"

"Just a little," he said. There was something in his ability to report on her failure to protect company resources that made her nervous about losing her position as librarian aboard *The Cullinan Diamond*. But there was also something in his voice that made her more than a little curious about him.

****

They walked what felt like half the ship's length to the staff canteen, talking about the shimmer that the Gold and White Ball still cast over the ship. She followed his lead through passageways she hadn't taken before, all variations on the theme of gold and blue, all mostly distracting her from her guilt over the laptop and her carelessness. Mostly.

But then barbecue brisket day crashed in front of them. How the cruise line managed to get that much smoked beef on the ship Amy wasn't sure, but she wasn't about to turn it down no matter how inauthentic it was, not after missing out on most of her breakfast. They scanned their badges and joined the line for the buffet lunch. Soft white bread lay out in bags cut down the middle. She grabbed a couple slices and scooped a spoonful of brisket next to them. Amy looked down at the containers of pickled jalapenos, and sliced onion, the coleslaw and potato salad, corn on the cob, and for dessert, banana pudding. "Goodness," she said in spite of herself. "I think I might be homesick."

"Me, too," Kevin said with a laugh.

They sat together at a small table under a flickering fluorescent light, the long kind that she'd learned to change by herself during her second week at the library back home. Back home.

"You said your son was at A&M this fall. Freshman?"

"Yes," Amy said. "Angus." The coleslaw was cool but almost slimy on the scratched melamine of her plate. She left that for a bit of the pickled jalapenos.

Her laptop, undergoing a virus scan, whirred next to her, so she wasn't able to jump onto her email as much as she wanted to do that right away. To download Angus's message. To download anything else he sent her.

"I missed driving him there by about a month. But he's going with his older cousins. They all pretty much grew up together, so I left him in good hands."

"Angus? Like the cows?"

"Like the cows, sort of. My ex-husband is a Brit who wanted to be a cowboy. I liked the name because it was my husband's grandfather's name. My ex-husband's. Silly, isn't it? But the name stuck." Amy watched the staffers coming and going, many of them filling paper containers to go, probably back to their rooms in the stomach of the ship where they could catch a sporting event or something. "The one bad thing about living so close to my family is that they protested to the name. Because of the cows. But there it is."

"It's good to have family around," Kevin said. "My kids flew about as far from Texas as they could go, but they do come home for a weekend during bluebonnet season. My ex-wife and I took bluebonnet pictures of our kids every year until they went off to college, pretty much."

Amy started to ask about his ex-wife. She wanted to ask Kevin a thousand questions about his past, his present aboard the ship, and where he wanted to go on it. She forked a too-big bite of brisket into her mouth instead. Sauce ran down the side of her chin. The meat was stringy and tough. "I never thought I'd have barbecue on a ship. Must have shipped it in frozen."

"Which leads one to wonder whether they managed to thaw it out." With the end of his bent metal fork, he pulled a piece of what looked like gristle from the brisket on his plate. "At least the food here is interesting."

"It could be better," Amy said. "Are these chocolate chip cookies in the banana pudding?"

"The food could be better," Kevin agreed. "From what I hear a floor below my accommodations, it would be good if they treated the staff as well otherwise."

"So I've heard, too," Amy said. "And seen. Are you joining the walk out?"

"I'd hate to lose my 'round the world' gig. But yes, I am." Kevin said. "This is my mid-life adventure, though. How often do you get to sail around the world on other people's money?"

"If you're Diane Westgrove Lewis, apparently you do that rather often," Amy said. "And she brought her sister, Wellie."

"Wellie Westgrove," Kevin said. "Like a boot."

"She was a dancer. Modern dance."

"Fascinating."

"Fascinating? Do you dance? Ballet?"

"Not ballet," he said. "On a post-divorce whim, I took all the social dance classes I could find. Waltz, cha-cha, foxtrot, Argentine tango, yes. And," he leaned in, "If you get a few Shiners in me, I'll even line dance."

"In boots?"

"I haven't gone that far," he said with a laugh. "Your laptop scan should be done. You might want to take a look at that email now." He logged out of the administrative account and turned the laptop toward her.

Amy set down her fork and logged in. She opened her email client, and dozens of messages downloaded, some of them waiting for her for days. Or at least since the night of the party.

"Angus," she said softly. "Angus, Brent Detweiler— "

"Brent Detweiler? The tech CEO?"

"He's playing publisher now, at least to the rich and famous."

"Yes, I've heard of him. Hard not to when I've been in IT as long as I have." Kevin shook the ice in his glass. "What a career. Started off as a programmer and worked his way up to the top. Then decided that wasn't glamorous enough."

"He blames me for Diane Lewis not remembering the painting." Amy shrugged and went back to her emails. "Angus, Stacey, Angus, Tiffany, Angus, Angus, Diane Lewis." She stopped herself. "Wait, this should show me the date and time the messages were sent, right?"

Kevin nodded. "That's how timestamps work on email."

"Okay, I knew that, but I'm feeling a little less technically savvy than I once felt," Amy admitted. She took a big bite of potato salad so that she could double check what she was seeing while she had her mouth full. "This is odd."

"The potato salad? Yes, it is odd."

Amy swallowed and grimaced. "That's odd too, but I mean that it's odd that Mrs. Lewis sent me a couple messages. Not much to them, just asking me to come see her so we could talk. One the day after the party and another one the day after that."

"So? Go talk to her tonight after you close up."

Amy looked up over the screen at Kevin. There was something in the nonchalant way he said it that reminded her of Neil. There was also something in the sweetness of his smile that reminded her of Neil, or of the Neil she thought she'd met while watching a golf game ages ago, but that was something she had to put away for now. "No, I can't."

"What are you worried about?" Kevin said. He was trying to give her the same pep talk Penelope had, except now it was all the more troubling.

"I can't, Kevin. She's missing."

"Missing?"

"Wellie, her sister, reported her missing last night," Amy said. She recounted the story about Wellie, the ghostwriter, and Diane's absence, all but Wellie's offer to dress her up and take her along to the Gold and White. Amy had never learned to dance, not really, so she couldn't possibly go even if she didn't have Diane to worry about. Anyway, that was for later, too. "I can't just go talk to her."

"Look, forward her messages to me," Kevin said.

He gave her his email address and told her he would do some forensic work on this too. "If she's still sending messages from a device, we can try to track her using that. It's not much."

"It's something," Amy said.

They finished their lunches and all too quickly left for their respective offices. "Keep in touch," he said as they parted ways at the elevator. Something in Amy fluttered. "About the painting, I mean. If anyone says anything odd around my office, I'll pass that along to you."

"I will," Amy said. She wanted to say more, but her mind was now on finding Diane Westgrove Lewis.

****

The library was once again packed in the afternoon. Someone had leaked Diane's disappearance to the passengers, and a line wrapped around the hallway to get into the library to see her painting. Which was, Amy knew now, not her painting. She opened the door and the hushed crowd filed in past her. Who would want word of Diane's absence spread so widely? Wellie, if that meant more sympathy for the worried sister, but would she need it in such an abstract way? There was Curtis, too, who needed to drum up publicity for the paintings he would sell in New York. Art from a missing artist would sell for a higher price, wouldn't it?

And Brent. The memoir, the dull book, as he called it, was just sitting there, right out of reach of so many people angling just to see the painting. Maybe the original painting was too boring in Brent's view? He'd know what sells, and a painting that was too challenging, too artistic, might not be what would work so well with the celebrity-memoir reading public. She focused on her suspects instead of her anger at what she knew so well after working in libraries for twenty years: most folks are deeper than people like Brent gave them credit for being. Especially readers, no matter what their favorite genre is. Back to Brent, though. If he could get enough people in line looking at the painting and, therefore, looking at the book, he'd be guaranteed to sell copies out of their morbid curiosity, perhaps.

No one seemed to want to look up books, so Amy sat down at her desk with the laptop. Every part of her mothering heart wanted to open up Angus's emails first, but she clicked on "write message" instead and dashed off a quick email to Tiffany instead. They might not have access to an arts database in Dawville, but Tiffany knew librarians who knew librarians. She had to hope this worked. She had to hope that maybe someone had kept a microfiche copy of the art school's newspaper or that some university had the archives of her mentors there. There had to be something, somewhere, that proved that *Venus Rising* as Diane Westgrove painted it was not the painting Diane Westgrove Lewis unveiled at the gala for it.

A quick internet search for *Venus Rising* and Diane Westgrove Lewis pulled up just about everything she'd read about the philanthropist and artist before they'd departed, except now more news appeared about the impending sale in New York. Nothing yet about the fact that she was missing, or at least nothing that showed up in the news feed search.

Give it time.

These things always showed up, didn't they?

Chapter Thirteen

"If I have to listen to that man rattling on about how the cruise line ought to commemorate Diane Westgrove Lewis's journey aboard this ship by buying his collection of her early works, I swear to you all, I will jump off this ship," Gemma said drumming her fist against the deck railing. "And I might pull him and his awful son over with me."

Richard shook his head. "Poor fellow will never see it coming."

"They never do, do they?" Penelope laughed. "All day, then?"

"Well, all morning, anyway. Until my docent duties ended at 3 p.m. or so."

They were all leaning against the railing, looking out over the north Atlantic, the cold wind off the ocean pushing them together so that they could keep warm and hear each other. "Wait, he was with you all day? And his kid?"

Gemma nodded. "The son was dressed up and everything. Looked every bit the Eton grad he wasn't."

"You're thinking about Diane?" Penelope asked her.

"When am I not?" Amy looked out into the vastness of the ocean around them, the great nothingness that stretched between London and New York.

"I thought you said you were able to get the messages from Angus now?" The chill in Penelope's voice made Amy shiver too.

"He's fine," Amy said. Maybe he was, but it didn't stop her from feeling guilty about it. "Diane, back to her. She went missing sometime yesterday morning. She missed her lunch with Erin Dunn the ghostwriter, and it sounds like they have a pretty deep friendship, so I can't see Diane just skipping out on that. Especially when Diane had so much weighing on her."

Behind them, the DJ called out to the crowd to shout in unison to the beat he was playing. The crowd's energy was high, even while hers was fading. Lights pulsed in time to the beat, and more and more people pushed their way toward the dance deck. This was a better place to talk than in the staff canteen where they might be heard. News of Diane's disappearance had gone around, and everyone had a theory. Only Lucia was quiet about the kidnapping.

\*\*\*\*

Which was the exact word Lucia had used. She'd met Amy in the hallway just as the library had closed. "Come in, let's chat," Amy had said, sensing the worry on Lucia's mind.

"I don't think this is a simple 'elderly person getting themselves lost on a huge ship' thing," Lucia had confided. "I think this is a kidnapping."

"What? Why?"

"Don't tell me you haven't considered it, Amy."

Amy had sighed deeply. The Princess Margaret roses glowed above them in the single sconce left on in the library. "I have, Lucia. And that's why I want to know everything."

"None of this came from me, okay? I'm only telling you this because I think Mrs. Lewis might be in more danger than staying overnight at the roulette table getting drunk and spending all her money like the old people usually do when they're 'lost'."

"What if you tell me something that I can't possibly have found out elsewhere?"

"Do you want to hear or not?"

"Sorry. I promise. None of this came from you."

Lucia had told Amy about what she'd seen.

The housekeeper had just come through the suite, though Lucia had instructed her not to clean Diane's room yet as she hadn't seen to replacing her gown in its bag along with all the accessories. Lucia had waited until the security team had gone through the rooms of the suite, as she was instructed, but as far as she could tell, nothing had been touched by the team. Everything lay in place as it had done—it hadn't looked as if Diane had done much of anything on the ship except lounge in the chair next to the window Wellie kept open for her. Lucia had felt sorry for the dazed old woman. Not her sniping sister, though.

She had opened the curtain in the bedroom to get more light in to work by. Earrings, cocktail rings, a necklace, the tiara all went back into the navy blue velvet from which they'd come. She'd rolled the gloves and stockings between tissue paper, and she placed the golden court shoes back in their box. She'd left the gown for last, as it required the most space for her to work. Easier to clear everything else out of the way first. That's when she had seen it: the length of pink satin ribbon on the floor, its edges frayed as if someone were worrying it or had used it for a bookmark.

"What's important about the ribbon?" Amy had asked Lucia.

"It wasn't in there the previous morning when I prepared Mrs. Lewis's gown," Lucia had said. She exhaled sharply. "I dropped one of the cocktail rings, which rolled just under the bed. There wasn't anything else under there but the ring. Took me a minute to find it, and I had to use my flashlight to spot the ring. I looked everywhere under there. This ribbon was lying right next to the bed, right near where I was looking the night before."

"Why, though, would some ribbon be significant?"

"You're the one trying to solve the puzzle," Lucia had said. "Not me. Anyway, I didn't want to take it out of the room, and I didn't want the housekeeper to touch it. I had my cotton gloves on anyway for putting away the jewelry, so I picked it up and put it into the nightstand drawer."

"What color pink?"

"About like that, but lighter. Like ballet pink."

Amy had thanked Lucia, and they left the library. She had been mulling over the ribbon when she met Penelope, Richard, and Gemma in the staff canteen for dinner. They'd briefly considered taking the conversation up to Penelope and Richard's suite, but Gemma demurred. "I'm allergic to cats, I'm afraid," she'd said.

"Is Carrington a secret at all anymore?" Richard had asked his wife.

"I didn't tell!" Penelope had pretended to look aghast.

"Neither of you said anything." Gemma had laughed. "You're wearing dark gray trousers, Pen.

Orange cat fur is going to show up on that, you know."

"We've gone through so many lint rollers." Penelope had shaken her head. "But they never quite get everything do they?"

\*\*\*\*

"You said Diane had so much weighing on her, Amy. What do you mean?" Gemma's question shook Amy out of her head. "She just has to sail and smile and eat until we get to New York. What could possibly be troubling her?"

"Don't ask me how I know this," Amy started. "But I know Diane didn't paint *Venus Rising*, or at least not the one in the library. She was right about that not being her painting. I can't say how I found out, but I did."

"Then I won't ask how you found out," Penelope said. "But who did paint the one in the library?"

"Or who had it painted for her?" Richard added.

Amy was chilled by the cold night air. The crowd behind her seemed not to register the cold, dressed as they were in their short dresses and t-shirts. "I'm sorry, I'm exhausted. I need to think this all out. And I want to spend some time with the emails I got from Angus."

"Very well, then," Penelope said. "Do get some rest. We don't want Beatrice complaining about you looking like you could barely string a sentence together at breakfast."

"Come now, Pen, that's not exactly what she said," Richard said.

"Not in so many words, true."

"I do need to be there, tomorrow especially," Amy admitted. "But I need coffee before I can hold my end of a conversation. I don't think I'm alone there, am I?"

Amy said her good nights to her friends on deck.

Gemma followed her inside the glass walls. "You're not getting away that easily from me," she said with a smile. "I need to know a few more things. And I think I can help you."

"Can we sit in the staff cafe?"

"I'd love a cup of chamomile after today," Gemma said.

They went into the staff cafe and ordered their drinks. After they'd received them, they sat down in a quiet corner. The coffee shop was, thankfully, still open but mostly empty this time of the evening. Amy sipped at her hot chocolate. The whipped cream was flavored with nutmeg, and she tried not to slip back into memory, all those nights she'd stayed up with Angus chasing some station from around the world or another or trying to spot some far-off object in the sky through his telescopes. She hadn't thought too much at the time about the radio and the telescope, only her time with her son those Friday or Saturday nights when he was allowed to stay up. Two big mugs full of cocoa and, and when he'd grown too big for marshmallows, whipped cream. "I'm sorry," Amy said. "I'm thinking about Angus."

"I'd be thinking about my kid too if I were you," Gemma said. "My Mum, when I went off to Uni, sent me a text every night before bedtime. Well, what used to be bedtime. You know how it goes." She twirled the sapphire and diamond pendant in her fingers.

"I do," Amy said. "That's a beautiful necklace. Are you a September baby?"

"March, actually," Gemma said. "But I love the color blue."

"Blue like the ocean," Amy said. "Like the ocean Venus is emerging from. You said you wanted to know more."

"I do," she said. Gemma wrapped her hands around the cup of chamomile tea. "I want to know where the original *Venus Rising* is."

"I don't know," Amy said. She took a sip of cocoa. Whipped cream dotted her nose, which she swiped at with the back of her hand. "Why?"

"Because, I told you I was with Curtis all day," Gemma said. She pulled a napkin from the dispenser on the table next to her and handed it to Amy. "I meant that literally. He asked if I wanted to see Diane's early work. I said sure, why not. He had me come by his suite for lunch, and he tried to show me some grainy pictures on a tablet. I told him off, said I couldn't possibly tell the cruise line anything about her early works if he couldn't show me in person. I was halfway out the door when he gave in and told me he had the paintings in the sitting room."

"Did you know that going in?"

"I had a feeling," Gemma said. "So, he takes a dozen early pieces out, all painted around the time she painted *Venus Rising*, and Amy, I was wrong about her."

"That good?"

"I can't say whether or not she would have made a career of it, but there was definitely vision there, and talent too."

"And you want to find the original painting because?"

"So I can see it for myself, mostly," Gemma said. "I don't have a commission for another ship, so I can't buy anything like Curtis seems to think I can. But I have contacts at galleries, that sort of thing."

"Are you going to help Curtis out?"

"As a rule, I don't help out anyone who compliments my 'tea with cream' skin then tries to touch my curls because 'he has never touched natural hair before,' no."

"Is there anything redeeming about this creep?" Amy warmed her hands on her mug. "Do you think he could be behind all this?"

"I didn't see any other paintings in the sitting room, but I don't doubt that he could have it stashed somewhere," Gemma said. "Then after lunch, he joined my next tour."

"So he couldn't have been with Diane, if he was with you all day?"

"Maybe not directly, but I wouldn't put it past him to arrange something, you know," Gemma said. "And there's that son of his."

"True," Amy said. The sugar from the whipped cream and hot cocoa were making her even sleepier. "Let's talk more in the morning. I think I might need your help on something, if my friend back in my hometown can come up with what I hope she can come up with."

They said their good nights, and Amy barely kept her eyes open in the long hallway down to her room. She was glad they'd be in New York the day after tomorrow, but that gave her only two more days to figure out the puzzle of the painting and the missing painter. She hoped Wellie was right, that Diane was hiding out in Raymond's suite to sulk. The alternative was something Amy didn't want to consider, even if

Lucia was probably right.

Amy slipped into bed. Her eyes closed, and she considered the responses she should have written to Angus and Stacey. If she had only known Diane was trying to contact her, though, those messages she would have jumped on first, wouldn't she have? Something urgent must have been on Diane's mind if she'd thought to contact Amy, especially after how badly the party went. Amy knew now that Diane had been right about the painting.

She dozed off for a few hours, then woke with a start. Roisin was still in her bed, so her alarm hadn't woken Amy. Perhaps the caffeine or the sugar from the hot chocolate woke her. Or the sudden sense that the answer was in the memoir. It was a little after 4 a.m.. She'd had enough sleep to make the day work. Amy rose and dressed as quietly as she could, grabbed her bag, then headed to the library. On the way, she grabbed a coffee and a muffin at the staff canteen, something she could eat while she read without leaving any traces on the book.

Even at this hour, passengers filtered through the hallways. Some had attended the ship's astronomer's nightly star-gazing parties. Others had been out dancing at the various clubs on board. She wondered how many were like her, unable to sleep, unable to leave the ship, searching for something that should have been obvious to her.

Inside the library, Amy took her coffee and muffin to the nook with the roses. She set her breakfast down, then pulled the key to the glass case from her desk. Through the clear windows of the library's doors, someone could see all the way to the glass case, so she chose a book with a somewhat similar cover to leave in place of the memoir once she'd taken it out.

The key slid into the lock quietly, and Amy held her breath and turned it. With a strange almost exhalation, the case opened. Amy took out the memoir and replaced the other book.

Beneath the light of the reading nook's pendant, Amy traced her fingers over the missing acknowledgments. The title page was still in place, so she'd start there.

Diane Westgrove, according to the memoir, was born in 1942 to the daughter of a jewelry heiress and the son of an English aristocrat. She was the third child and the elder daughter to a family who'd defined itself against its origins in the sun of southern California. Her father, Quentin Westgrove, was sent to Los Angeles by his father after Quentin's older brother died in the First World War. Quentin made use of his connections in England and its then-empire to build an import company that ultimately made him exceedingly and independently wealthy.

Her mother, Isolde, was the only child of a Boston jewelry designer who'd made his fortune at the turn of the century. When he died, he passed the business on to one of his nephews instead of Isolde, who'd shown great talent as a designer in her own right in her father's studios. Upset at her mother, whom she felt was behind the slight, and tired of the Boston climate, Isolde fled to Los Angeles with what money her father had left her. She set up a studio of her own there. Although her business never took off to the level her father's had, Isolde designed pieces decadent and imaginative enough to catch the attention of all the wealthy young people of the day. At a party, she met Quentin, and they were married three months later. Quentin's parents were, of course, aghast at the match, but they were soon won over by the charming Isolde. She sold her business shortly before the birth of their oldest child, Alfred.

Their childhood—that of Alfred, Giles, Diane, and Jacqueline—was one spent in the southern California sun in winter and in the north of England during the summers they spent on Quentin's parents' estate. In spite of their parents' various business successes, none of the Westgrove children succeeded at much other than being known as the Westgrove children. Alfred joined the Navy after college and remained there for the duration of his unremarkable career. Giles returned to England for good to become an Anglican priest in a quiet rural parish. Diane showed promise as a painter, but she gave up on that dream. Wellie was born after Diane, and a few sentences remarked in her early talents as a dancer. Not much was said about any of her siblings, other than to acknowledge their presence in her early life. Which was not, judging by the slim chapters of the early years, a significant one.

Diane married in 1967, by which time she'd given up on her chances on a career in art. Amy had hoped to hear Isolde's take on Diane's decision, but it wasn't in the book. Amy crossed off the possibility that anyone could have been upset about her childhood and youth because there wasn't much there to say, it appeared.

After this, though, the prose became more vivid and the details more telling. It wasn't exactly a thrilling read and definitely not a titillating one, but the arc the ghostwriter found for Diane's life after her marriage was at least interesting. She'd had her first child two years after her marriage, and this change shifted how she saw herself. Diane's presence in the world shifted from heiress to mother, according to the book. And that shaped how she saw herself as a philanthropist. The arc was pretty simple: Diane wanted to see herself as more than just a donor for good causes. She wanted to do good works herself. She shook off her old haughtiness—she and Wellie must have been quite alike at some point—and learned to be gracious, empathetic, and humble. That was all there was to it, all 300 pages of it, including a rather expansive section in the middle that showed photographs of Diane's life, mostly after her marriage. By the time she'd finished the book, Amy had five minutes to spare before opening time.

She rose to return the book when she heard a knock at the door. Quietly, she peered around a shelf to try to see who was knocking. Another three sharp raps made her nearly drop the book. Quickly, she stuffed the memoir beneath her jacket and walked briskly to the library door.

As she unlocked it, she heard a muffled exclamation. In pushed an especially ruffled Raymond Entwhistle, looking as if he'd gotten less sleep than Amy had. "Thank goodness you're here," he huffed. He closed the door behind himself and locked it.

"Mr. Entwhistle," Amy started.

"I need to talk to you, Ms. Morrison." At first, Amy thought he'd looked over at the painting, but then she realized he was looking at the copy of the book that had replaced the memoir instead. She pushed the copy of the memoir tighter to her stomach. "It's about Diane."

"What else would it be about?"

"I'm afraid the security team are rather insistent about an interview with me," he said. "About my aunt's missing persons case."

"And you don't want to talk with them."

"It's not that I don't want to talk with them." Raymond's voice shook. "It's just that I don't wish to speak with them in my suite."

"And why have you come to me?"

Raymond's eyes narrowed a bit. "I need your help." He held forward a wrapped chocolate bar in his hand. "You see, I didn't wish to get caught, so to speak."

"Chocolate?"

"It's illegal chocolate."

"Explain."

And he did. Raymond Entwhistle, in an attempt to help a dear lady friend from years past, as he put it, brought with him a hundred cases of British-made chocolate into the US for sale, all without going through the proper channels. Or any channels. The details of the cases of chocolate he mentioned flew past her sleep-deprived brain, but the gist of it was that his dear lady friend who could use a bit of help at her British goods shop in New Haven would take delivery as soon as they docked in New York. "So you see, I'm in a bit of a pickle here."

Amy wanted to laugh, but she thought better of it. "You want me to hide a hundred cases of chocolate bars in the library?"

"Something like that," he said. "Or somewhere."

"Why did you come to me, in particular?"

"Because you seem so nice to Diane," he said.

"And she said she'd seen something elegant in you that she thought you should nurture."

"She did, did she?" Amy looked at the doorway. "Oddly enough, Wellie said just about the same thing." A few people had lined up already, some of them clutching books to return before the voyage ended tomorrow. Before they'd have to wake up from this dream. "Diane—when was the last time you saw her?"

"The day after the party," he said. "And then, only briefly. I'm sure if you've spoken to Wellie, she has thoroughly filled your ears with every incriminating possibility regarding my involvement with Diane's disappearance, but sadly, I have no idea where she is. I'm hoping to find somewhere to stash my sweeties so the security team can clear me and move on to something more productive."

Amy waved to the people outside, one of whom had knocked on the door. She felt the book slip from beneath her jacket and caught it with the cover facing outward. "I was just—"

"It's okay. I want to read it, too." Raymond glanced down at the book and then waved the chocolate bar. "Shame if Brent Detweiler finds out if you read it."

"Are you trying to blackmail me?"

"No," he said. "I'm trying to tell you that it's in both of our interests that we help each other."

"Fine," Amy said. "Give me the morning. I'll figure it out."

"How about I cause a bit of a diversion for you?"

"Perfect."

He slipped the chocolate bar into her hand then ran to the door, pretending to work on the lock and speaking loudly about doing so until Amy had time to get the memoir back in its glass case. She returned the book just as the passengers began to filter in. She slipped the chocolate into her jacket pocket. A milk chocolate bar with toffee, Angus's favorite. If she couldn't figure out where to put the boxes of chocolate, at least she might possibly buy a few off Raymond to send to Angus once they were all ashore.

Raymond seemed less and less like a suspect. He'd shown her his hand, hadn't he? But so had Curtis, if indirectly, by showing Gemma the actual paintings. And Gemma had shown her willingness to put herself in peril of a sort to solve the same puzzle Amy was trying to work her way through. But did what they showed her mean anything? Raymond could be a brilliant actor. Gemma could be using Amy's lack of knowledge about art against her. And Curtis, well, putting the paintings in front of Gemma might have been part of his plan all along. Amy might have been an attractive diversion.

Time was running short.

There were too many diversions, and Amy needed to stay focused. Even if she'd become one of them.

Chapter Fourteen

The queue for the library hadn't been for the books, as it turned out. Amy checked her laptop—still no news from Tiffany. At least her internet access was still working. So she stood by the painting, acting if not as a docent, then as a tour guide to a place that had been badly reconstructed. Like the Italian restaurant Neil had taken her to when they had first met, with its pretend Roman ruins. At least the staff weren't dressed up as gods.

Amy shook off the memory and stood by the art and the memoir beside it. "Good to see so many people here," she said to the group of women in line next to see the painting. They were all in long linen dresses, sandals, sunglasses holding back their hair. Maybe they were pretending to be Venus, or at least in her entourage.

"Well," the red-haired one began. "How could we miss it? The publisher, that delicious Brent guy, he starts talking to Gina, there." Gina held up her hand. She was pretty much the opposite of Venus in the painting, dark and voluptuous in her beauty. "He comes over to our table in the lounge and buys a bottle of rosé and starts to chat her up. Then he tells us all about the painting, how Diane Westgrove Lewis painted it. We know her name from the charity events she did in LA, where we're all from. Never knew she painted."

"Not many people did," Amy said. "Aside from her mentors. And her family."

They moved up as the people in front of them moved on. "I don't know," the third one said. "I'm not into art, but this doesn't seem all that. Not like he said it would be."

The women shrugged and left the library. The rush, mostly women, as it turned out, turned into a trickle. Amy didn't want to think about how much Brent Detweiler spent last night, buying wine for women roughly in the forty to sixty age bracket, exactly the demographics of the audience for Diane's book. She'd heard of worse, authors desperate not to fall off the mid-list blanketing libraries they had no connection to with news of their latest book. Publicity departments pulling stunts to get their authors seen on the most coveted social media accounts. But it all came down, for Amy at least, to whether someone would like the book or not. The wider they cast their nets, the more disappointed readers they'll get in the end. If it's about finding the ideal reader, then that was another task entirely.

A ding from her email program called her back to the librarian's desk. Amy shouldn't have left the laptop open, even if she had locked her screen, especially with the rush, but she'd hoped to hear from so many people. Angus and Stacey most of all, but any of her nephews or nieces or her parents would have been good. Or Neil, though their communication had fizzled out to next to nothing after they had separated. There wasn't much to say, was there? Since it was Neil's sister who'd told Amy about the job, she didn't need to tell Neil much more than his sister had already told him. And what was she longing to hear from Neil? That he'd spent the weekend learning to ride western-style? That he'd found a great new barbecue place near his apartment? That he was, at the very least, thinking about her? The woman she'd become after he'd left? Or the woman she'd always been, but he hadn't seen?

She opened up the email program to find another message from Angus. His first messages were mostly pictures of his set-up dorm room, of him and his cousins on campus, and of his radio antennas, a loop that he set up on his desk and a long wire that he taped to the window. He was pretty far up in the tower he was living in, which made him happy. And that made her happy, even if she didn't understand his hobby. She tried hard never to idealize Angus, to see in him something that he wasn't. This message contained a selfie at the cafeteria along with several other students who weren't familiar to her. Good, she thought, he was making friends. With the laptop's camera, Amy took a picture of herself holding the chocolate bar, and she replied with that and a note that she'd send him a case once she was in New York.

Amy never understood the appeal of British sweeties over American candy, which she wasn't fond of after childhood either. But to Angus, it was a part of his British home in Birmingham, a part of his extended family that he saw too infrequently. A week over summer spent reacquainting himself with cousins he'd seen last the year prior. At least the kids all had chocolate in common, and their Gran kept them well supplied for the week. His relationship with his British cousins was not as close as his relationship with his American ones, but at least it was built around something they all loved.

And what could be better than that?

\*\*\*\*

"My dear, I have come to discuss our little misunderstanding, shall we call it?" Amy had been so lost in her email that she hadn't noticed Curtis Jenkins entering the library. He leaned against her desk, his leg pushing against the surface and his left hand splayed flat upon it. Two gold rings clanked against the desk, one his latest wedding band, and another with what looked to be a series of channel-set sapphires on his little finger. "I fear our evening didn't end as well as it ought to have."

"I think our evening ended exactly where it ought to have ended, Mr. Jenkins. Now, unless you have a book you'd like me to find for you or you have a book you'd like to return, you'll have to excuse me." Amy went back to her laptop, furiously typing into a blank email message the lyrics to Trisha Yearwood songs because that was all her exhausted brain could come up with on the fly. "I do have work to attend to."

"Of course." Curtis smiled broadly. What possessed Lily or his first two wives to marry him she couldn't fathom. Must have been the money, which he was losing at quite a rapid pace, if the stories going around the internet were true. "But, hear me out, my dear. You only sampled a bit of the cuisine chef has to offer. And you've only seen a very tiny bit of my collection of early Diane Westgrove paintings."

"Are you asking me back to your suite?" Amy kept her eyes on the laptop screen. "Because I must decline if that's the case."

"Must?" Curtis shook his head and clucked his

tongue. "Such a strong word."

"Sometimes, strong words are necessary, Mr. Jenkins."

"Ah, you have spunk," he said. "I like that. I especially like that in your Texas drawl."

Amy looked up. "I do not have a drawl, Mr. Jenkins." An imposing figure in a matronly gray suit caught her eye in the hallway. "Tell me, then, exactly why do you want me to return to your suite?"

"Ah, yes, I'd like you to return to my suite, and," he paused, "I'd like to show you a few things of various kinds. And then, I'd like you to talk to your friend, the one who put the art show together. I want you to bring her to me. Delicious little thing, isn't she? Anyway, I have something that might be of interest to both of you."

Just as Amy stood up to shout a few stronger words, Beatrice Taylor entered the library and marched straight toward Amy's desk. Her face went from angry to congenial in the moment she must have recognized who Amy was just about to shout at. "Mr. Jenkins," Beatrice cooed. "What a lovely surprise to see you here in the library. And how is that delightful son of yours?"

"Mrs. Taylor, charming to see you as well." Curtis lifted himself from the side of Amy's desk. "Alas, Ms. Morrison was unable to locate the volume I sought, and I'm meeting my son for lunch shortly. So I must bid you adieu." He took Beatrice's hand and kissed the back of it.

"I do hope you have a delightful lunch, Mr. Jenkins," Beatrice said with a titter. "It's such a joy to see parents bringing their children aboard ship. Such a thoughtful idea, giving him this journey as part of his gap year."

Curtis nodded at both women and left. Before Amy could express her disgust at the whole exchange, both before and after Beatrice had arrived, the assistant entertainment director resumed her angry mien. "Unprofessional, Ms. Morrison, simply unprofessional. First you fail to report to me this morning before breakfast, and then from what I sense, you just had a rather terse exchange with an elite-level passenger." Beatrice hugged her clipboard to her gray blazer.

Amy closed her laptop. "Mrs. Taylor, I do apologize for my absence this morning. You'll be able to check on my whereabouts as I scanned the lock on the library. There were books that were in the wrong places, and I came by early to sort that out."

"I will be verifying your story later, of course. The previous librarian would never have allowed the books to become mislaid in the first place." She looked down at her clipboard, then made a note. "As regards the conversation you were engaged in a moment ago?"

For a moment, Amy considered telling her supervisor about the mystery of the forged painting, about the troubles she'd had with her internet connection. But no, it was too soon. She needed to know what Curtis had to tell her. And she needed to figure out who would have blocked her internet access and why. If she played her cards right, maybe she wouldn't have to tell Beatrice any of it at all. "It was a misunderstanding," she said. "I had brought a book to his son, and I'm afraid it might have been misplaced. I'll go to his suite over my lunch break to see to it that the book is found."

"One more misstep with a passenger," Beatrice

said while looking over her reading glasses, "especially an elite-level passenger, and you'll be off this ship as soon as we dock in New York. Besides, as the saying goes, you'll catch more flies with honey than with vinegar. So try to be a bit more cordial next time a passenger has a problem with a book."

"I will be," Amy said. She looked over at the painting, and the forged Venus looked passively back at her, as if she too were someone who'd stepped into someplace she shouldn't have been.

****

"That's checked out, I'm afraid," Amy told the elderly gentleman in a dapper suit. "We do have a few other titles by the same author, or I could find you something on someone similar." She looked up at him from the writing desk, her best customer service smile disguising the anxiety of hiding a hundred boxes of British-made candy bars in her own closet as well as the closets of a half-dozen of the housekeeping staff she'd bribed with a whole series of Polish science fiction translations, romances, Spanish poetry, and whatever else ended up on the ever-lengthening list by the time they got to New York.

The man shook his head. "Ah, you see, it was just that I had a bit of a wager with another gentleman aboard ship about an anecdote related in this particular book," he said. "You'd be doing me a great kindness if you could track it down for me." He looked over his shoulder and then back at her. In a low voice, he added, "And I'll be happy to treat you to the finest bottle of your poison of choice."

"Tempting as that may be," she said, "my beverage of choice is tea. I'm rather dull that way. Anyway, I do

197

need to start tracking down books before they end up going ashore. So no need to treat me with anything."

"If you can find the book, you'll find waiting for you here the finest Darjeeling the region has ever produced," he said with a wink. "Good day, then. And thank you, in advance."

He must have had some wager. Amy was curious about this Darjeeling, though maybe not so curious that she'd willingly go to Curtis's suite to pick up the book she'd brought for Cole. Who knew—maybe it had gone overboard just like whatever it was she saw flying into the sea that evening she'd had dinner with his father.

At noon, Amy closed up and, shaking her head at herself, went up to the elite suites. She didn't want to see Curtis—not yet, anyway, until she figured out what he wanted from her and Gemma—and she very much didn't want to run into Wellie. What Gemma had said disturbed her. Of course, she knew he was not the sort of man she should have had dinner with, staff around or not. But it was the fact that Gemma was able to see through him more clearly than she had—she'd known just what to say to get him to fold. And he did. The secret out about the paintings' presence on the ship, maybe he'd be more willing to show Amy the early works, too. After all, he hadn't asked for Gemma to keep quiet about it. Or Gemma hadn't mentioned it. That would be too important for her to have left out.

Amy stood outside Curtis's door and inhaled before she knocked. Though she'd hoped he would be at lunch with his son as he said he'd be, she had her quick few words ready, and she didn't want to spend any more time in the suite than she had to, even if she was curious about the paintings.

She knocked.

No one answered.

She cleared her throat, lest the words get stuck there, and she knocked again. This time, to her relief, the housekeeper, Jagoda, opened the door, the same one who'd cleaned up after the "sea bird" incident. "Oh, hello, Amy," she said. "Mr. Curtis is out for lunch. With his son, you know."

"Good," Amy said. "Look, I just need to grab a book that Cole borrowed from the library. Have you seen it?"

"The book you left the other day?" Jagoda tilted her head toward the sitting room. Her graying blonde hair was pinned tightly to the top of her head, which emphasized her motion. "It's been in the same spot the whole time." She shrugged and went back to cleaning the bathroom.

Amy went into the sitting room. The book was, in fact, right where she'd left it. She looked behind her for the housekeeper, paused, then looked at the place where the painting cases had been. The chair had been moved, though there were still enough pieces of furniture in the room—including a rather large cabinet—to stash a painting in, behind, or between. Amy opened one of the cabinet doors. The hinge squeaked a bit, and she shut the door too quickly with a rather loud clatter.

"He took those down to storage," Jagoda said in a half-whisper. "To get them ready for, you know, New York."

Amy jumped. "Oh," she said. "You startled me."

"I was thinking, after all the rumors, you know, that you might be looking for the paintings." She folded her arms over her apron, the cleaning cloth that stank of ammonia and perfume resting on her elbow.

"I just," Amy started. "I just needed something to leave a note on. To let Cole know that I'd taken the book."

"You want to do something like that? Let him know that you've been snooping around for the pictures?" Jagoda cocked her head.

"You're right," Amy said. "That would be—"

The housekeeper shook her head. "I'll tell him that his valet took the book back for him. If he misses it. Which I don't think he will. He never moved it, so?"

"So," Amy agreed. "Thank you."

"I'm adding a few books to your list," she said with a smile.

"You do that," Amy said. "Yes."

She grabbed the book tighter to her chest and ran out into the hallway.

Right into the ghostwriter.

"Oh, I'm sorry," Amy said. But Erin didn't seem to hear.

"You've got to help her," she said. She was shaking, pale, and wide-eyed. "I found her."

"Who? Mrs. Lewis?"

Erin nodded. Amy saw the opened door to the suite.

"Where? In there?"

"I don't know how," Erin said. "I came up to look for Wellie, just in case she'd missed something from the other day when Diane disappeared. And I found Diane in her chair on the balcony. Please help. She doesn't look like herself at all."

Amy ran into the suite. She dropped the book on the entryway table and rushed out to the balcony.

"Where have you been, Mrs. Lewis?"

A half-croak escaped from her mouth before she could open it wide enough to speak. Weakly, she tried again. "Here, I think."

The old woman looked out at the ocean, the bright sun burning on the water. Her lips were cracked, and her hands shook. Around her sleeve was a long string in ballet pink, as if someone had shredded a satin ribbon. Perhaps a ribbon off a nightgown? Amy called out to the ghostwriter to get her some water. When she returned, Amy said to stay with Diane until Amy came back.

Amy dialed the number for the security team, then hung up. She called the emergency services instead and told them about the dehydrated, sunburned, and windburned Mrs. Lewis, who probably needed more than just water, by the looks of it. They told her they would be on their way. After she hung up, she dialed the security team once again and explained the situation.

"Did no one check the closet on the balcony?" Amy asked them once they'd arrived. The medical team were already at work, getting Mrs. Lewis onto a stretcher, hooked up to an IV in an attempt to rehydrate her as quickly as they could.

"Ms. Westgrove said that she'd seen Mrs. Lewis go out," the security team member said. "We had no reason to suspect she'd be in the balcony closet."

"Speaking of which," Amy said, "can someone track down Ms. Westgrove? I'm sure she'll want to know her sister has been found."

"Ms. Westgrove is on her way, in fact," the security team member told her. The other one had gone out to the balcony once the medics came through the door. "She was not happy that we'd disturbed her luncheon, as she called it. But she seemed pleased with the fact that Mrs. Lewis has been found safe."

The medics wheeled Mrs. Lewis out, with the ghostwriter beside her, holding her hand. Good, Amy thought, good that they have each other. That was family, wasn't that? "She's safe then?"

"She's alive," the security team member said. "Safe, we're still working on."

"You've had days, haven't you?" Amy said. She wanted to say a thousand other things, but she stopped herself from doing so. "If it's all the same to you, I think I'll wait for Ms. Westgrove here. Unless you need to talk to her first."

The security team member shrugged. "We've talked to her many, many times over the past few days. Nothing new after the first interview. And we're not interrogating the wealthy sister of an honored guest aboard the ship. You're welcome to talk to her first."

Amy looked at her watch. She had half an hour before she had to be back at the library. Ten minutes to walk back to the library gave her twenty minutes left here, really. Her stomach churned in its emptiness. Ten minutes to wait here, so she could pick up a sandwich at the staff canteen.

With five minutes to spare, Wellie Westgrove strode into her suite, looking as if she'd just finished some exquisite dessert accompanied by the finest espresso. She looked at Amy, then over at the security team. "I suppose you'll want to interview me again? I really ought to be with Diane, wherever you lot have taken her."

"Yes, we will want to speak with you, Ms. Westgrove," the remaining security team member said. The other one hadn't returned from the balcony yet. "Interview is probably not the best word. We would be happy to speak with you here, or we can go to the security office. Whichever will be more comfortable for you, ma'am."

Wellie looked over at Amy, a slight smirk pinching her lips. "Do you usually bring a librarian to your final interviews? I'm hoping this one will be the last one, so I can get back to tending to Diane. My sister has memory problems, you know." Wellie sat down on the sofa and looked up at Amy and the security team member, both of whom were standing up. Her cocktail ring caught the light from the lamp beside her.

"We can't guarantee this will be your final discussion of your sister's whereabouts, Ms. Westgrove," the security team member said. "But we hope not to have to disturb you again."

"Very well, then," Wellie said. "We can talk here."

The interview was useless and perfunctory, at least in the few minutes Amy had heard before she had to go back to the library. Amy stood up and made her excuses to go. The first security team member called the second one out to the balcony. The second one produced a plastic bag, into which the first one dropped two segments of pink satin ribbon. Ballet pink.

She grabbed the book she'd come for and rushed back to the library. On her way, she thought of what Curtis had said about Diane's life being free from scandal, at least after her sister's fall. If only she'd had a few minutes to talk to Penelope and Richard, to sit down and write it all out, then she might be able to think it all through. For now, though, there were two people who would benefit most from the scandal that was Diane's kidnapping, faked or real.

First was Brent Detweiler, who was in need of something to call attention to the life of the woman whose memoir he'd panned as boring. Scandal could mean sales. And second, on the topic of sales, Curtis could really use the publicity around Diane's disappearance. If she were to appear in the news as the victim or perpetrator of her own absence, then buyers might flock to his auction of her early works.

But why make it look like she'd faked the kidnapping? To call attention to Diane Westgrove Lewis' lack of credibility? Brent might benefit from that, if it looked like there were things she left out of her story. Maybe he could get that titillating book about her after all, even if it wasn't one she'd written herself, and even if it strayed from the truth. Curtis, on the other hand, was the clear winner here. If her credibility was called into question enough to make people doubt her memories on the night of the party, wouldn't it stand to reason that she might have sold him paintings that he wasn't supposed to have? In particular, the real *Venus Rising*?

Chapter Fifteen

Amy hastily unlocked the library door. Kevin was there, in the golden hallway, waiting for her. His assistant, Montague, was at his side, tapping in something on a tablet and looking around the doorframe "Nothing out here," he said to himself more than to his supervisor.

"You probably don't come bearing good news, do you?" Amy asked as she opened the double doors for the passengers who would be by shortly. She caught her reflection in the glass of one of the doors, just below the etched cursive announcing the hours of the library. That the library closed for arrival and departures. Something in the angle of her face made her jaw seem more set. She pushed a stray hair from her cheek and moved the heavy doors into place. "Am I downloading pictures of nightgowns again?"

"You? Probably not," the assistant said. His accent couldn't have been more posh. "Unless you've been going to the shops online. We received another complaint about data usage, and we're here to check it out." He walked in through the door and sat with his tablet under the painting. A few passengers came in behind Kevin and Amy. "This time, it was a passenger, said he'd noticed the problem first after he'd had a bit of an altercation in the library."

"Amy, have there been altercations in the library?"

Something in the deep smoothness of Kevin's voice made Amy momentarily forget that Raymond Entwhistle and Brent Detweiler almost came to blows in front of the fraudulent painting. "Or anything else odd happening in here?"

She inhaled and thought for a moment before the scene came back to her. Amy motioned toward the painting. "Other than this?"

Montague looked up from his tablet. He narrowed his blue eyes at the woman in the slinky silver dress and said, "Smoking."

"Could I please have a word with you at my desk, Mr. Park?" Amy half folded her arms around her. She was still carrying the book that she had taken from Curtis's suite, which made the gesture all the more awkward. "About my laptop?"

Once at her desk, Kevin apologized for his assistant's crude assessment of the painting. "It's a fake, then?"

"I'm sure of it, now," she said. "I'll tell you more about that later. Um, would this passenger having data problems happen to be Raymond Entwhistle?"

"That's him."

Amy told Kevin about Raymond's altercation that morning with Brent Detweiler, and that Raymond's aunt had been found safe on her own balcony. She left out Raymond's subsequent meeting with her. If the problem was what she now suspected it was, she'd ask Raymond to leave a half-dozen bars of chocolate in the IT offices. "Wait, wasn't Brent Detweiler a tech guy before he went into publishing celebrity tell-all's?"

Kevin nodded. She'd nearly kicked herself when she realized it. Yet another technical failure on her part.

"Keeps his hand in the game—literally—by competing in hack-a-thons. Wins a fair number of them, too."

"So Brent Detweiler put the strappy nightgown downloading program on my laptop to keep me quiet about the painting," Amy said. "Then he hacks into Raymond's account to, what, keep him quiet about— what? About their fight?"

"That's for you to figure out," Kevin said. "I'm just here for the technical sleuthing."

"You could have just sent your assistant," Amy said. She smiled, genuinely, not just her customer-service expression of openness.

Kevin furrowed his brows. "To be honest, I'm having a bit of trouble with that one. He's related to someone in the cruise line higher ups, so I can't outright fire him. Which I don't think I can do under British labor laws, anyway." He looked over at the assistant, who was tapping at the tablet between obviously checking out Venus.

"So British labor laws protect you if and only if you're related to someone high up in society?" Amy felt a pang of disappointment at Kevin's answer, but she needed to focus on what was in front of her. "I've decided that I am going to walk out with Lucia and the others."

"You're going to buy books in New York City anyway, aren't you?"

"And the gala to celebrate the auction of Mrs. Lewis's work," Amy said. "I'd been invited before we set sail for New York. So it's rather disingenuous of me to say I'm walking out when I'll be working. Sort of."

"Sort of," he said. "When and where is this auction? I might drop in."

"Are you an art fan?" Amy asked. "I should introduce you to Gemma, who curated the art on the ship."

"Not in particular on the first, just curious," he said, looking over at his assistant. "And I had the pleasure of meeting Ms. Williams just before we departed. Her brother is a network engineer."

"I didn't know that," Amy said. She hoped she'd have time to tour Gemma's choice of art works before the curator disembarked in New York. Along with Curtis, Cole, Brent, Erin, Wellie, Diane, Raymond, and a hundred cases of chocolate. Time was running out.

The assistant came over to the librarian's desk. "Nothing here to speak of," Montague said. "I still think your prime suspect must have hacked in. I can't find any hardware here that isn't supposed to be here." He showed the tablet to Kevin.

"Well, we got what we came for," Kevin said. "If not proof of what he did, then proof of what he didn't do. Good to see you again, Amy."

"You too," she said. And she held back what she was going to say about how good it was to see him, which was far more than just that. "Thanks for keeping me in the loop. Even if the loop was my fault, sort of. Mostly."

"Entirely," he said with a smile.

She suddenly realized that she hadn't thought of Neil for a while, which, she supposed, was progress. Not the sort of progress she needed to make right now, but at least Mrs. Lewis was safe.

All that was left was to figure out who'd want her missing for a day.

And who would want to fake her most famous

unseen painting.

And who would want to profit from the real one.

Amy sent an email to the man who wanted the book she'd retrieved from Cole. She opened her laptop not just to do that but also to make sure everything was still working for the most part and to see whether Angus or Stacey had answered her replies full of apologies for missing their messages and assurances that she hadn't been lost at sea. As Diane seemed to be for a while.

Erin came into the library just as the wind-down before closing began, when so many of the passengers would be on their way to getting dressed for drinks before dinner, energized by the glamour the evenings promised. Not the ghostwriter, though. "I wanted to thank you for helping me," she said to Amy. "And for helping Diane."

"Is Mrs. Lewis going to be okay?" Amy asked.

"Diane is dehydrated and shaken, but she should make a good recovery," Erin said. "It helps that she was in relatively good health before all this began. For her age, I mean."

"Good health?" Amy closed the laptop. "Wellie, that is, Ms. Westgrove seemed to think she was declining, or at least her memory was."

"I never saw any sign of significant impairment in the months we spent together. Or after that, in doing everything we did to prepare for this trip, the auction, the media," Erin said. "It's unusual that I'm so involved with the memoir still, but Diane wanted me along on this part of the book's journey too. She said she trusted my understanding of the publishing industry, since I'd been in it for so long."

"Did Ms. Westgrove seem happy to have Mrs. Lewis back?"

"You know, I thought I heard her say something about Diane doing this to herself before Wellie realized I was there. Or maybe she knew I was there and she wanted me to hear it." The ghostwriter paused. "It's like something out of a novel, so unreal that Diane would fake a kidnapping."

"Why would Diane fake her kidnapping?"

Erin turned toward the painting. "I don't know, maybe to lend some legitimacy to the fact that someone replaced her art with this forgery?"

Silence hung over the library too long before Amy broke it. "I should get your novels for the library here," Amy said. "To commemorate the journey."

"Good luck with that," Erin said with a flat laugh. "The first two are out of print. Number three maybe you can find a copy of through the distributor, but number four never came out. My editor left my publisher, and no one at the press wanted to take up the story of an eighteenth-century farmer's wife who must face the turbulence of life in a new country after the death of her husband in the Revolutionary War."

Amy winced.

"Yes, it was as dry as it sounds." Erin laughed, brightly this time. "But she spoke to me, and I followed her story. It happens. Novels get trunked. I'll sell another book."

"You're working on one now?"

"Yes, but it's not the story of a twentieth century philanthropist, if that's what you're wondering."

Amy inhaled deeply. "Books aside, I need your help now," she said. "You're the only one who saw

*Venus Rising* who can vouch for Diane. I need you to come forward with that information to help me solve the puzzle of the forged painting and Diane's kidnapping."

"So you don't believe that she did this to herself either?"

Amy shook her head. "You're the key, though. If you can convince someone to look for Diane's original painting, if it's on board somewhere, then maybe we can get to the bottom of this."

"I couldn't," she said. "Who'd believe me? Besides, Brent is convinced that this is the painting that Diane did just before she shut down her career, which means that if I go against him, I won't get another job through his company. Or anyone else's, if his bluster is as powerful as he says it is."

"Isn't the truth bigger than that? Bigger than Brent Detweiler and any sway he might have in the publishing industry?"

"The truth about one painting isn't bigger than the fact that my literary career is all but over, Amy. At least it's not bigger to me."

"But couldn't Diane arrange something for you, a grant through one of her foundations, if you were to vouch for her?"

"That's not how it works," the ghostwriter said. She dropped her head as if she were looking at the place in her lap on which her hands lay clutching at each other. "Diane stays out of the process for choosing which artists and projects get funded. If she stepped in for me, then that would look bad for the rest of her work. She's been incredibly transparent about her philanthropic mission, and it's important to her to keep that reputation. And besides—" The ghostwriter trailed off.

"Besides?"

Erin inhaled and breathed out a shudder. "I don't want to ruin our friendship by asking. She means so much to me, and she's been so kind to me. People like Brent look at me and think that I'm just a waste of money. Diane thinks I'm talented, in my way."

"I'm sure you are," Amy said.

Erin thanked her with a shaking voice.

Her laptop dinged. She opened it, expecting the old man to have thanked her for the book, but instead she saw Tiffany's name at the top of her email queue and the subject "Microfiche of an article from the art school's newspaper, dated about the right time" at the top.

"Oh, hold on," Amy said. "Excuse me for a second here." She opened the message, which contained a large image. The image failed to download at first, but on trying again, the email client completed the download.

It wasn't exactly what she needed, but it was a start.

"Look at this," Amy said, her voice a whisper. "It's Diane. She's in front of a canvas. Who's this with her?"

"Who sent you this?"

"My best friend," Amy said giddily. "The best-connected small town librarian in Texas, that's who."

"There's a caption," Erin said. "Can you enlarge it?"

Amy tried, but the text was blurry. "Okay, Tiff, huge thanks, but did you give me the text?"

Another ding on her laptop made Amy minimize the image window. A second message had arrived from

Tiffany. "This is good, it's the caption in close up. Listen to this: Diane Westgrove in the background with her mentors in front. Nothing new there. Who is this that's covered over by the men sitting in front of her?"

Erin shook her head. "Can you get Tiffany to send a higher resolution picture of Diane and her canvas?"

Amy typed in the message. They waited five minutes, and then Tiffany delivered.

"Does this look familiar?"

Erin gasped. "It's hard to say I'm completely sure, since it's black and white, but that looks like *Venus Rising*, the one Diane showed me."

"But we still can't see who else is with her. Someone else who could say that this was her painting or not." Amy clicked on the enlarge button on her image viewer, but the man's shoulder didn't move away from the person behind him. "We can't tell who this is by the hair, can we?"

"Probably not," Erin said. "But maybe Diane remembers? I'm sure she would."

Amy printed off copies of all three images. "I'm about to go to see if I can talk to Diane. Want to come along?"

The ghostwriter gave Amy a dejected smile. "Brent wants to treat me to dinner at Le Bœuf du Duc, I think just to keep my mouth shut. I can't cancel on him. Besides, this might be my one and only cruise, and when am I going to get five-star cuisine in the middle of the Atlantic Ocean again?"

"Go," Amy said. "Have a good dinner. And get dessert. I hear it's fantastic."

"Which dessert?"

"All of them," Amy said, thinking back on the

tasting menu she'd suffered through with Curtis. "Will I see you at the auction in New York?"

"I'll be there," Erin said. "Good luck."

"Thanks," Amy said. They walked out together, and Amy locked the door behind her. As Erin caught an elevator descending to the restaurant desk, Amy called out, "Good luck to you too. I will try to get your novels. Especially your new one, even if it is about the wife of an eighteenth-century farmer."

Erin lifted a hand in acknowledgement, which Amy just saw as the door closed and, behind it, the young woman once again disappeared.

Printouts of Tiffany's discovery in hand, Amy nearly ran from the elevator she'd taken up to the elite suites, but she stopped herself. She couldn't just go barging into Curtis's suite, accusing him of stealing and hiding *Venus Rising*, the real one, anyway. Instead, she stopped a floor below his and ran down the hallway to Penelope and Richard's suite instead.

Amy banged on their door. Breathless, she nearly tripped over Carrington, whom Penelope was trying to keep inside as she opened the suite door to Amy.

"What is the matter, dear?" Penelope scooped up the ruffled cat. "Another suspect?"

"No," Amy said. She put the papers down on the writing desk. Richard put on his reading glasses and joined them. "It's the real *Venus Rising*, or at least it's the painting that would be the real version."

"These things are no help," Richard said touching the temple of his glasses. "It's all a bit of a blur to me."

Penelope stroked Carrington's ears. "It's hardly conclusive, but I do think I see a young Diane Westgrove painting something." The cat let out a plaintive meow.

"Sorry, Carrington," Amy said. She scratched him under the chin. He started to purr. "Here's the thing, though. I have a witness who saw the original."

"Ah, someone in the photos, then," Richard said. He slid his glasses into his shirt pocket. "That proves it's a forgery."

"Not so simple," Amy said. "I'm pretty sure everyone besides Diane Westgrove Lewis and the model have passed away, unfortunately." She looked down at the painting again. What seemed so clear to her in the library now seemed to be an illusion. Like Venus rising over the water, which Brent Detweiler intended to add into the photos of the unveiling later on. "But there has to be something to this. In a larger context, I mean."

Richard nodded. "Now you're headed in the right direction, dear. Take it from one who's spent more years in the dust of archives than out of them. You need confirmation from another source."

"I know that," Amy said. "I'm about to go get that, if I can."

"From whom?" Penelope asked. She sat down on the sofa. Carrington leaped from her arms to the floor. He padded over to Amy and began to rub his cheeks on the ankles of her tights. "And what kind of confirmation?"

"From Curtis Jenkins," Amy said. She told them what she knew about the other early Diane Westgrove paintings she'd seen along with Gemma's opinions on the matter of her talent as a painter. "It has to be Curtis Jenkins. He's got other works of hers. He'd know what he was looking for, wouldn't he? And if he found it, he'd know the value of it."

"But Amy, why would he want to take it in the first place?" Penelope looked toward the window. Through it, Amy saw the fading light of evening's approach. "What did he think he'd do with it once he had it?"

Richard chuckled. "You know, Pen, Curtis Jenkins doesn't strike me as the sort of fellow who thinks things through all that thoroughly."

"You think he might have snatched it up opportunistically, then hid it away?" Penelope shook her head. "That's impulsive, isn't it?"

"Cole," Amy said suddenly. "I wouldn't put it past Cole. He did get expelled for what I can imagine were worse things. And anyway, like father, like son, right?"

"Maybe," Penelope said. "But Angus, from all you've told me, is nothing like Neil."

Which was true, but beside the point. "We're running out of time," Amy said. "If I'm going to confront Curtis about this, I have to do it tonight. He's already begun packing up the other paintings to be unloaded in New York. I don't see why he wouldn't put *Venus Rising* among them."

Penelope and Richard looked at each other for a long moment. At last, Penelope nodded, Richard shrugged, and Carrington rejoined his mistress on the sofa. "If you do talk to Curtis about this tonight," Penelope said as she smoothed the cat's orange fur, "you must call us the moment you return to your room. Please."

Amy promised she'd do so. She picked up the printouts and walked toward the door. "I have to talk to him. I don't know what I have to lose if I do."

"How about your job? Your chance at adventure?"

"I know that, Penelope." Amy held the papers out, looking once again at the painting in the picture. "But if I don't resolve this, then I've failed at my job already. I was responsible for making sure the unveiling went as planned. It didn't, and I can't fix that. But I can figure out what happened and bring that to light. It won't change what happened that evening, but it might reassure my employers that I do have some capabilities as a librarian and host."

"Go then," Richard said softly. "And call once you're back in."

"I will," Amy said. She had to solve this, if only to reassure herself that the failure the night of the party hadn't been entirely hers.

****

Around her, Amy sensed something about the gold of the ship pressing against her. She loved it, the filigree and the piping, everything in gold. But now, something about it all felt wrong, as if it were hiding something from her. Amy felt her heart beating harder with each passageway she'd gone through. The papers shook in her hands. She stopped for a moment, took a deep breath, and closed her eyes.

So much about Curtis Jenkins told her that he could have replaced *Venus Rising* with a fake and that he could have tied up Diane on her balcony. The pink ribbon sealed it for her—of course, he'd choose something soft and almost sensual to restrain her with. That was his way. Where had he even gotten the ribbon? Something of Lily's that he'd brought along? Amy shuddered. She stopped in front of Curtis Jenkins's suite door and looked down at the crumpled papers.

Maybe this would work.
It had to.

Chapter Sixteen

Amy knocked on Curtis's suite door. No one answered. For a moment, she thought it better to run from here, to run to Diane's suite and check in on her.

No, if Amy was going to confront Curtis about the painting, it had to be now.

She knocked again.

After a moment, Curtis opened the door. "What a pleasant surprise, Amy," he said. He opened the door wide. What was left of his hair was plastered to his fleshy white scalp. Around his middle, he'd halfway pulled on a plush navy blue robe. She could just make out the script of *The Cullinan Diamond* stitched in gold between the collar and the sleeve. "You, my dear, have caught me while I'm freshening up before dinner," he said, his voice low. "You're welcome to wait in my sitting room, of course."

"No, I'm sorry, I can't." Amy folded the papers in half. From inside the suite came the blaring of a sporting event, the yelling of the announcer piercing through the roar of the fans. "I'm sorry to disturb you."

He shook his wet head. "You haven't disturbed me at all, Ms. Morrison. Amy. Do come in. Chef just sent up a tray of canapés. Please, come in and enjoy while I finish up. Dinner will be served in my suite at half-past."

"No, I can't," Amy said. She fought the urge to run

to the stairs.

"You must. I insist," he said with a half-smile rumbling up his lips. "I have something to show you."

"What is it?"

Curtis Jenkins laughed. The stridency of his voice managed to echo even off the velvet walls of the hallway. "If I tell you, darling Amy, then it would spoil the surprise, now wouldn't it?"

Cole started to shout something unintelligible from deep inside the suite, his voice matching the intensity of that of the sports announcer. If he stayed in the suite too, and staff would be by shortly with more food, then perhaps she'd be okay inside Curtis Jenkins's suite. Besides, Amy could hold her own in a fight, or at least she could with all the over-filled book carts she'd wrestled around over the years. Not that she thought there would be an altercation of any physical sort. Amy was new to sleuthing, and she realized that she had no idea what to expect.

"All right," she said primly. "I will stay in the sitting room until you've finished up, and then you can show me the, well, the whatever it is you want to show me."

As she crossed into the suite, Curtis stepped back and let the robe fall open a bit more. She hoped that wasn't what Curtis wanted to show her. Grimacing, Amy covered her eyes with the papers and darted into the sitting room.

Around her, everything had been replaced or repaired. No sign of the earlier upset remained. Even though Curtis and his son had been here for days, nothing of them marked the room. Perhaps Cole's room would be different, strewn with clothing and drink glasses, dishes still bearing the remnants of breakfast and lunch. Amy didn't want to look inside. She almost felt sorry for the young man, who lacked in Curtis the kind of role model Neil had been for Angus. Even if Angus had never understood his father totally, at least Angus respected him. Loved him. And the respect and love went both ways. How damaged Cole must have been by his father and the world he'd created around them both. Men like Curtis damaged people. Taught their kids to damage people. To lie to them.

To steal from them.

"Dad?" Cole stamped from his room over to his dripping father, who was heading back to the bathroom. He looked angry enough to hurl the TV remote he was wielding through whatever obstacle might come between him and his father. Amy breathed in and stood behind the doorway so that he wouldn't see her. There was assurance number one out the door. Cole would be no help if Curtis wanted to do anything untoward to Amy. "When's food getting here?"

"Dinner will arrive in a quarter of an hour," Curtis said. "But you will not be joining me."

"No, Dad, I need to see the end of this game. It's important. And I'm starving." He tapped the remote in his fist. "I need to know how this game goes."

"Then you'll have to order your own dinner, son," Curtis called out from the bathroom. "If you're old enough to have placed bets last year, even losing ones, you're old enough to place an order for pizza now, or whatever it is you eat here."

"I don't have time to talk to the food help," Cole said. "I need to eat now. And I need to talk to Frank about the end of this game. Now."

"Frank?" Curtis bellowed. "You were expressly forbidden to talk to Frank as part of your rehabilitation. Did you place a bet on this game?"

"Dad, I can't talk," Cole said. "I'm taking whatever you ordered. I'm talking to Frank."

"How much?"

"There's another game on in an hour, and I need to talk to Frank," Cole said, his voice spiraling up in what must have been despair. The announcer yelled. The crowd yelled. Cole howled. Something crashed into something breakable. Amy held her breath. The "sea bird" would come crashing into the suite again, angrily, forcefully.

"How much, Cole?"

Curtis rushed out of the bathroom, fully dressed. His scalp was blotchy red, as was his face. He went into Cole's room and emerged with Cole in front of him, one arm pinned behind him and the other scrabbling to free himself. With strength Amy couldn't have guessed he'd had, Curtis managed to open the front door of the suite, drop his son into the hallway, and slam the door closed again before Cole could get up.

Her second assurance, that she'd be able to fend off any physical attack by him, got tossed out the door along with his son.

"Dad! Dad! I don't have a key! I need to talk to Frank!"

"Then go talk to Frank from the Sapphire Lounge," Curtis bellowed. "I never want to hear that man's name again, do you understand me? I am not paying this time, son."

Amy peeked around the sitting room doorway. Curtis raked a hand through his hair and sighed. "Ah, there you are, my darling. Afraid dinner's not formal tonight, but it will be a treat nonetheless."

"Is Cole all right?"

"It's nothing," Curtis said. He smoothed down the placket of his shirt and strode over to the sitting room. "Just a disagreement. Father and son."

"I can go," Amy said. "I can come by later."

Curtis took her by the elbow and led her to the dining table. In the light of the early evening, the suite seemed far less glamorous than it had when she'd been here for dinner before. "Please," he said. "I would appreciate company after learning that my son has just gambled away who knows how much on who knows what sport. He's had rugby on, so I should have known."

Amy sat. The white damask of the cloth that lay across the dining table echoed the white silk of the dining chairs. So much evidence could be visible on their rich surfaces, like spilled wine. Spilled Cabernet. The papers were folded in her lap, crumpled along with her nerves. "Fine," she said. "I'll have dinner with you. But there's something very important I need to talk to you about, too, Mr. Jenkins."

"As do I, Amy," he said. His voice showed none of the anger that he'd just addressed his son with. "Please, let's not be so formal, Amy. Do call me Curtis."

"Curtis, then," Amy said. "Curtis, I have something very important to talk to you about." She took the papers from her lap and smoothed them out on the dining table. The image of *Venus Rising* had gone from a vague impression to a creased blur.

"So you've said," he said. "I have something very important to tell you. But I can wait. Ladies first, yes?"

Amy looked down at the papers. If he confessed, or at least gave her a bit more to work with as far as the paintings he'd shown Gemma, then she wouldn't have to use her tenuous link from the art school to the fake in the library. She smiled and turned on what she had of a Texas drawl. "You've got me curious, Mr. Jenkins. Curtis, I mean. Please, you go first. I'm listening."

"Good," he said. "Give me a moment." Curtis moved toward the large closet and inserted a key into the lock. The mahogany door shuddered as he turned the key. "I do so hope you'll appreciate this." At that moment, the dining staff knocked on the door to the suite. "Hmm. That's dinner. You'll just have to wait, my lovely librarian."

Amy held her smile but shuddered inwardly. Like the doors. "Patiently, of course."

The dining staff rolled in a cart, which held enough food for Curtis, Cole, herself, and about a half-dozen others besides. There were two waiters dressed in white jackets with the cruise line's logo embroidered on their lapels, one who handled the food and another who prepared the wine selections, of which there were at least four.

"There is a pizza, sadly," Curtis said. "Pepperoni. At Cole's insistence. Now I know why he wanted to be able to eat alone in his room. But, enough of that. For us, my darling, there is lobster ravioli to start." He ordered the staff to lay out the dishes under their metal domes on the sideboard.

The scent of a dozen warm and well-seasoned things distracted her from her task at hand. The waiter brought her a plate of ravioli along with a stemmed glass for white wine and another for red. "Tonight, we have a chardonnay to accompany the starter."

"None for me, thank you," she said.

"Oh, but I directed the sommelier to send up the ship's best," Curtis said. He motioned for the waiter to pour the wine into his glass. He drained half of it as soon as the neck of the bottle cleared the path between him and his glass. "Do try the lemon butter sauce, Amy."

"It's kind of you to offer," she said. "But I'm not hungry, thank you." Her stomach turned anxiously in protest. The lemon butter drew her down to the plate in front of her. She pushed it away gingerly.

"It's not kind of you to allow me to eat alone." Curtis sliced one of the ravioli in half and lashed it with lemon butter sauce. "Especially when chef sends up such delectable dishes."

"Do you usually order so spectacularly for Cole and yourself?" Amy asked in a low voice after the waiters had returned to the sideboard.

Curtis laughed. "Only aboard *The Cullinan Diamond*," he said. He finished off the appetizer, and the waiter who'd served him the dish retrieved it and brought another. "Ah, steamed mussels. Amy, you must join me for these."

"Chenin Blanc, sir." The second waiter brought forth another white wine glass and a bottle wrapped in a white napkin.

"Amy, surely," Curtis said between bites of mussels. "Surely you must try the Chenin Blanc. A varietal you've never experienced before, I'm sure."

"You're correct there, Mr. Jenkins," she said. "And no, thank you, to the mussels, either. As I said, I'm not hungry." At least the brininess of the dish muted her queasiness. "Shall we talk about what you wanted to tell me?"

"Ah, that."

A loud knock cut him short. "Dad, Dad," Cole shouted. "Let me in. They won't serve me at the Sapphire Lounge."

"What did that infernal boy try to order, underage as he is," Curtis mumbled.

"Sir, shall I open the suite door?" The first waiter motioned to the entry.

Curtis shook his head. "Put the pizza in the boy's room," he said. "Let him bawl another minute. Does him good to know who's in charge around here."

"Very well, sir."

"You were saying, Mr. Jenkins," Amy said softly. "What you were going to tell me about."

He glanced over at the sideboard, on which were four more dishes plus a dessert selection. "Let's not spoil dinner. Or my dinner, since you've refused." Once the first waiter returned, Curtis requested the next course. "Lobster bisque," he said. "A favorite of mine. And this particular Sauvignon Blanc."

"I don't want to spoil your dinner," Amy said. "But I don't see how talking about your revelation will ruin food and wine as good as what's in front of you."

"How would you know if you don't try it?"

Amy smiled her best customer-service smile. "You're a man of impeccable taste, if I may say so."

"You may. And you should."

"Then what you wanted to show me should also be in impeccable taste?" Amy looked up at him. She was careful not to show too much interest in him. Particularly if it was true what Richard had discovered about his impending divorce from his ostensibly beloved Lily.

Curtis laughed. A salmon wrapped in phyllo came next. "You've talked me into it, haven't you? Such a southern charmer you are, naughty girl."

A shudder ran through Amy's spine, and she forced herself not to break her smile. "How about you show me what you have for me to see?"

"Very well then," Curtis said. He dismissed the waiters with instructions not to allow his son back into the suite. They rolled the cart back into the hallway. "Now that we're alone, follow me," Curtis said to her. He rose and returned to the locked cabinet.

In the hallway, Cole shouted a stream of expletives at his father. "I'm not dressed for dinner, Dad. They won't serve me anyway without my card. Let me in, please."

Amy shook as she followed Curtis. She'd grabbed the papers too tightly, and she didn't dare look at the mess she'd made of them. Slowly, Curtis unlocked the cabinet and removed a case. Amy recognized it as the one in which the painting of Wellie had been half visible from. "Now, I'll need you to stand back, my darling librarian. Over at the chaise should be fine."

She drew in a breath and obeyed. "All right," she said.

"Good." Curtis opened the case. The painting of Wellie grabbed her more than it had on her first half viewing. "This, before you, is an early Diane Westgrove original."

"It's beautiful," Amy whispered. She cleared her throat and tried again. "Just beautiful. But why are you showing me the painting in person this time?"

Curtis's body seemed to crumple before her. "Listen, darling, I need a favor. I've seen you and Gemma together. Yes, I've watched you. I need you to convince her to buy my collection. The whole lot. It's all as good as this."

"I can't," Amy sputtered. "I can't do that, and you should know it. Besides, why would you want me to ask Gemma a favor like that? I've only just met her a few days ago?"

"Women have a way of talking," Curtis said. "To each other. Among themselves. Surely, you must know what I mean?"

Amy shook her head. "I think you're attributing a power to me that I don't have." She looked down at the painting again. "Wait, what happened to the auction you have set up?"

Cole began to pound on the door. "It's nothing for you to worry yourself with," Curtis muttered. "Will that blasted child shut up?"

"I could go talk to him for you," Amy said. "If you think I can."

"No one can," Curtis spat out. He breathed in and resumed in his smoothed voice. "Now, will you talk to her or not?"

"On one condition."

"I don't allow for conditions," Curtis said.

Amy stifled a laugh. "You must be pretty desperate to unload the paintings."

"Not at all," Curtis said. Cole shouted again, and Curtis's face reddened. "You've seen how good they are."

"I've seen one," Amy said.

"You've seen two, if I may correct you. The ones I

have are far more technically and artistically superior to *Venus Rising*."

"To that one, maybe."

"What do you mean, that one? That one in the library is an early Diane Westgrove too, just not as good as what I have. You have to see that, Amy." A bit of spittle foamed at the corner of his mouth.

"Maybe," Amy said.

She slipped past Curtis and opened the door. Cole nearly slammed into her, racing through the doorway.

"Cole Jenkins, *stop*," she said in her best upset mother tone, the one that would halt Angus ten yards away and make him blanch. "Before you go running off to your room and hide. Come over here."

Cole slunk back from his doorway. "My pizza's getting cold."

"From what I see," Amy continued in her mother voice, "is that you have a microwave not fifteen feet from you."

"Ms. Morrison," Curtis shouted. "What is the meaning of this?"

Amy ignored him. "Cole, tell me this." Though a good head shorter than Cole, she stared him in the eye. "Why does your father want to unload the paintings on the cruise line?"

"Do not say a word, Cole, or I'll cut off your allowance."

Amy looked down from Cole's face for a moment. She looked back up with a forgiving face. "Cole, son, you're upset with your dad, aren't you?"

The young man nodded.

"Can you help me?"

He nodded again.

"Not one word, Cole, or I'm done with you."

Amy lowered her voice. "Cole, do you even have an allowance anymore? For your dad to cut off?"

The young man shook his head. "Dad, you were already done with me years ago," Cole said to his father. He turned his back on Curtis and sat down. "The auction house thought Dad's paintings wouldn't sell because there was the charity auction. They called him before we left. He cut off my allowance already."

"Thank you, Cole," Amy said. "Now go eat your pizza. It's probably still nice and warm under that metal dome."

Cole rushed back to his room.

"Well then," Curtis said.

"Well then," Amy said. She smoothed out the papers as best as she could on the coffee table in front of them. "Tell me where the real *Venus Rising* is."

"It's in the library."

"Not the fake one you arranged, Mr. Jenkins. The real one."

Curtis's face went from reddened to absolutely mottled. "Just what are you trying to say, Ms. Morrison?"

"I have a picture of the real *Venus Rising*. Here." She pointed to the creased image of the now unrecognizable Diane Westgrove and the model in front of her. "You faked the painting in the library and kidnapped Mrs. Lewis."

"You have a tattered printout and no evidence." He fanned himself and sat on the sofa.

"You have motive and the means to carry out the forgery and the kidnapping," Amy said. "And now that I know why you've been pestering Gemma, I have more than plenty proof."

"You have no such thing." Curtis tipped his head on the back of the sofa. "Is this what you came here to talk to me about?"

Amy grabbed the papers and folded them as best as she could. "I was coming here to look for more evidence too. Between the painting you showed me and what Cole told me, there's no reason to doubt what I said."

"Have you told anyone your little theory about me?"

"Maybe one," she said. "Or three."

Curtis narrowed his eyes. "You told people that I stole a painting and kidnapped the artist? I could sue you and the cruise line for slander. In fact, I will."

"No," Amy said. Her life aboard ship, either as a success or a failure, fell to pieces in her mind. "It's all there. You can't deny it."

He laughed. "I will sue you, and I will see to it that you never work anywhere ever again."

"Aren't you showing just how ethical and honest you are?" Amy pulled her arms tight around her, further crushing the paper.

"Do you think I'm stupid enough to steal a painting from Diane Westgrove Lewis and try to sell it?" Curtis laughed again. "I might be unwise in the ways of the heart, but I'm not stupid in business."

"Then how come your business is failing, Dad?" Cole shouted from the safety of his room. "Again."

"You don't know the first thing about my business," Curtis shouted back.

"You don't know the first thing about what I know, Dad."

Curtis stood up and shot toward his son's room.

As quietly as she could, Amy slipped from the suite into the hallway.

In, she realized, terrifying defeat.

Chapter Seventeen

Still gripping the crumpled papers, Amy raced to the stairwell. She ran down three flights before needing to stop and catch her breath. The gray cold wall of the stairwell pressed its metallic back against her. She'd gone forward with her assumptions too quickly, hadn't she? She'd been too quick to presume Curtis Jenkins could have pulled off the forgery. He wasn't the cunning businessman she'd thought he was. Instead, he was a miserable man whose world was falling apart around him. Which left her back where she'd begun. If he didn't have the original *Venus Rising*, then who did?

Amy inhaled, righted herself, and started back down toward her room. If nothing else, she had to call Penelope and Richard to let them know that she'd returned from the ordeal in one piece, even if her theories about Curtis Jenkins had not.

Call or, if they were in anyway, knock. Amy went down one more floor and opened the stairwell door back into the golden hallway. It wasn't like the dim stairwells at so many libraries that opened up to well lit stacks. She went from dimness to dimness, even if the latter had the luster of gold about it.

In the hallway, passengers in couples and groups crowded together over events programs and schedules. Some were already dressed for dinner, in long gowns and suits. Tomorrow would be the last night of this leg, and for many, it would be the last chance to dine under the glow of a chandelier, the ocean slipping past beneath them, the light of the moon just out the window. Or the light of Venus and all the beauty and glamour she offered.

Amy slipped by them as quickly as she could, her lanyard and badge clanking against the soft elegance of the music issuing from the well-hidden speakers above them all. She stood outside the suite door she'd sought out and knocked. No answer. She tried again, gripping the papers even tighter. This time, Richard answered the door.

"Amy, dear, you look as if you've run all the way here," he said. A wriggly Carrington peeked out from under his arm. "Sorry it took a moment to catch this fellow. Edyta said he's been getting braver about the door when she pops round. Come in, please."

"Oh," Penelope said as Amy slipped into the suite. "It didn't go as planned?"

"Nothing is going as planned," Amy said. She laid the crumpled papers out on the coffee table and fought the urge to pound on them with her still-shaking fists. "Curtis Jenkins doesn't seem to be our culprit after all. He's still a creep, and he's still a terrible dad. But after seeing him this evening? I don't know. He looks so defeated and dejected."

Carrington, free from Richard's arms, waddled over to Amy. "I think the old boy is trying to cheer you up."

Amy uncurled her hands and reached down to pet the cat, who was rubbing his cheeks against her ankles. "Either that, or marking me as his." She sighed. "How could someone so awful be innocent?"

"Just because he is innocent of this one crime doesn't mean he's not an awful person," Penelope said. She was dressed in a long peacock blue gown, and her gray hair, usually worn straight behind her ears, floated above her shoulders in a low chignon. In evening makeup, Penelope looked like an altogether different woman. She hadn't looked this dazzling the night of Diane Westgrove Lewis's reception. "Instead of chiding yourself for jumping to the wrong conclusion, look elsewhere. Focus on your other suspects."

"You were about to go out," Amy said. "I'm sorry. I'll go."

"No, Amy, sit," Richard said. "I'm not dressed for dinner yet. Good thing with all this orange cat fur on me now. How about I go get gussied up while you two talk?"

Some fleeting sadness crossed Penelope's face. "We should talk," she said. "Let's go through who's left on the list."

"Who's left?" Amy thought for a moment. "Just one person. One who makes any sense, anyway. Brent Detweiler."

"Makes sense, yes," Penelope said. She cocked her head, and the light caught the diamond studs in her ears. "He'd have the most to gain from making a scene during the painting's debut."

"And, who else could have sabotaged my internet access?" Amy explained what she'd learned from Kevin and what she concluded about Raymond Entwhistle's technical problems as well. "But, I don't know, there's something so sudden and needlessly cruel about it, isn't there? Brent Detweiler could have found a dozen other ways to cause a stir around the painting's debut. Or any other event aboard *The Cullinan Diamond* while he and Diane were aboard. Someone wanted Diane to look bad."

Penelope nodded. "There's your question, then. Who would have been angry enough at her to make her look so confused?"

"The way Curtis went on with his son, I could believe that he'd be capable of that anger," Amy said. Carrington hopped up on the coffee table, planted himself in the middle of her papers, and began to groom his rather massive belly. "But I don't think he'd be capable of putting all the pieces together. Maybe he was clever enough to buy the early paintings, but getting *Venus Rising* was beyond his abilities."

Richard, dressed in a tuxedo, emerged from the bedroom. "One thing we haven't asked is how the chap got those early paintings in the first place."

"You do look dashing, my darling." Penelope shooed the cat from the printouts. "Gemma asked him that exact thing after he pestered her about the cruise line buying the lot. Again. He said he'd bought them not long ago from a buyer trying to get rid of the lot for cheap."

"Wait, someone dumped them on the market?" Amy picked up her papers again. "Not that long ago?"

"Ah, there's the act of a tormented soul," Richard said. "Or at least a soul who wanted—"

"Revenge?" Penelope stood up. She went to the balcony. "There's an interesting idea."

"Who would want revenge on someone who lived a dull life except for almost making a career as a painter," Amy pondered. "She's done so much good for so many people, hasn't she?"

"Has she?" Penelope tapped her hand on the glass of the doorway. Amy hadn't noticed before, but she'd had her nails done in a flattering shade of dusty rose. "Aside from those whose artistic work she made possible, whose programs and charities she's funded. Who else?"

Amy's stomach dropped. She hadn't thought to ask that question. She didn't want to ask that question. "I'm sorry, Richard, you said Penelope and I needed to talk?"

Penelope shook her head. "No, I'm sorry, dear. I was too focused on the mystery at hand. Richard and I have decided New York will be our last stop on the ship. We wanted to tell you sooner, but we didn't want to interrupt your work on solving the puzzle."

"You're going out tonight," Amy said quietly. "It's a farewell dinner…"

"Of sorts," Richard said. "Captain Patel invited us up to his table at Le Bœuf du Duc after he heard we were considering leaving. We wanted to leave at port in London, but he convinced us to stay on one more leg."

"I'm sure you've given Beatrice a shock," Amy said. "Well, I won't keep you."

"Will you join us?" Richard said. "We're not seated for another half-hour. We thought we'd go up to the Sapphire Lounge as soon as we'd heard from you. But here you are. We can celebrate your continued journey after ours has ended for other adventures."

Amy stifled a sob. "I've pretty much lost my job. When Curtis tells Beatrice, I'm out."

Penelope slipped on her wrap and picked up her pearl-beaded clutch. She took Amy by the arm and led her to the door. "You get dressed, then. Meet us at the

Sapphire Lounge in twenty minutes. Come along, Richard. We're about to invite another guest to dinner. One who can help us resolve all this. The good captain won't mind."

Back at her own room, Amy found the door slightly ajar. From inside, a deep voice spoke to someone she hoped was just Roisin. Could Curtis have sent his son to the staff floor to threaten her? Or worse, could Curtis have come himself? Beatrice's voice was higher, more reedy than Roisin's but Amy didn't trust her senses at the moment.

****

She breathed in and flung the door open. "Just tell me what I need to do to make this right." The words came out too fast. "I don't want to lose my job, and it's not like I won't leak what you tried to do to me and what you said to Gemma to the media."

"Ara, Amy, what'd you make the bags of?" Roisin sat at their small table, her head in her hand. Just across from her sat the violist Amy had seen earlier. Beatrice's lovely violist, so like the former librarian. He held Roisin's other hand softly. "I've never seen you up to ninety before."

"Oh, I'm interrupting," Amy said. "I'm sorry."

Roisin shrugged. "Time for you to go, dote. I've been up a donkey's age anyway." The violist stood up and kissed her on the cheek before excusing himself and slipping out the doorway.

"I had no idea, Roisin," Amy said. "Is this new?"

"Very," the pianist replied. "As in two days ago. I'm dizzy. I can't wait until we get to port so I can have a good chat with my sister about it." She yawned and stood up. "I'm off to the jacks for a bit."

As soon as Roisin had closed the bathroom door, Amy opened the closet and pulled out the dress she'd worn the night of the painting's debut. She changed as quickly as she could. Her librarian bun would have to do, as would her daytime makeup and earrings. She grabbed her wrap and her evening clutch and stood in front of the mirror for a moment.

Just as she was about to leave, Roisin called out, "Beatrice came by to talk to you. Didn't say what she wanted."

"Thank you, Roisin," Amy said. "I'm going out. Goodnight."

And it was high time Amy called her sister for a chat, too.

\*\*\*\*

Outside the Sapphire Lounge, Amy felt the urge to run to Beatrice, to tell her all about the failures she'd had during the trans-Atlantic crossing, overestimating her technical and sleuthing skills. At least she had some ground to stand on claiming she could fix computers. Her sleuthing skills, on the other hand, had never been fully tested. Had she suspected Neil of cheating on her, she would have readily gone to whatever lengths she needed to go to in order to find out the who, where, what, and why of it. But he wasn't living a fantasy life with someone else. It was that the fantasy life he'd tried to create with her had finally crumbled. Which was, she reluctantly admitted to herself before their divorce was finalized, never a mystery to her. It had only been a matter of time when he'd seen through it too.

If she had any chance of salvaging the fantastic turn she'd taken getting the job aboard *The Cullinan Diamond,* then she'd have to act now. Once through the blue glass doors, she felt her resolve return to her. If the rest of the ship was a vision in gold, then the Sapphire Lounge was a dream in deep blue. Penelope and Richard sat in a blue leather booth near the entrance. Dressed in sky tulle, looking both impatient and reluctant, Gemma sat beside Penelope.

"She has arrived, and just in time," Richard said. He stood up to greet her.

"Just in time to hear the plan, I hope?" Amy had forgotten the papers, but they were useless to her now, weren't they?

Penelope shook her head, then smiled and raised her hand. Amy turned around to see Captain Patel and his wife. Curtis Jenkins, still looking defeated, trailed in behind him. Penelope and Richard greeted the captain and his wife. "Amihan," Penelope said. "I wish we could have spent more time with you this leg of the journey."

"I wasn't expecting to see you here, Ms. Morrison," Curtis muttered. "Or you, Miss Williams."

Gemma glowered. "Pen and Rich tell me you're in need of some, let's say, assistance."

"Cole isn't joining you?" Amy asked. Either Curtis ignored her question, or he was too focused on Gemma.

"I am in need of no such thing," he said. Even in the very blue light of the Sapphire Lounge, Curtis Jenkins's face shone a deep and livid red.

"I do so enjoy our dinners at Le Bœuf du Duc," Amihan said. "It reminds me of the posh restaurant officer's table where I first met Rahul."

Curtis eyed her. "The young officer Rahul falls in love with his waitress?" He sneered.

Amihan met him with a flat gaze. "You're right in

that at the time, Captain Patel, as you may address him, was a young officer. I, however, had just begun my career as a maritime lawyer at the cruise line for which we both worked."

Curtis mumbled and hung back as they left the Sapphire Lounge.

They all walked down the golden hallway together to Le Bœuf du Duc. Richard maneuvered the captain and his wife slightly ahead of the rest. "Have I ever told you about my work on the Torstenson War between Denmark and Sweden in the 1640s?"

Penelope took Curtis's arm. "Mr. Jenkins, I'm so glad you could join us."

"Such delicious company," he said in a low voice. "How could I say no?"

Amy wanted to say something about having his second dinner spoiled by his quite large first, but she watched Penelope instead to follow her lead.

"It's our last night before we disembark," Penelope said. "And I thought since we hadn't had a chance to talk with you, it was now or never."

"I've always been a now or never kind of man, Mrs. Percival." He placed his hand on his heart.

Amy looked over at Gemma, who shot her a look, then raised her eyes to the gold-paneled ceiling.

"Don't you mean, Dr. Swift?" Gemma asked him flatly. "Curtis."

"Well, then," Penelope said as she patted Curtis's arm with her free hand. "Now's the time to ask, it seems. Ms. Morrison and Ms. Williams have told me that you have brought a delightful art collection along with you on this voyage."

"Ms. Morrison, you say." He glanced back at her.

Amy froze for a moment, then nodded.

"And Ms. Williams," Penelope continued. "You must tell us all about the paintings when we're all seated for dinner."

"Must I?" The back of Curtis's neck grew splotchy. "I don't want to talk about my art collection tonight. Unless you have a buyer for it." He glanced back at Gemma.

"Alas no," Penelope said. "We want to know where you got the paintings, Mr. Jenkins. And which ones you have."

"Oh, no," he said. His neck went from splotchy to red. "What has Ms. Morrison told you? It's all lies."

With her head cocked back slightly, giving her an air of height above what she already had, Penelope laughed. "For now, I'll believe what you tell me. But you must be honest with us. Completely."

"Or?"

Penelope nodded at Amy.

Curtis shook his head, "Or what?"

Amy froze for a moment. She willed her feet to keep up with the others. She willed her heart to keep beating. It was now or never, as Curtis Jenkins had said.

Gemma saved her from speaking. "Mr. Jenkins," she said primly, "If Ms. Morrison, an astute woman, I'm sure you'll agree, came to the conclusion that, quite frankly, I came to independently and Dr. Swift came to, then do you not think that authorities investigating the crime of Diane Westgrove Lewis's kidnapping and the whereabouts of the original *Self-Portrait as Venus Rising from the Sea* will come to the same conclusion?"

"What are you saying?" Curtis shoved Penelope's hand from his arm. "Get to it, you infernal women!"

At last, Amy spoke. Penelope and Gemma had set her up, but she needed to drive the point home. Curtis's home. "Yes, I accused you of a crime that I now think you're incapable of."

"Oh?" he harrumphed.

"You don't have the means. Or not anymore," Amy continued. They were nearly at the grand golden entrance to Le Bœuf du Duc. "I know—we all know—that you're being sued for divorce by your third wife."

"So what?"

"For infidelity," Amy added.

"Ah, that."

Penelope nodded at her, and Amy continued. "You might easily go to the cruise line and tell them what I accused you of." She held her breath for a moment, then pushed on, moving through the swift current of everything she needed to get out. "Which would easily cost me my job. But I could just as easily bolster your wife's case by testifying about the dinner you set up for us, ostensibly so I could see your art collection, which you never showed me. I'd be more than eager to testify about the part in which you were fondling my wrist and saying some things that were rather unprofessional."

"What are you saying?" Curtis must have been struggling to keep his voice down.

"She's saying spill it, or we run to your wife's legal team," Gemma said. "And I'd be rather glad to add in a few words about your not-so-micro microaggressions."

"Fine," Curtis said. "What do you want?"

"What we want," Amy said firmly, "is for you to tell us over dinner how you acquired the early Diane Westgrove Lewis paintings, from whom, and for how much."

"On one condition," Curtis said.

Penelope raised an eyebrow. "Are you asking for conditions now?"

Curtis shook his head. "Help me convince Diane to buy the paintings. Once she found out I had them, she made me an offer. It wasn't high enough. That's why I set up the auction in New York." He put the heel of his hand to a sweaty temple. "I need to sell those paintings, and the auction house pulled out. Said they wouldn't make much off those paintings now. I've been a crappy husband and a crappier father. No, I've been a miserable failure of a father. You saw that yourself, Ms. Morrison. I need to sell those paintings. At least make back what I spent. You gals could easily smash whatever defense I have against Lily, and I need the money to fix what Cole messed up."

The three women exchanged a long look. Amy spoke after a moment, just after they'd crossed through the gilded doorway. "I'll ask," she said. "She's sick and resting up in the medical suite for now, so I can't talk to her before she's discharged, I'm sure. But if Mrs. Lewis does buy them, it must be at cost. You don't get to earn a dime, got it?"

Curtis nodded. The hostess greeted the captain's party, and they were led to his table at the side of the restaurant nearest the long window overlooking the roiling ocean. Beneath the silver and crystal chandelier whose center blue stone was cut to the same rose shape as St. Edward's Sapphire in the Imperial State Crown, Amy hardly noticed her dinner, paying attention instead to the conversation as she ate.

Curtis spilled the whole story in detail, about how he was contacted by an anonymous source who'd heard of his situation and who was willing to help him. Why the anonymous source was willing to help he wasn't sure, but he was desperate. All he had to do was go to a run-down warehouse in the north of England to pick up the art, which was stored in cases marked with a sharp-beaked sea bird, from the manager of the gallery who'd acted as an intermediary. "It's a razorbill," the gallery manager had told Curtis. "Sort of an unofficial emblem of the Westgroves."

Like a seabird diving into her consciousness, the image of the razorbill struck her. She remembered where she'd seen it before, not only on Diane Westgrove Lewis's brooch the night of the reception, but also in the one place that made sense.

"This has been so lovely," Amy said halfway through the entree course. "I am so sorry, but I'm feeling a bit unwell at the moment."

"You're not coming down with something, are you, dear?" Richard said.

Penelope smiled at her. "She'll clue us in later, won't you, Amy?"

"Tomorrow," Amy said. "Everything will be better tomorrow."

With that, Amy said her goodbyes and walked out the door of Le Bœuf du Duc. When she was out of sight of the doorway, she hitched up the hem of her skirt and ran all the way to the library.

When all this was over, she told herself, what she needed was a long weekend in bed with a few romance novels and a long talk with her sister.

Chapter Eighteen

Amy opened the library, her hands steady. Once inside, the door locked behind her, she grabbed a flashlight from her desk and made her way over to the painting, the fake *Self-Portrait as Venus Rising from the Sea*. There, on the wooden stretcher of the canvas, was burned the image of the razorbill, a black and white sea bird with a sharp beak. The same bird Curtis had noted on the other early Diane Westgrove paintings. The bird Diane Westgrove Lewis herself wore in brooch form the night of the reception for the unveiling of what should have been the real piece that could have made her career as an artist.

Amy checked her watch. Late for her to be out and to have slept well enough to make it past Beatrice for breakfast at the elite's table. She had to. Tomorrow by this time, the perpetrators of the crimes of hacking, art fraud, and kidnapping would be somewhere in the glamour of New York City, and the glamour of the ship and its Transatlantic Crossing far behind them.

Quickly, she printed off copies of the images Tiffany had sent her along, this time, with the nightgown images Kevin had found on her laptop, a list of the meanings behind giving certain types and colors of flowers, and a picture of a razorbill in flight.

A knock on the library door startled her. Amy wasn't expecting Zuzanna or any of the other staff. She clicked the flashlight off and crouched down. The knocking grew louder, more urgent. The fabric of her dress gathering around her waist, Amy crawled along the floor. "Amy," a voice whispered hoarsely. "Amy, I know you're in there. I saw someone moving around in there. Let me in. Please."

She looked up. Through the gold glass, Amy saw the unmistakably shaggy figure of Raymond Entwhistle pacing the short distance between the walls of the hallway. Her heart steadied. She stood up and tried to smooth the fabric of her dress back down, but the static that had built up kept the waves she'd made crawling on the floor in place. "Thank goodness, it's you, Raymond," Amy said.

"I could say the same about you, Amy." He looked at her rumpled gown. "You haven't been unpacking them in your evening gown, have you?"

"Them?"

"The sweeties," Raymond whispered. "I need them back in my suite tonight to pack away for tomorrow."

Amy gasped. She'd forgotten all about that. "I'll need to go gather them up from the closets I stashed them in," she said. "I should change first."

"I have a cart just down the hallway," Raymond said. "Can we start with the ones in the library?"

"Please," Amy said. She unlocked the tidy supply closet in the library, in which the previous librarian had stored anything but contraband, and they unloaded the small unmarked boxes from the shelves to his cart.

"May I walk you to your room?" Raymond asked. "Am I allowed on the staff deck?"

"That would be useful, actually," Amy said. "I think we need to talk, anyway." After taking as deep a breath as her rumpled and increasingly uncomfortable evening dress would allow her to do, Amy filled Raymond in on her suspicions, leaving out her accusation of Curtis. "I think I need one more favor from you."

"Anything," he said, the cart jostling beneath his hands. "Especially if it means unraveling the mystery about what happened to Diane. Wellie still won't let me see her."

"Still?" Amy watched the gold light above them dim slightly to mimic the lower light outside. "Can you come to breakfast tomorrow? I need to convince Brent Detweiler to meet with me just after."

"Won't you be at the library?" The cart ran over a bump and protested loudly.

Amy shook her head. "We're closed on disembarkation days. So that the books don't disembark too."

They took an elevator down to the staff floor. "I'm afraid I can't," Raymond said. "I need to pack all these in my steamer trunks after I do inventory. I'm trying to get off ship as quickly as I can." He nodded toward the boxes.

The elevator doors opened with a sigh. "I understand," she said. "I'm this way."

They clattered down the hallway until Amy stopped suddenly outside her room. "Oh," she said. An untied bow tie, one worn by the musicians aboard the ship, lay across the handle of her door. "You know what, I can pack up just fine in this," she said.

Raymond chuckled knowingly. "Do they still do that at university?"

"There, I don't know," Amy admitted. "But

apparently, we do that here."

They rattled the cart back down the hallway and down one floor. Music blared from the rooms, and Zuzanna and Edyta waved her over. "You're straight from a party?" Zuzanna raised her plastic cup.

"Something like that," Amy said. "We're here for the boxes. And for the list of books I need to get in New York."

Jagoda handed her a small notebook. "We consolidated. Made it easier, you know?"

Amy flipped through the pages. "I will be shopping, won't I?"

"Anything Amy can't get in New York, I'll have shipped to your next port of call," Raymond said.

Zuzanna facilitated the collection of boxes of chocolate, and soon the cart was full. "All here," Raymond said, tallying them up. "I am in your debt." He bowed deeply, and he and Amy clattered back up to her floor.

As the elevators opened again, Amy bid Raymond a good night. He shook his head. "You go check," he said. "Your roommate might still have company."

The bowtie lay still across the handle of her door.

"I'll knock," Amy said. After she did so four times with no answer, she ran her hand through her now disheveled hair.

Raymond cleared his throat. "You could stay in my suite for tonight. The sofa is a pull-out bed, and there is bedding in the closet."

"Oh, no. I couldn't."

"I am a gentleman," Raymond said. "And I could use a hand with these."

"The last time I trusted a man who told me he was

a gentleman, he tried to make a move on me after drinking a bottle of champagne," Amy said.

"Champagne? Horrid stuff," Raymond said. "Not much of a wine drinker myself, either. A stout now and again, but only with my fellow birdwatchers." He straightened the collar of his worn green shirt. "I could tell you a thing or two about how to spot a capercaillie in the Scottish highlands."

"I'm sure you could," Amy said with a laugh. "So you really are a birdwatcher?"

"It is that obvious, then."

They clattered up the hallway with the cart. "Raymond, can you tell me anything about the razorbill?"

"The ones off the coast?" The cart squeaked to a stop. "Or the one flying on the back of a certain picture frame?"

****

The strange bed and the odd feel of the long t-shirt Raymond had given her for the evening might have kept her from falling asleep, but rather it was thoughts about tomorrow kept her up. True to his word, Raymond had given her the bedding and the t-shirt and locked himself in his room for the night after telling her more than would ever have been useful about the feeding habits of the razorbill, a bird emblematic to Isolde Westgrove.

When the alarm on her phone woke her, Amy guessed she'd had maybe a couple hours sleep. Raymond was up packing his steamer trunks, placing the cardboard boxes beneath rumpled sweaters and hiking boots. "I hope I didn't disturb," he said. "I'll excuse myself so you can—" he motioned to the bathroom.

After Raymond had gone back into his room, Amy got up and went to the bathroom. She'd hung up her dress on the shower curtain hoping that some of the wrinkles would fall out, but if anything, the gown looked worse in the morning light. Which was even more unsettling when she realized that the regal jewelry theme graced even the regular passenger decks. Raymond's bathroom was, in fact, a veritable parure, a matching set of earrings, bracelet, necklace, and brooch with a tiara serving as crown molding. Maybe it wasn't quite that, but the glossy blue tiles and metalwork of the faucets and knobs certainly called to her mind the aquamarines set in gold of Queen Elizabeth II's Brazil Parure. Maybe she had read a bit more about royal jewelry back home in Dawville than she'd realized.

Dressed, she emerged from the bathroom and called out to Raymond. "Are you sure you won't join us for breakfast?"

"No, but I do wish you the best of luck," he said. She'd need it.

Amy unlocked her door and swung it open harder than she meant to. She'd run through the hallway, worried that someone might spot her in the wrinkled and wilting gown she'd quite obviously worn the night before. Thankfully, everyone else in the hallway was either still asleep or already at work. At least the bowtie was gone this morning. She changed as quickly as she could, the rose cardigan set that set off her light brown eyes nicely, Neil had told her once. She took out a pencil skirt but put it back. She grabbed a pair of camel trousers instead.

She was struck with how tired she looked, but also

how much like Stacey she had become. She'd always thought her older sister favored their mother more, but as she and Stacey moved farther into midlife, Amy could see in herself her mother *and* her sister now. Tired maybe, but also determined. If there was a word that described them both, it was determined. She emptied the contents of the canvas bag Angus had given her onto her bed and slipped the printouts from the library into it.

Late for her morning check in with Beatrice, Amy rushed to the waypoint. A few musicians lingered around nervously. Beatrice was in full "housekeeper to a grand estate" mode, barking out to no one in particular rules of conduct that must be obeyed at all times. "This includes any public display of affection with other members of staff. You might be talented musicians, but do not forget that you are staff on this ship, here to serve the guests and not to entertain yourselves. What you do on the staff floors is your business, of course, but there will be no snogging on passenger decks."

Amy stifled a laugh. All right then, Roisin and the violist.

"Mrs. Taylor," Amy said softly. "Am I to join breakfast?"

Beatrice looked at her with a sneer. "You don't need my permission to grab a take-away from the staff canteen." She returned to her clipboard, writing something furiously on the top of the page.

"Please," Amy tried. "I'd like to speak to the ghostwriter, and to Brent Detweiler. It's important."

"If it's important," Beatrice said sharply, "then you may send an email. Marked urgent."

"It can't wait," Amy pleaded. "I need to talk to them before we debark."

"Then you may use the phone in the hallway. It's your day off, but some of us have work to do." Beatrice turned and focused on the lingering musicians.

Well, then. If Amy's job was in jeopardy already, she figured, she couldn't lose it twice.

She ran to the cafe. Slightly out of breath and hungry, Amy nearly ran into Richard and Penelope, on their way out. "Please tell me you're not leaving," Amy said, her voice at the edge of breaking.

"Afraid so, dear." Richard patted her on her shoulder. "You're feeling more lively than last night?"

Amy nodded. She craned her neck awkwardly at the same time, trying to see who was at the elites' table in the back of the cafe. "Particularly lively, since I'm about to get fired."

"Fired?" Penelope turned to look back into the cafe.

"Or maybe not, if I can hurry," Amy said. "Was Wellie or Brent in with you this morning?"

"Brent is still at the table." Penelope looked back toward Amy, her mouth in that half-open moue as if she were about to ask Amy something troubling. "But Wellie wasn't there, at least not for the last hour or so."

Richard laughed. "Brent and Curtis are having a bit of a row this morning."

"What about?" Amy shivered. The music faded above her, as if they were pulling away from the trans-Atlantic dream into the reality that they all faced in New York.

"The bacon," Richard said. "Of the fried pork and the metaphorical kinds."

"Curtis was angling for a word or two about his paintings in the press alongside the media attention Diane will get for her book." Penelope yawned. "Excuse me. It was a late night. Anyhow, Brent informed us that Wellie insisted Diane recuperate in their suite rather than in the ship's medical suites."

"Diane," Amy said. "Wait. She's recovering *with* Wellie?"

"So the gossip goes," Richard said. "We'll see you tomorrow night at Diane's gala preview?"

Amy nodded absently. Her friends said their goodbyes, and Amy charged into the cafe.

"Please, just a mention," Curtis said. Three empty plates lay in front of him. "Just a note that they're available."

"Mr. Jenkins." Amy stood before the empty chair at which Richard or Penelope must have sat moments ago. "May I join you?"

"Amy, please do," Curtis said. He motioned for the waiter who brought her a cup of coffee. With a motion she only half-registered, he removed the plates in front of Curtis. "I was just asking Mr. Detweiler here to put in a good word for me with the press regarding Mrs. Lewis's paintings. That can only be good for us both."

Brent huffed. "The librarian," he said. "At least it's not the ghostwriter."

"Mr. Jenkins, before you go to the trouble of convincing Mr. Detweiler to act on your behalf, I should tell you that I haven't spoken to Mrs. Lewis yet." Amy poured milk into her coffee then added a packet of sugar to it. She stirred slowly, then took a long, lingering sip. "So I might be of more assistance to you than Mr. Detweiler ever could."

"You?" Brent looked at his watch. "I need to finish packing. I'm done with this guy anyway." He crossed his arms and leaned back in his chair, his expensive techie watch tucked into his elbow.

"Mr. Jenkins," Amy said, cutting him off just as he tried to speak. "I told you last night, in error, that Mrs. Lewis is still in the care of the ship's doctors and nurses in the medical suite. I was wrong. She is, as Mr. Detweiler mentioned, in the care of her sister."

"It's good to be with family when you're not well," Brent said. "Plus I'm sure the ghostwriter is there. She's always lurking around the old woman. It's pathetic. Like she wants to be part of the family."

"Mr. Jenkins," Amy said after taking another long sip of coffee. "How is your son, Cole?"

Curtis rose. "I think I ought to return to my suite. I'm just next door to Mrs. Lewis's, so maybe I ought to drop in to say my farewells."

"A goodbye party," Brent said.

"I'm afraid it might be if we don't hurry," Amy said. "Mr. Detweiler, how much are you depending on Mrs. Lewis's connections to the media to promote her, as you called it, boring book?"

Brent shrugged. "It would be of use."

"Of use?" Amy drained the rest of her coffee. It wasn't breakfast, but at least it was something in her stomach. They would reach port in less than half an hour, and disembarkation of the elite-level passengers would begin not long after that. She had no more time to lose, even if she lost her job. "And if something terrible befell her on the ship?"

A dry smile rose on his face. "Hasn't it already? Her memory lapse? And faking her own kidnapping just to get attention?"

"No," Amy said softly. "I mean actually terrible."

Brent's eyes widened, and he stood up, clattering a fork against a plate as he brushed into the table. "My suite isn't far from theirs."

**\*\*\*\***

Quickly, they went up to the elite-level suites, Curtis following behind Brent and Amy. Brent mumbled an excuse for not going straight into his suite. He should check up on Diane if she's in with the ghostwriter. Or worse, Raymond.

"I think you should go in first, then," Amy said suddenly. "You're the one with the most reason to see Mrs. Lewis."

"What if that Raymond Entwhistle guy is inside?" Brent scratched at his chin. "You don't know what a man like that is capable of."

Amy fought the urge to roll her eyes. "If Raymond is in there holding Mrs. Lewis and Ms. Westgrove hostage, then you're the best one of the three of us to do something about it. You're bigger than I am and more," she paused and waved her hand in search of the right words, which she failed to find. "More than Mr. Jenkins."

"More what, Ms. Morrison?" Curtis's face mottled.

"Just more," Amy said. "Let's not do this right now. Go in, Mr. Detweiler. Please."

Amy grabbed Curtis's arm and led him to the bend in the hallway where she had watched Erin twice before. Brent knocked. Wellie met him and led him inside.

"Now what?" Curtis pointed toward the stairwell. "I can grab the fire extinguisher and rush whoever it is you're worried about in there."

"Mr. Jenkins," Amy said in her best customer service voice. "That won't be necessary. Please go to your suite and ask for a security team to meet us here."

"But you'll be all alone," Curtis said. He stood too close to her and whispered at her with bacon-laden breath. "You'll be defenseless, and a woman like you needs to be protected."

"Please, Mr. Jenkins," Amy said backing away from him. "We'll all be better off if you return to your suite and call the security team. To defend me. It's worth the risk of leaving me here alone."

He squeezed her upper arm tightly and nodded. "If you think it's worth the risk, I'll go." He ran toward his doorway and fumbled with the card. Cole opened the door for him, and Curtis pushed him out of the way as he went inside.

The security team would be on their way soon. And Brent was inside with Wellie and Diane—he'd do what he needed to do to ensure Mrs. Lewis's safety. Amy could walk away now, plead with Beatrice so that she could keep her job, do what she needed to get Kate to pull strings at corporate headquarters. She could even ask Curtis to put in a glowing report on her behalf.

But, she reminded herself, working on board *The Cullinan Diamond* was a risk in the first place, a risk of losing the safety of her life in Dawville and her place at the local library. Taking this job was a risk that she might finally find herself. Losing it meant she might never do so.

Going inside the Westgrove sisters' suite was the biggest risk of all, then.

And it was a risk she was willing to take.

Outside the suite, Amy paused. She listened to voices within churning in a troubling way, but she couldn't put her finger on it. A man's voice chimed in. Amy took a deep breath, then knocked.

After a moment more of the voices rolling together, Raymond answered the door. "You've got to help us," he said quietly.

Behind him, Amy heard clearly what she couldn't parse from behind the door.

"Raymond, thank goodness you're here," Amy said. She straightened herself as upright as she could be under the weight of her exhaustion. "Of course, I'll help. That's what I'm here for." She patted the canvas tote at her side.

Raymond peered around the hallway and ushered her in. Diane was lounging on the sofa with the curtains drawn. Brent and Wellie were in chairs on either side of her, trying, presumably, to get her to talk. "They've been like this for almost an hour now, Diane and Wellie," Raymond said to her. "I don't know what she wants from my aunt. And Brent, what does he want, rushing in just as we're trying to get off this infernal ship?"

"I think I know on both accounts," Amy said. "Look, I need you to do me a favor."

"You and I are getting thick as thieves with favors, aren't we?"

"I might not use that phrase," Amy said. "But sure." Quietly, Amy asked Raymond to go retrieve a couple items for her from the library, items that would be of use to resolving the puzzle. "And if anyone asks, tell them I lost this in the hallway outside your aunt's suite," she said as she handed him her badge.

If this was going to work, she needed it to work now.

Chapter Nineteen

"Good morning," Amy said with as much relaxed confidence as she could muster. Which wasn't much, but it would have to do. "Raymond let me in. He needed to run an errand, and he asked me to send his excuses."

In the morning light, Amy was struck by the detail in the most exclusive suite aboard the ship. When she'd been here the night Wellie reported Diane missing, Amy had been so focused on the older woman's safety, she hadn't registered how the space would be lived in. The cream-colored sofas were covered in a subtle print, a repeating linked circle design. Every wall had either a mirror or some glossy surface to reflect the light from the balcony back into the room. Only a sliver of light from outside pushed through the drawn heavy drapes.

No matter, since the glow from the fixture above them all illuminated the scene well enough. A hint of blue shone on the glass tabletop between them all, as the light fixture's rectangular blue crystal ringed by smaller white round ones echoed the configuration of the Prince Albert sapphire brooch. Which, if Amy remembered correctly, was given to Queen Victoria and worn by the Queen Elizabeth II. So many details Amy could get lost in, from her tours of the ship weeks ago when she was first hired to the long history of discord between the sisters in front of her now. This was all about getting behind appearances, wasn't it?

"Sad excuse for a man," Wellie said. She sat back and waved as if dismissing even the thought of Raymond. Something regal in her gesture reminded Amy of a minor royal waving from a far-off balcony. "Coming in here and asking Diane all these questions about who tied her up. As if she could remember in her state."

Diane's eyes were glassy and unfocused. She muttered something, but Wellie just patted her hand. Diane shook her head and closed her eyes. Her other hand ran over the linked circles on the sofa's fabric.

Brent stood up. He tossed the rectangular sapphire pillow that had been behind his back onto the sofa on which Diane lay. The pillow's white tassels reached in what seemed to Amy like protest at the older woman's feet. "Tying herself up in the balcony closet and getting stuck there—what a ridiculous thing to do." He scratched his head, at the point where he was going bald just in the back. "Though if I'd known about her memory issues before we signed the contract, there is no way I would have gone through with this. And look at her—how can she be of any use to me with the press now?"

"Wait. Memory issues?" Amy asked.

"Yes, like forgetting what her painting looked like," Brent said. Wellie barked out a laugh. "If I'd known that she was going to make a scene like that, I would have never allowed the launch of her book aboard this ship. Even though it is a brilliant idea for a book launch."

"Not much of a launch," Amy said. Beatrice's warning to her after her confrontation of Curtis in the library rang in her ears, but she knew honey would not trap the intended fly in this case. "Especially if you don't let anyone actually read the book."

He threw up his hands. "On sale date has always been the Tuesday after we reach New York. It's embargoed until then, and I can't break my own embargo."

"Not even for reviewers?"

"You're asking a lot of questions, Amy." Wellie smiled in the luxurious gloom. Her cocktail ring—a different one this morning—caught the sliver of light from the curtains. "Maybe, Mr. Detweiler, you've had an embargo breaker here on the ship. Someone you trusted to host Diane's book debut party."

Diane moaned in her half-dozing state.

"If someone had reason to read it," Amy said, "then I think breaking an embargo is justified, don't you think, Mr. Detweiler? Especially if that reader couldn't access the internet to say anything about said book? Especially if she realized someone was in danger of—"

"What are you getting at, Amy?" Brent cut her off.

"I did read the book," she said. "And with some expert technical help, I found out why I couldn't access the internet. Why I couldn't even get the emails from Diane asking me to come see her the day after the gala."

"Oh," Wellie said as she waved her ringed hand. "She probably just wanted to thank you for the lovely party. It was nice, even if she ruined it for you."

Diane reached for something. Amy followed her hand, her finger, really, to the coffee table.

"Mr. Detweiler, do you know what these are?"

Amy pulled the papers from her bag and set down the pictures downloaded to her laptop.

He shook his head.

"This is clever," she said. "Sort of. The cruise line is in negotiations to buy your publishing company. If the book fails, the talks fail, don't they? I think you were warning me to stay away." She opened the curtains to let in more light. Though the sun rose on the other side of the ship, the lights off the water and the lights on the side of the ship made the images clearer. "I think you were trying to tell me that if I said anything about how boring the book was, you'd make sure I'd get the 'pink slip.' It would be clever, if it weren't so cliché."

"Why would I do that?"

"That's what I want to find out from you," Amy said. "I have my suspicions, but my suspect must be you. How many hack-a-thons have you won this past year, Mr. Detweiler?"

"So what if I win programming competitions? That I can still defeat the best and brightest coders to come out of the Ivy Leagues doesn't prove anything. Even if it is impressive," he said. He looked down toward his arm and placed a hand over his techie watch.

"You're right," Amy said. "It is impressive but it doesn't prove anything. Oh, but it does prove that you really ought to freshen up the way you express yourself. Pink slip. Does anyone use that phrase to refer to getting fired anymore? A good ghostwriter should be able to solve your problem, don't you think?"

A knock on the door interrupted them. "Oh, don't," Wellie said. "It's probably just housekeeping. I'll send them away." She grabbed her cane and went to the door.

After making her way to the front entry, she shouted that she didn't want to be disturbed. Of course she didn't want that. She made her way back to the chair and sat down again.

"There, that's taken care of. We really need to get that Lucy girl back in here to ensure we're packed and ready to disembark. Diane will come home with me, of course. My New York home. She wouldn't be able to make the trip back to Los Angeles, or at least not with her memory issues. Poor lamb would get lost." She took a drink from the crystal flute on the coffee table.

Diane moaned again.

A glass of water that had left a ring on the glass overlay was the only other container on the table except for a small vase of dark pink rose buds.

"How beautiful. Are those Princess Margaret roses?" Amy asked Wellie.

"Unfortunately," Wellie said with a smirk. "Though they look just like Queen Elizabeth buds. Ancestor rose to the Diane Lewis hybrid. They're tawdry things, but apparently you can't get something as simple as yellow carnations here from the florist unless you tell them what you want before you're on ship."

"They're charming, I'm sure." Brent looked out to the water. "Can we get some air in here?" He opened the balcony door. A cool breeze wafted in, bringing along with it the smells of salt and the faint whiff of ship's exhaust. Amy thought of the sea bird that had supposedly ransacked Curtis's suite.

Another knock on the door was nearly drowned out by the sound of waves and the ship's engines. Amy must have been the only one to hear it. She excused herself for a moment and went to the door.

She held her breath and looked through the peephole. Outside stood Raymond with the two things she needed. "Shh," she said as she opened the door. Raymond handed her one of the items she'd requested. She nudged the door a bit and set what Raymond had delivered to her on the threshold to keep the door open just a crack. Raymond gave her a thumbs up.

"Who is it this time?" Wellie shouted.

"Just housekeeping," Amy said. She smoothed the fabric of her trousers and sat down. The printouts she had brought with her fluttered in the breeze. "I asked them to come back another time."

"Good," Wellie said.

"Now, Mr. Detweiler," Amy said. "Back to the download script that you put on my laptop. I think you were worried that you'd left a copy of an exceedingly dull memoir—the one that would get your publishing company back on track financially—in the hands of a curious reader, didn't you?"

He banged his fist against the balcony door frame. "So what if I did? One bad review from you, and sales would plummet. I needed a good debut. You blabbing about the book would have done us in. And I couldn't have that."

Amy nodded. "You made two mistakes there, Mr. Detweiler. First, I don't think the book is dull at all. Mrs. Lewis's story might not be as fast-paced and compelling as the latest starlet's confessional, but she and the ghostwriter, Erin Dunn, did a fantastic job of finding the story of Mrs. Lewis's convictions that she should do right by the world through her philanthropy.

She's a fortunate woman in many ways, and she's known that all along. She's never taken advantage of it."

"Is that so?" Wellie smirked.

Brent turned back toward the sitting room. "Fine, that's one. It's good for women who've reached mid-life looking for a feel-good story about someone who does something nice for the world. What's my next mistake?"

"Two was blocking my internet access," Amy said.

"I confessed already," he said. "It's not a crime. And you left your laptop sitting out, may I remind you. I'm not alone in making mistakes on this cruise. Can we move on?"

"I should explain before we do move on," Amy said. "After I was able to access the web again, I asked a friend—a librarian, of course—to look into the issue of Mrs. Lewis's painting. Now, you, Ms. Westgrove and Mr. Detweiler, won't even entertain the idea that *Self-Portrait as Venus Rising from the Sea* in the library is not her original work."

"And what did you find?" Wellie asked. She looked toward one of the mirrors on the wall, as if posing again for the painting Curtis had shown Amy of the dancer at the barre.

Amy flipped the pictures of the pink slips over. She passed the pictures beneath them first to Brent. "You would have had a sensational story there, Mr. Detweiler, if I'd found out sooner. As soon as this hit the news, you would have had lines around the corner at every bookshop and orders by the thousands online."

"What am I looking at?" He flipped through the three printouts.

"Archives from the art school newspaper, dated just before Mrs. Lewis finished *Venus Rising*. You can see the mostly completed work in the background, along with the model she used." Amy pointed at the head just behind Diane's mentor.

"What do you mean?" Wellie grabbed her cane and stood up. "Model? The painting is a self-portrait. I'm sure she said as much in that supposedly dull book of hers."

"That's what you'd like us to think," Amy said. Brent fluttered the papers in his hands. "Raymond, can you come in now?"

"Raymond?" Wellie took another drink from her flute. "What does that twit want?"

"It's not what I want," he said. Raymond set the painting on a chair, propped up so that the woman in the slinky dress faced them. He gave the book that had propped the door open to Amy. "It's never been about what I want."

"Don't be coy, Raymond," Wellie said. "You've wanted to be in Diane's will since the first time you met her. Haven't you?"

He shrugged. "I am, in a sense," he said. "Diane offered to include me as an heir to her estate, but I declined. I asked her to make a donation in my name if she wanted to do something to honor our relationship. So that's what she's going to do."

Wellie barked out another laugh. "Hmm, the Raymond Entwhistle Fund, I presume?"

"Hardly," he said. "It's a thousand dollars to a local school arts program I donate that much to yearly already. Which is about half of what your ring cost you, I'd imagine."

"Let's get back to the painting, shall we?" Brent ran his hand through his hair again. "What's this about me missing out on a sensational story, Amy?"

Amy set the pictures next to the fraudulent painting. "I have at least one witness who can verify that the painting in the school photograph is the real *Venus Rising*. And another who can vouch for the fact that this looks nothing like Mrs. Lewis's other early work."

"Oh, come now," Wellie said. "You can't prove anything from those things. You don't know how many people there are in the world who'd gladly bilk a sick old woman out of her money."

"You're right again, Ms. Westgrove," Amy said. She held up the book. "You were right, Mr. Detweiler, when you were worried I'd read the book. I did read the book. Well, not all of it." She flipped to the missing acknowledgments section. "There was something missing in the book that made it impossible to complete."

Diane reached toward Amy. She sat down next to the old woman.

"Whoever you hired to paint this, Ms. Westgrove," Amy said, "must not have had access to the paintings your sister did in art school, or those she'd done after. Or you hired them to make a cheap copy of her original ideas. To make her look bad. Juvenile, really."

"Whatever are you going on about?" Ms. Westgrove looked over at the painting. A sudden gust from the open balcony doors chilled the room. "Why would I have any idea how my sister painted?"

Amy took the pictures from Brent and handed them to Wellie. "Because you were the model for *Venus*

*Rising*, weren't you? You were Venus, not Diane. When she slighted you, when she claimed to be the woman in the painting that was going to make her famous, you were irate."

"And? It was a long time ago, Amy."

"And it was just before your accident," Amy said. "I don't know what your sister said about you in the acknowledgments, but it must not have gone over well with you. After all, she should have acknowledged you as *Venus* years ago. The least she could have done was make that right in her memoir. But she didn't, did she?"

"Fine. I'm Venus. I've always been Venus, and I've lived the sort of life Venus might have if she'd been the indomitable heiress I am. Can you blame me?" Ms. Westgrove looked down toward her rings. "I was irate, as you said. I went to the party that night when we were both so young, to have a good time, to forget about what she'd done to me. Or what she hadn't done. We were both going to be famous. Diane Westgrove the painter, and her muse Wellie Westgrove, the modern dance phenomenon. But," she said as she looked up again, "Diane decided to give up art, and I got drunk and fell down a flight of stairs. That was a long time ago, and what I did was just what she deserved."

"Let me ask you another question," Amy said. "Yellow carnations. They mean that someone has been rejected. Or disappointed." Amy turned to the printout of the yellow carnation and the explanation of its meaning.

In her chair, Wellie shook one finger up at Amy. "You bookish lot read symbolism into everything. What proof do you have that they'd mean anything to me in particular other than my love of golden things?"

"This might convince you." Amy took the painting and turned it backward and upside down. "That marking, right there, burned into the wooden stretcher, is a razorbill. Your mother was fascinated by the bird, found in northern England. She designed the brooch Mrs. Lewis wore on the night of the painting's debut. And I have it from a source that it's an unofficial emblem of the Westgrove family."

"Where did you get that nonsense from?" Wellie demanded.

A tremor of a smile passed Diane's mouth. Wellie blanched.

"The same source that will be of use when the identity of the party who sold Curtis Jenkins a collection of early Diane Westgrove paintings," Amy said. Her heart was pounding beneath the canvas bag she held to her chest. She thought of Angus for a moment before she brought her attention back to the old woman roiling against Amy's revelations.

Wellie shot up from her chair. She left her cane behind and grabbed the painting. Before anyone could reach her, she'd gone to the balcony and flung the painting over the railing, into the ocean. "You have no evidence now, do you?"

"You didn't." It was Amy's turn to feel sick. She gasped despite trying to will herself back to calmness. The pizza box. Which wasn't a pizza box or a towel after all. Her worst suspicions were true. "Ms. Westgrove, did you throw the original *Venus Rising* into the ocean a few nights ago?"

"You have no evidence of that, either," Wellie said.

"Oh, but I think I do," Amy said. "That night, I was on Curtis's balcony, having the chef's tasting menu. I thought I'd seen a pizza box flying from the ship. But it was the painting, wasn't it? I talked to your valet, Lucia, after, and she confirmed that there aren't any pizza boxes on ship."

Diane let out a choked cry.

Wellie barked out her laugh again. She leaned against the frame of the balcony door. "If you could be so kind as to bring me my cane?"

"No," Raymond said. "I think I know what happened now, why Aunt Diane has been so unwell." He picked up Diane's water glass.

"You going to have a drink?" Wellie smiled. "You're always following after Diane. Why not? *À votre santé*." Wellie looked grandly up toward the sapphire light fixture. A gift of love, The Prince Albert brooch, wasn't it? There was not much love in this room. "To your health, Raymond."

"Not a chance," Raymond said. "Aunt Di, has Wellie been drugging you?"

Diane inclined her head slightly.

"Then this is evidence," Raymond said in a more aristocratic cadence than Amy had heard him use before. He gripped the glass tightly.

"Evidence of what?" Wellie's cocktail ring flared, just as the sun flared off the waves. "Your fingerprints are all over the glass too now, you know. It's evidence of nothing."

"It is evidence, though. Evidence that I will sue you, Ms. Westgrove," Brent said. "I'm calling the security team."

"No need," Raymond said. "When Amy asked me to get the book and painting, I knew something was fishy. They were already in the hallway. So I asked them to follow me and stay around the corner until I went inside. They're outside the door as we speak."

"Well, then," Wellie said, floating across the room on dancer's feet, "at least I get some media coverage from this. It's been four years since my last very public and very expensive divorce—expensive for him anyway—and I've been dying for some attention since then." The security team came in and escorted Wellie Westgrove from her suite.

Wellie, head raised, gave the room one last look, one that she must have given Diane as she was posing for Venus decades ago. Wellie Westgrove might have aspired to be Venus, goddess of love and beauty. She may have had plenty of romance in her life, but like the Venus of myth, she was denied a childhood story, at least by Diane's memoir. And like the Venus of myth, and Aphrodite before her, Wellie had no intention of being less beautiful, less admired, less anything than anyone else.

After Wellie's grand departure, the medical team came in with their gear and began to attend to the drugged philanthropist.

Tears in her eyes, Diane smiled and held Amy's hand. The medics put the older woman on a stretcher, and Amy held on to her hand all the way to the medical suite.

Diane Westgrove Lewis might not have written the most fascinating memoir ever, but her story was nothing short of sensational.

Brent Detweiler would see to that.

Chapter Twenty

The ship was docked in New York City for a few days for shore excursions and to allow members of the staff and officers to attend Diane Westgrove Lewis's gallery opening. Lucia led the walkout of valets and housekeeping staff, which wasn't unexpected to the higher-ups on board the ship. The cruise line sent Lucia a concerned message—they'd talk with her and the others in her group if she agreed to return to the ship. They did, and negotiations were set up between the groups. For Lucia, it wasn't a total victory, as she'd told Amy, but at least they'd made more progress than they had at similar walkouts in the past. Time would tell if they would get the increased pay and better conditions that they'd asked for. Amy would do what she could to pitch in, following Lucia's lead.

Amy ran into Roisin leaving their room with the violist. "So sorry about the other night," he said sheepishly. "We were caught up in—"

"No, dote. No need for that." Roisin kissed him on the cheek. "Amy," she said with a gasp. She held up her left hand, on which was a souvenir ring from one of the ship's cheaper gift shops. A sapphire surrounded by diamonds. Amy's stomach fluttered for a moment thinking about the light fixture in the Westgrove suite and its nod to The Prince Albert sapphire brooch.

"You're engaged," Amy said with her own gasp.

"After just two days?"

Roisin laughed. "It's worse than that. We got hitched. It's just a plastic ring, I know, but I had to have one just like the one Kate got from Wills." Roisin looked over at her new husband. "We'll get a proper one on shore. Anyway, Captain Patel did the honors since we're on the water. And it was three days we were courting, thank you very much."

The ring the Duchess of Cambridge received on her engagement was also that of the Princess of Wales, Amy recalled, but the two young people in front of her were of a different generation. Just as she and Stacey were so unlike Diane and Wellie.

The violist laughed. "What have you been telling people, darling?" He shook his head. "We've been on this boat together, what, seven months now? And we were friends at conservatory for four years before that."

Roisin mocked an angry face at her husband. "Don't you go spoiling my adventure now, dote."

Amy congratulated them and slipped into her room. She gathered up all the gifts Angus had sent along and placed them gently back in the bag. Much as she wanted to hold each and every small thing, she knew she should save them for another day.

****

As the library was closed for the day of debarkation, Amy spent the rest of morning with Erin, perusing all the local independent bookstores the ghostwriter had haunted during her year in the city as a fledgling writer. "It wasn't until I went back home to Ohio that I got myself together as a writer," she told Amy during a walk between bookstores. "I wanted New York to be something for me, but I wasn't anything for

New York. Besides," she said with a smile, "it's nice to celebrate publication dates with family and friends who've supported you since you were a little kid with a dream."

They found all the books Erin recommended for the library as well as everything on the staff's list. Which was long. They ended up calling on one of the porters to meet them halfway through their shopping trip and again at the end. It was, Amy thought, pretty successful.

The security team turned Jacqueline "Wellie" Westgrove over to the FBI in New York City upon arrival. What would happen to her next depended upon their final investigation, which would take place over the days during which the ship was docked. Lucia had helped her pack up all her jewels and clothing and expensive perfumes to send to Wellie's daughter by her second marriage. Apparently, there was another daughter by the first marriage, but relations were not as smooth there, or so Amy had been told by a far more lucid Diane.

Mrs. Lewis was escorted to her hotel by Raymond Entwhistle and his voluminous luggage. Amy hoped the chocolate hadn't melted in the city's summer heat. He'd given her three small cases of Angus's favorites as a thank you, which she'd mailed off to him at college along with a letter on ship's cottony white stationery with the navy blue logo. She'd apologized for her silence and related the story of the art forgery and kidnapping. He'd be the talk of his dorm for a few days, anyway, once the package reached him.

The Darjeeling tea had arrived at the library as the older gentleman had promised. Amy thought for a moment about sending it to Angus too, but she decided to save it for herself. Amy brought the tea to Penelope and Richard's suite the evening after they'd docked. Gemma was there too with her fiancé, Keene, who'd boarded in New York. "We didn't want to tell anyone until after the voyage," Gemma told them. "He's one of the artists whose work I selected, which wouldn't have looked above board, even though we hadn't met until after I'd purchased the work for the ship at a gallery here in America. Besides," she looked sweetly at him and twirled her pendant, "I wouldn't want to spoil the debut of the ship's collection with anything as exciting as an engagement. Mine especially."

****

The next evening was the gala event: the opening of the Diane Westgrove Lewis retrospective and auction preview. Diane dazzled in her long silver gown in the softly lit ballroom. Refreshed and away from Wellie, she seemed to have recovered and was now swanning her way through the crowd at the gallery opening, at which many of her paintings were on display for the first time. Put away for the night was the Diane Westgrove Lewis who strove to be in the background of her work. She was elegant, graceful, the center of the room. Amy was heartened—that's how it should have been her whole life, shouldn't it?

Her paintings lined the walls of the ballroom, each hung with an explanatory card to the right. Amy marveled at the paintings, so unlike the *Venus Rising* in her library. She should have known sooner, shouldn't she have?

At round tables between the paintings and the ballroom floor, pink Diane Westgrove Lewis hybrid rosebuds glowed in their tiny vases. A band played somewhere in the background, its singer crooning standards over the piano's insistence and the interplay of the upright bass and the drums.

Penelope and Richard were their dashing selves. "You must have been to hundreds of these things," Amy said when she found them at their table. Richard motioned for her to take a seat, which she did. "You both look perfectly at home."

"Maybe not hundreds," Penelope said. She raised her champagne flute to her lips and took a sip. "But we've been to our share. And how could we miss this one?"

"Ah, my dear," Richard said. "They're playing our song. Shall we?"

"Which song is that?" Amy asked.

"Any song I can get my wife to dance to is our song," he said with a wink. Penelope and Richard rose and glided toward the dance floor.

Amy smiled and raised her champagne flute to them. The ghostwriter waved at Amy and crossed over to her. Erin, so often dressed in dove gray and shades of smoke, was stunning in a long burgundy velvet and lace gown that looked as if it had come from the 1960s. "You'll never guess," she said, glowing. "Diane had this gown flown in from her wardrobe for me. Can you believe it? It's Givenchy. I never dreamed I'd wear a vintage couture gown like this."

Amy suddenly felt conscious of her dress, the same one she'd worn the night of the party for Diane. She'd done her hair differently, of course, and had a far lighter wrap. No one would notice, not with the low lights and the art, would they?

Gemma and her fiancé joined them. Tomorrow, Amy would join Gemma and Keene, for a tour of the art aboard ship which had been overshadowed by the real and the fake *Venus Rising*. "Won't you look at Curtis and Cole over there, like father, like son. Someone should warn those poor girls."

"Do you think he would have made anything off Diane's early works?" Amy asked. "Diane has agreed to buy them at the exact price he bought them for."

Keene shook his head. "Market's flooded with Diane Westgrove Lewis now," he said. "It would have been better for him to auction them off before this event. Might have saved everyone a bit of a hassle with the art forgery too."

"Wellie would have found another way to get back at her sister," Gemma said.

"It's sad, really," Amy said. "If Diane would have been honest then about who the model for Venus was, then Wellie might not have gotten herself so drunk and fallen down the stairs. Maybe she blamed Diane for the loss of her career, too."

Gemma shrugged. "Maybe Diane wasn't completely honest about why she'd decided not to pursue a career in art, either. She was jealous of her beautiful younger sister, her father's favorite, but not enough to see Wellie lose what she loved most. So Diane tosses her career over too as a means of penance."

"They were never close," Erin said. "Diane let me read some letters. If Brent knew about the animosity between them before and especially after Wellie's fall, then he'd be furious. There's a tell-all of the worst sort. But it would have been a best seller."

"Then why not go for the whole truth?" Amy asked.

"Because it might sully the good work she did do," Erin said. "We didn't want to do that. I didn't want to do that."

Across the room, Amy spotted Kevin. He and his two assistants were there together. Kit wore a short silver gown not a far cry from the strappy pink things downloaded onto Amy's laptop days before. Kit leaned on the arm of Montague, the one Amy had met in the library. Kevin stopped to converse with one of the officers while the assistants made for the dance floor.

Gemma tapped Amy on the arm. "Who are you gazing at like that?"

"I'm not gazing," Amy said. She turned away but looked back.

"Yes, you are," Gemma said. "Is that Kevin from IT? Oh, my, he's dishy. Amy, Amy, Amy." She raised an eyebrow and nodded.

"All right, then," Amy said. "He is dishy, but technically, we're just colleagues. He fixed my laptop, that's all. Anyway, I just got a divorce, and I'm supposed to be tending to rebuilding myself for a while until I'm ready to start dating again."

"Who told you that? Your therapist?" Gemma asked with a laugh.

"My sister," Amy said. "Which is close enough. She said she read it in a magazine."

"Your sister won't think you're in over your head if you have a drink with him," Gemma said.

"And a dance," Keene added.

"Or two," Erin chimed in.

"You're all getting ahead of things, aren't you?"

Amy said. She could feel her cheeks growing pink. Though not quite the deep pink of the nightgowns or the Princess Margaret roses, thankfully. "He hasn't even come over here to say hello, and you're all presuming quite a lot, aren't you?"

Erin looked over into the crowd and then back again. She laughed. "Amy, I think you're about to be said hello to."

Kevin walked over to the table. "I thought I'd stop by over here, since the pair I'm chaperoning have decided to ditch me. And Regina is in better company than mine." He motioned over to his two assistants, who were locked in a dance that was nothing if not close. Regina, the receptionist for the IT suite, sat at a table with a young officer. Richard and Penelope, on the other hand, were gliding together, dancing both to the music and with each other. "Good news, Amy. I've wrangled you unlimited data aboard ship. Don't misuse it, okay?"

"No shopping for personal items, especially," she said. "Got it."

Amy introduced Kevin to the ghostwriter and Gemma's fiancé. "I think you've met Gemma, is that right?"

"Touring the ship with the head of the cruise line's VP of Luxury,' Kevin said. "I remember. You said we needed more art down in the offices, as much as the passengers did in the lobbies. I'm inclined to agree."

"I'm glad to hear it," Gemma said. "I know a few artists whose work would suit your needs." She smiled and elbowed her fiancé.

The ghostwriter looked up. "On the topic of artists, I think Diane is coming over."

She floated over, a vision in silver, if not Venus, then some other venerable goddess. Perhaps even Juno herself.

"Amy, I'm so glad you're here," Diane said. She sat next to Amy and took her hand. "This—all of this— is how it should have been at the library. At your first gala on ship. I'm only sorry Wellie ruined the moment for you."

"And you, too," Amy said. "Your paintings are amazing. If I'd only known what to expect, I would have figured it out sooner."

Diane shook her head. "Amy, dear, that was my fault. You can live your life pretending to be one thing while hiding another, and, somewhere along the line, something will fall apart. For me, it was never repairing what little warmth there was between my sister and me. You have to figure out what will matter before it's too late."

Amy looked out into the crowd. "So was the square I saw thrown into the water the real *Venus Rising*?"

"I'm afraid so," Diane said. "I'd had it photographed just before the trip, but having that isn't the same." She turned to Erin and said, "That was when you saw the painting, my dear. No, let's focus on the here and now. Two things I cannot believe tonight. First, is that you look just the spirit of the couture house that made the gown you are wearing, Erin. I have more Givenchy, and alas, I have neither a daughter nor a granddaughter who care a whit for 1960s fashion. Second, is that Brent Detweiler won't leave me alone until we've signed a deal with him for a tell-all about the events aboard ship."

"We?" the ghostwriter asked.

Diane smiled "Who else would I trust with my story? Besides, I'm not going to sign anything unless you get a three book deal, whatever you want to write. And when I tell him later that the project just isn't working, my fault of course, even with a brilliant ghostwriter such as you are, I'll remind him how well the first book is doing. I failed Wellie long ago, and I won't sell her out now."

"You failed her?" Gemma asked.

The older woman's face tightened for a moment, and she gazed at the ceiling. "We argued the night of her fall," Diane said. "Just before she left for the party, we argued about a half-dozen unimportant things. We were really arguing about the fact that she was younger and more beautiful and Father's favorite of the four of us, and I was feeling hurt by her success. And she was feeling hurt by my engagement to my late husband."

"Can I ask one more puzzling question, Mrs. Lewis?" Amy asked.

"Just one," Diane said, recovered from her moment of what looked to Amy to be grief.

"Was Venus in your painting a self-portrait, or was it Wellie?"

Diane was quiet for a while. The sounds of the band and the crowd filled her silence, but still, Amy kept her focus on the older woman. "This is the problem with answering that question," Diane said at last. "The face was mine, as much as it was anyone's. But I couldn't get the pose right, I couldn't get Venus coming out of the water at just the angle I wanted. I tried modeling that myself, but it was no use. I asked a handful of my friends at the art school to give it a try, but I couldn't quite get it. Oh, I used a hand here and the curve of a hip there. Wellie heard me complaining about it to our mother. And when Wellie called me to ask if she could pose for me, well, I was desperate, wasn't I? She got it, just perfectly, as soon as I told her what I wanted. So, in a way, Wellie was Venus. But Venus wasn't entirely her."

"Why not mention that in your memoir?" Amy asked.

"Ah, so you've read it?" Diane shook her head with a smile. "Brent was right about you. Well, I didn't mention it because it didn't seem important at the time. I said I used multiple body models, which was true, but nothing about Wellie." She was quiet for a moment. "Maybe I should have."

A waiter brought drinks to the table. Diane took a champagne flute and raised it. "To all of you, and," she motioned toward Amy, "you for solving the puzzle, Amy, and you, Erin," she motioned to the ghostwriter, "for helping me find my story, my dear."

Diane stood up with the help of her cane. "And now, let's go find Brent and tell him his good news." Erin took Diane's arm and steadied her. They walked off together into the crowd. Amy felt a sudden pang at the loss of the painting, but like Diane, like Erin, Venus would rise again in another form. That's just what she did.

Gemma stood up and grabbed her fiancé's arm. "I feel like dancing," she said.

"Oh, I don't know," Keene said. "I'm rather enjoying this champagne."

She shot him a look. "Love, it will be here when we get back."

"Fair enough," he said. Amy watched them walk to

the dance floor.

"They're quite the couple," Kevin said. "And I think I'll have to take her up on her offer to find some art for the office. We could use some sophistication down there. I'll get Regina on it as soon we we're all back on board."

"It's not so bad in your office, is it?"

"The suite could definitely use some gussying up," Kevin said. "Gemma's selections aren't as fantastic as pictures of kids in bluebonnets, but the walls down there need something."

The lights lowered just a bit, and the band started in on an old standard Amy loved, "The Best is Yet to Come." She smiled softly to herself. "I used to sing this song when I was driving to college," she said. "It made me feel more certain of things, I think. I thought of the 'you' as some more realized version of myself. Is that weird?"

"Not at all," Kevin said. "It's a good song."

"It's a wonderful song," Amy said with a laugh. "Even though Sinatra would never have approved of me as a duet partner."

"It's still a wonderful song," Kevin said. He set down his champagne flute and stood up. "Shall we?"

Amy's heart fluttered. "I couldn't," she stammered. "You know how to dance, and my repertoire is pretty much the hokey pokey and the chicken dance."

"I'll lead," he said. "It'll be fine. It's not the chicken dance, but most of the people on the floor are just winging it, anyway."

"Is that a pun, Mr. Park?"

"You're laughing," Kevin said. "Which is a good start."

"All right, then." Amy stood up.

He took her hand and led her to the dance floor. Amy held her breath for a moment as she felt his arm sliding across her back in a gentle embrace. She laid her left arm across his right, set her right hand in his, and exhaled. "See, not so hard," Kevin said in that deep voice of his that sounded to her like a faint glimmer of home.

"Well, you're right that it's not the chicken dance, but I like it."

"Good," he said. "I like it, too."

Everything felt suddenly clearer to her. What she wanted to tell Angus the next time they spoke, about how she left only because she was so sure that he was certain of himself. What she wanted to tell Stacey, about how much her presence in Angus's life and Amy's own meant to her. What she wanted to tell Penelope and Richard, about how much she wanted them to stay on board the ship with her, for a little while longer at least. What she wanted to tell Lucia, about how much she admired her for her leadership. And, most of all, what she wanted to tell herself about the life she could lead.

The ship, the library, the music, the art, the vibrant people around her—that was what she wanted for herself.

When she came home to Dawville, eventually, she would tell her parents and Stacey and Tiffany and everyone else all about the adventures she had.

But for now, the music buoying her, her friends nearby, and Kevin's arm around her and her hand in his, she couldn't think of a better place to be than right here, waiting for the next part of her journey to begin.

## A word about the author…

Tammy D. Walker writes cozy mysteries, poetry, and science fiction. As T.D. Walker, she's the author of the poetry collections *Small Waiting Objects* (CW Books 2019) and *Maps of a Hollowed World* (Another New Calligraphy 2020). When she's not writing, she's often reading, trying to find far-away stations on her shortwave radios, making poetry programs, or enjoying tea and scones with her family.

Find out more at her website:
https://www.tammydwalker.com

## Acknowledgments

Many thanks to Laura Larsen Cox, Bonnie Sharp, and Pam and Dave Fisher for their thoughts on an earlier draft of this novel as well as to Morena Stamm at The Wild Rose Press. To Valerie Reiss and Wendy Van Camp, who help me stay focused on my creative goals, much appreciation. I'm also grateful to Joy and John Walker, Carrie Phillips, and Brandi Ford for our travels around New York City, London, and Paris, and to Carrie especially for her insights into cruises. And to Justin Fisher, who travels with me through life, much appreciation and love as always.

CPSIA information can be obtained
at www.ICGtesting.com
Printed in the USA
BVHW050800180123
656507BV00015B/115